THE FISHER GIRL

ELINOR TAYLOR

For Joseph.

WAY BACK WHEN

They carve Diamond into four, each with a gate to elsewhere.
North has the cloud-wrapped floating islands.
The oceans sparkle in the East.
South Gate opens to a land of resources, albeit a hellish one.
While West leads to an odd spherical world Danny thinks of as home.

PART ONE

1. MARIE

It was a widely held view in Marble Falls that one shouldn't put much faith in the words of a goblin. Nobody knew where this had come from. There was certainly no evidence trail leading back to a specific event.

Marie had her suspicions.

She was ten and a half, now, a big girl, and received not much more than a cursory wave from the woman on the sofa as she stuffed an apple and the last slice of blueberry cake into her backpack, a carton of milk for later, and went out the back door.

'Have fun, Hunnybun,' her mother said, not taking her eyes off the screen for a second, mesmerised as she was by her favourite Bradley Gimble, phone in hand, poised to dial in with the fierce conviction of someone who knows–KNOWS–that the grand prize of a ski holiday in St Moritz has their name written all over it.

'Home before dark,' her mother added. An afterthought.

The door swung shut and, as often happened, the little snail-shaped knocker fell to the floor on the outside stoop. One day her father would fix that, Marie thought. But first (came the inevitable follow-up) he'd have to stop being quite so dead.

This inner dialogue was fleeting, matter-of-fact. It wasn't something that troubled her any. And after fifty yards or thereabouts she dipped down and crawled face-first into the hedgerow that marked the boundary of their raggedy, overgrown garden. Another thing her father ought to hurry up and fix.

The hole seemed narrower to Marie than it had previously. Maybe the hawthorn had grown some, or maybe she had grown some, either way it was a squeeze. She scrambled deep into the thicket, her backpack catching on brambles, tough and sharp as barbed wire. Regardless, she pushed on.

Finally, when the branches thinned a little, she got a hit of an aroma so instantly familiar, so wonderful (toasted chestnuts and fresh bread, the sweetest rose hip tea) that she thought she might actually cry.

She didn't, of course. Rather a waste of good tears that would be. She allowed herself a brief misty-eyed moment before blinking it off and crunching through to where she believed her old friend, happy as a bumble bee to see her, would be waiting on the other side.

2. THE QUIET

Ordinarily on a day like this, the forest would be alive with noise. It was all coming back to Marie, now, in glorious and vivid waves of colour: the sounds, the smells, the people. The girl wondered how she could've ever forgotten.

Travellers were commonplace on the path. Perhaps on their way to celebrate the harvest or to sell handwoven goods at one of the market stalls that were known to appear at times, ad-hoc, along the banks of the stream. Creatures and woodland folk alike ought to have been busying themselves with the myriad autumnal tasks that fell into one of three categories: clean up, stock up, or wrap up. Lest anyone doubted winter lurked around the bend.

'Best be ready or pay the piper!' is what Dale would've said, had he been there to meet her at the gate like he promised.

Marie would smile and nod–she was good at smiling and nodding–all the while wondering who this piper chap Dale spoke of was. Or how paying him might help you eat or keep warm in the lean, cold months.

The more Marie thought about it, the more she remembered that Dale said a lot of things she didn't fully understand. But she felt sure that he was funny and kind and made the best plum pudding in the world (this or any other), and that he was so much better company than Barbara.

Thinking of Barbara (it was after her father's death that Marie began to call her mother by her first name) led Marie to worry about the attic. Had she pushed the steps back, nudged the self-closing hatch up so it sat flush with the ceiling? Did she hear it click? She decided she had. Too late to go back, anyway.

Onward.

Something in the forest felt amiss. Still, Marie padded down the dirt track as she had supposedly done many times before, choosing with care when to stay on the path and when to detour through the trees. She vaguely recalled it being wise at this time of year to steer around the oaks, with their gnarled trunks that looked to be growing faces where the lower branches had once been.

But even the squirrels were being uncharacteristically reserved, which she doubted was due to a shortage of ammunition. (She'd learned the hard way about the squirrels of these parts and how easily irritated they could be. How they'd chitter and take aim from disjointed boughs, targeting unsuspecting passers-by with a warning acorn or three. They were not the Disney kind.)

Where was the hustle and bustle? The girl looked about. Where was the noise? Whoever thought the walk to Faretheewell could be so quiet?

Still, it didn't cross Marie's mind to turn around. Not then, anyway. It didn't occur to her to slip back through the bars of the iron gate, scramble through the hawthorns and go home. Even this too-hushed place that felt like it was holding its breath was preferable to yet another afternoon watching quiz shows with her mother.

But she didn't like it. She didn't like it one bit.

3. A TROOP

'The thing worth remembering about fairies of the North is that first and foremost they look after their own. The notion of them as benevolent is laughable. That they spend their days fluttering about on gossamer wings, sprinkling magic dust on the needy, is a fallacy brought about to protect the minds of the young.

'Anyone who's ever had the misfortune to come up against one (or heaven forbid more) of these nasty little specimens will tell you, you'd be well advised to run as fast as you can, as far as you can, away. Or better still, not cross paths with them in the first place.

'Fairies have an agenda. And you'd better hope it doesn't involve you.'

Journal of George Fisher
'On this day 18th March 1991'

***

The 3rd Faretheewell Division awaited instruction. The greens among them felt Marie coming down the track from a hundred spotted heifers away. The air had a way of shifting, you see, when people moved through it. They'd raise the alarm and scoot back into the barracks utilising their tactical size advantage, each being no bigger than a dragonfly.

But the people were gone and the air had been still for such a long time. Whoever it was must've come through the gate. No other explanation.

'Damnit!' Capt. Borealis smacked her hand on the desk, her wings humming in tense anticipation. 'I said we should weld it shut. Now look.'

So she sent a squadron to check who this person was that sent out ripples, what they were up to, and if they had anything worth taking.

'Stay stealthy,' Borealis said.

'Yes, Ma'am. '

'Your priority is to gather intel and return.'

'Yes, Ma'am.'

'And, A Troop?'

'Yes, Ma'am?'

'Don't come back until you know what the FUCK is going on.'

4. FINE

Marie found it less worrying if she sang, so she arranged a tune to the beat of each step. Time and distance passed much faster that way. There was a song her father used to sing when they went walking, and though the details escaped her, even the vaguest memory of it buoyed her a little and she picked up the pace with practically no additional effort whatsoever.

The aroma of chestnuts grew stronger. And something else, something like roast chicken.

A couple more turns, she thought. Then she'd see the little house come into view. The cottage with the sparkly clean leaded windows, the roof made of thatch.

Wood smoke gave the forest a gauzy filter. Dale must've lit a fire knowing she'd be hungry when she arrived. Though how he'd known to cook but not to meet her at the gate was a conundrum she chose not to delve into too deeply.

Marie's tummy grumbled.

'Left, right, left, right,' she sang.

She couldn't recall Barbara ever going on a walk. To be honest, Barbara didn't do much of anything. Consequently, her mother didn't know the words to her father's songs, so it was down to Marie to remember them. And she tried to remember, she really did, to keep at least something of him alive. But over time, as happened, it all sort of slipped away.

'No, no, no,' Marie told herself, working the words into the tune of the song she made up as she went along, with an extra stamp and a stomp added into the forward motion of her feet for good measure.

'Chin up, girl,' she said (not sang) with a sniff. 'On. We. Go.'

She passed the old well, then a blackened tree stump long since eviscerated by lightning, and a small clearing furnished with lichen encrusted standing stones in shades of mustard and grey. It was the same yet somehow not.

She tried to shake off the feeling of being observed, tried to convince herself that she was fine, that this was fine, that there wasn't an obvious gaping weirdness hovering on the periphery.

Left, right, left.

Fine, fine, fine.

No-one was watching. No-one was following. Just a couple more turns was all.

5. PSSSST

Okay. Marie stopped and spun in a full circle. She definitely heard something that time. She lowered her backpack, slipped it down so it dangled from the crook of her arm. If she had to she reckoned she could take out almost anyone with a quick spinning thwack. The milk carton might explode, but that was a price worth paying.

'Who's there?' She said to the silent forest.

No answer.

Marie checked her digital Dora watch: nearly lunchtime. It seemed later. Darker. It wasn't only the woodland canopy or the scudding autumn clouds that dimmed the light from above.

The haze in the air was almost chewable. Visibility had dropped to no further than a half dozen trees distance from where Marie stood on the winding dirt path. Something was dreadfully wrong.

'Pssssst.'

It came from over there, by a tumble-down pile of stones which Marie guessed had at one time long ago been a wall.

Something moved.

'Who is it?' Marie said, trying her best not to let her voice tremble. 'I know you're there.'

A small hand appeared from behind the stones and gestured for her to go closer, closer, closer than that.

Marie, who was nobody's fool, did as the hand suggested. Not because she wasn't afraid (she was quite afraid), but because she found in life the scary stuff was always less scary when you could see it. This, she believed, could be said of most things.

She stopped at a small mound of shrivelling ferns, a spit away from the fallen wall, and put her hands on her hips. It's what she did when she wanted to show someone who was being silly that she wasn't having any of it, thankyouverymuch. And right then it felt appropriate.

'Why on earth are you hiding?' she said.

'Shush!' came the reply.

'I will not shush,' Marie said. 'You invited me over.'

'Will you please be quiet?" the voice said. 'They's listening!'

'They? Who's they?'

'Shhhhhhh!'

The hand appeared once more. It pointed a finger, jabbed it toward a darker patch of forest where something hovered, something tiny, that disappeared the moment Marie turned to look.

And it was then that Marie realised, whoever was hiding behind the fallen down wall, whatever their reasons for calling to her, they were far more afraid than she was. A fact that was equal parts reassuring or alarming depending upon your point of view.

6. MUGGINS

After a while it became apparent that the person hiding had no intention of showing themselves. So Marie put her best foot forward, stepping tentatively over to the fallen wall. As she rounded the stones she saw who she thought at first was a small man crouching there. But, in a blink, she saw that it was something else, not a man at all.

'Hi,' she said to the little creature. 'I'm Marie. Who are you?'

Well, Marie knew a goblin when she saw one and this was most definitely, almost certainly, a goblin. She was 98% sure.

She had it in mind that she'd met one before when she was small. The memory, faint as it was, clouded in time, was of sitting on her father's shoulders, of being excited and thinking how clever her daddy was as he explained to her about this wonderful, new, and magical thing.

Of course, having now lived a whole ten years Marie was smart enough to know that through the eyes of a baby all things were new things. And that all new things were magical. Back then she'd as likely have squealed with delight at a conker falling from a tree as she would've had a spaceship crashed on the lawn. Still, it wasn't often you met an actual goblin and by Marie's reckoning she'd now somehow managed it twice.

'Who are you hiding from?' she said, squatting down so she wasn't towering over the little fella. He didn't look so bad, she thought. Quite sweet, actually. Soft eyes and if she didn't know better she'd say he had an honest face.

But then, Marie reminded herself, untrustworthy goblins couldn't help their nature any more than a bear or a cat or a weasel could. Even as she asked the question she made a mental note not to believe a single word he said.

'Have they gone?' The goblin clutched his chest and glanced nervously over the stones toward the dark patch of forest. 'I don't sees 'em,' he said. 'Can you sees 'em? Cunning beggers, they are. Just when you think they've lost interest: wallop! There they goes again with their scratchy nails an weeny feet. All 'Fetch this, Muggins,' an 'Do that, Muggins.' Like I gots nothin better to do than whatever they sets their bastard froggin hearts on.'

Marie blinked, not knowing how to reply to the goblin's tirade. She made a fair guess that was his name, though: Muggins. A name that rang bells like she'd heard it before.

7. THE FOSS

It had been a summer of rainstorms. The ground beneath the boy's feet slid away as he trudged through the fields, dodging sheep shit and thistles, a small kit bag slung on the diagonal across his back. A song haunted him. It went around and around and had a knack of working on his stomach in ways that would oftentimes lead him to throw up. How he wished he could reach in his ear and pull it out. Or simply forget.

It was never just music, he knew. Never just a song. It was a threat, a warning to grab what you could and run away and hide. So when at last he did run he knew exactly where to go. Yet the song followed. Seemed there was no getting away from his own mind.

The leaves hadn't started falling yet. It would be another week or three before true autumn blew in. The boy was glad. The coverage made him feel safe, swaddled in a blanket of red and crispy copper, hidden from prying eyes and a multitude of possible harms.

The old man would be on his fifth or sixth bottle of stout by now. Soon he'd be calling for the boy, looking to find reasons for his rage in his only surviving child. If Danny were home, and not traipsing through the wilds, the hate would fly from his old man's mouth like an explosion of coal dust, as if the mines had become a part of him somehow, blackening his insides. And Danny would cower, or, if he couldn't help himself, cry.

Not this time, the boy thought. Nor ever again.

Slip, slide, on he went. The fading light gave way to a world of shadows. The boy reached into his pocket and pulled out a torch he'd found in the old man's toolbox earlier that day. Please, God, he thought, tapping the handle against his hip. Please, God, let the batteries be okay. And they were, if only for a while.

He followed the stream uphill toward the pool, the waterfall, the small clearing, and the cave where he'd spend the night. That was enough for now. He'd figure the rest out tomorrow. Any stray ramblers would be long gone, either home to their beds or warming their socks by a crackling fire in one of the public houses down in the nearby village. There'd be nobody to see him scrabbling into the cave. Nobody to question why a small boy might be out alone in the dark. Nobody, most importantly of all, to take him back to his father.

A smile, then. The first in a long while. He'd never known how it felt to be free.

***

The boy was spotted long before he got to the falls. The silent alarm went up and dozens of pairs of eyes followed him keenly as he weaved through the trees, stumbled and fell up the poor excuse for a trail.

In darkness, tiny hands stifled laughter, little elbows dug into adjacent ribcages to shut them the hell up, each time the child tripped over a root, or, unaware he was being watched, let go of a well-rounded fart.

'Is he the one?' they whispered. 'A boy! A boy!' They congratulated themselves on just how perfect he was, giddy with the endless, palpable *soons*.

Soon the child would be at the cave. *Soon* he'd be theirs for keeps. And *soon*, after so much waiting, so much wanting, it could finally begin.

8. BIG BADA BOOM

'Hello? Anyone there? Hellooo?' Marie spun in circles on the path with her arms outstretched, palms up, to prove a point. The forest didn't respond. Course it didn't, she thought. To imagine otherwise was ridiculous. 'See?' she said to Mister Muggins, who had steeled himself enough to peek over the fallen down wall.

'Just us?' he said, eyes darting from tree to tree. 'You knows that for sure?'

'Just us.'

It took the better part of an hour to calm the nervous creature enough that he agreed to step out into the open, by which time Marie's tummy had begun to growl. 'Hungry?' she said.

The question was rhetorical. Already she'd scanned their surroundings, calculated the direction of the breeze, chosen a nice level patch of ground where the smoke wasn't too thick. She proceeded to lay down the same old emerald green tablecloth she'd used to wrap up the fruit.

A sound caught her attention, deep in the forest and movement drew her eye. Something (or more than one something) didn't want to be seen but was doing a terrible job of it. She decided against telling Muggins this, given his fragile nature. He wouldn't handle it well.

The instant the little girl sat down and unzipped her backpack, Muggins, catching a whiff of a lunch opportunity, all but forgot how frightened he was supposed to be. Each time Marie pulled out a new picnic item and placed it on the ground, his gaze followed: apples; cheese; a plate of cooked sausages.

The goblin's eyes widened. They fixated on, and coveted, every aspect of the feast. So much so that he drooled. The cake was the clincher. Marie kept that for last, savouring the grand reveal. The moment it hit the plate, Muggins scurried across to join his new best friend on the tablecloth and picked up a napkin and tucked it, bib-like, into his collar.

'Milk?' Marie said, after taking a moment to contemplate how this little goblin chap A) knew what a napkin was for and, B) had the manners to use one.

Muggins pushed an entire sausage into his mouth, which was still full from the cheese before it, and therefore led Marie to revise her view on his manners.

'Aye, go on,' he said, his words muffled. He lifted a plastic beaker toward Marie so she could pour him a milk. 'Where you off, then, girly?'

'To see my friend,' she said. 'Dale. Do you know him?'

'Can't says I do.' He reached for another sausage. Marie passed him the entire plate. 'What's he look like, this Dale? He goblin or other? Whereabouts is he? Not right you be wanderin'. Not right you be 'ere at all.'

Marie was about to describe Dale's appearance, but she paused, unable to. Not because she couldn't speak, but because at that moment she couldn't picture him, neither his face nor stature, which was the worst kind of strange. Dale was nothing but a blur.

She centred herself with a deep breath.

'I'm going that way.' She gestured along the path, the way she'd been going before the goblin's *Pssst* interrupted her. As she pointed, Marie noticed for the first time that the route ahead was considerably darker. Had it always been like that? She couldn't think, couldn't remember.

Muggins stopped chewing. He put down his plate and gulped what remained of his mouthful. He looked to be choosing his words with care. 'You wants to be going home, now, girly,' he said, with a serious hush that was new. 'I appreciates your kindness. I does. But back is best, now. No place for you, not down that way.'

'I'm worried my friend is-'

Marie had barely spoken the words when a fearsome screech ricocheted off the trees, out from the deepest and darkest part of the forest. Both the girl and the goblin froze. The explosion that followed rocked the very earth beneath them.

Marie covered her ears but it was already too late and her head buzzed with the intense shock wave of sound. The impact knocked her over and it took her a few seconds to realise that Muggins was waving his arms around and saying, or rather shouting, something to her.

Slowly, the buzzing quietened and Marie's hearing returned.

'Go, now!' Muggins was saying. 'Hup. Hup. Come on, biggun. On yer footsies.'

The explosion. It had come from the direction of Dale's cottage, Marie's most favourite place, with its sparkly clean leaded windows, its roof made of thatch.

The goblin's growing distress was evident. He tugged at the girl's sleeve and pulled her toward the path that led back to the gate, the hedgerow, home.

But, as the ringing in her ears subsided Marie was as calm as she'd ever known herself to be. There was not a scrap of doubt in her mind about what she had to do.

'No,' she said.

Muggins stopped pulling at her sleeve, then. 'You gots to go,' he whispered.

'Sorry, Mister Muggins, but no.'

She stood, brushing off bits of woodland that the explosion had rained down on her. 'I have to find my friend,' she said. 'He's in trouble, I just know it.'

And with discussion on the matter closed, Marie set off down the path to Dale's cottage, leaving the goblin, picnic and all, behind.

9. WELCOME TO NEW DIAMOND

The cottage was gone. Just gone. All that remained were glowing embers and odd structural sections, beams and the like, from which flames still licked up at the air.

Marie stood as close as she could to the smouldering footprint of what had been her friend's home. She examined the coals, subconsciously checking for bones, but also for shards of coloured glass from the beautiful windows she'd always loved so much. She wondered if her friend had been inside when the place went up. Had he been alive, then? Which begged the questions: was he dead, now? Did he suffer? And the loudest question of all: who did this?

A powerful urge came over her to drop to the ground and pound the dirt with both fists and feet, to scream and wail for all the woods to hear, and were she still small she would've done it. Not that tantrums ever solved anything, Marie knew all too well. But, holy macaroni, sometimes it felt good to get these things out, to give physical form to the anger and frustration inside.

Years ago, if she was in a supermarket or a car park with her mother, anywhere where people might gawp and form opinions, Barbara would say, 'Oh, don't mind her. She's just having one of her moments.'

The grownups would laugh and shrug in the way that grownups do. And they'd go about their day, not recognising learned behaviour when they saw it. Not realising that the kid acting out on the floor wasn't the only member of the household to handle life's challenges that way.

A moment. Yes. She needed a moment.

But rolling around in despair would hardly help Dale, now, would it? Besides, she was a big girl, she had words and (what was it?) coping mechanisms. Another thing she'd picked up from her mother.

A sharp tug on her skirt made Marie start and she turned to see the goblin, Muggins, leaning against her backpack. He was out of puff having dragged it all this way. She slumped down next to him and the two of them watched the fire burn, the smoke rise and drift into the surrounding trees.

'Why?' Marie said, to herself more than anyone.

The goblin placed a small, tentative hand on hers. And they sat like that, not another word spoken, for a while.

10. HUMMERS

This was not the North lands, it was becoming abundantly fucking clear.

Capt. Borealis had begun to question the rural recruits' commitment to the cause. In her experience, it took a unique style of encouragement to get soldiers to fight against their own kind. She wasn't averse to doing what needed to be done, quite the contrary, but she had neither the time nor inclination to play the long game. Not in this shithole.

'Where is she?' Borealis said, in a controlled fashion which made A Troop–and Green 5, especially–nervous.

'She's with a goblin, Ma'am,' Green 5, said.

'A goblin? Or *the* goblin?'

'The goblin, Ma'am,' Green 5 said, eyes down, fighting the urge to flit back a ways. 'She's with the goblin. I apologise for my initial lack of clarity, Ma'am.'

Borealis pondered this response. Sorry was not good enough

Before the power shift reached the forest of Faretheewell, or even the wider Diamond area and its capital city of Must, there had been no call for an army. Borealis could not fathom such a thing. She knew there had existed an unwritten pact between those living near the gates and those beyond them. And that it had stayed that way for a thousand spoken histories. But it was an alien concept to her, to manage borders of that magnitude by trust alone.

Since the earliest recollections it had been understood that the temperate forest of Diamond West was the territory of local fairy folk, by virtue of the winged ones' affinity with nature and privacy, both of which could be found across the vast swathes of dense woodland, near impossible to access from outside. Some aspects of this Borealis understood: ownership, segregation, utilising natural defences. Just not the greens' lackadaisical approach to protecting what was theirs.

She felt a profound contempt for the fairies of Faretheewell. Though sly as any of their outer region counterparts, they seemed to have no appetite for inviting trouble from the people, even when those same people began moving in.

She wondered how much it had rankled when the foreigners arrived through the gate with their stalls and wares, and formed well-trod paths through the untouched woods, and rasped their saws through the trees in order to build ugly, towering homes to live in.

On fairy land.

At that time, legend went, an agreement was forged by all parties that a distance would nonetheless be kept as it was well known, even then, how fairies liked their space. Still, boundaries were crossed from time to time, favours asked, deals brokered, and spells cast, for a reasonable fee, naturally.

And so it went that the fairies and people, and on rare occasions trolls and goblins and other outer types, settled in places they maybe didn't belong for the simple reason that they chose to. And that was deemed okay. After all, wasn't every Diamonder an immigrant or born of immigrant parents? Even fourth, fifth, sixth generation? Even those that considered themselves otherwise?

Half-arsed motherfuckers, Borealis thought. Why had they not organised, killed a few bigguns and scared the greedy sons of bitches off? The welcoming ethos of Faretheewell had been its death knell. She wasn't inclined to feel sympathy for those that brought hardships upon themselves.

None of this had any business bothering the captain. And yet, it did.

She was no Faretheewell native. Hell, no. She was a Hummer to the core, second wave, which made her one of, if not the longest serving of the Western garrison. Sent in to take care of business, after the cannon fodder were done.

In short, Borealis took no shit. So her reaction wasn't any great surprise to A Troop when they returned with the unacceptable news of a little big girl wandering the locality in clear violation of martial law.

That Borealis raised a hand to Green 5, summoned her near, grabbed her by the back of the neck, was almost expected. They'd come to learn that failure was intolerable. They'd braced for it.

Even so, when the captain called on her borrowed magic, sparks arcing between her fingers, cleanly severing the soldier's head so that her body dropped the height of a brown heifer and crumpled on the floor below?

Well, no amount of bracing themselves could've prepared A Troop for that.

11. THE SKYLARKS

After the execution was over, and Green 5's corpse thrown into a poor man's ditch to be eaten by whatever crawling or scurrying things stumbled across it, the winged Eryl and the wingless Mae took it upon themselves to be the first to find the girl. It seemed to them that the only way to avoid such a fate as befell Green 5 was to prove their worth to the Captain. Though they weren't convinced even that would be enough.

Borealis was notorious for her changing moods and capricious rules. What kept you in her good favour one day might easily be the thing that got you grounded or dead the next.

Mae learned this to her cost. The keloid scars that spanned the height of her shoulder blades throbbed as she remembered how it felt being on the receiving end of Borealis's wrath.

Eryl's back tingled, too, connected as they were, attuned to each other's senses since the womb.

Nobody within the garrison saw them sneak away. The best place to start, they guessed, would be the immediate vicinity of the West gate where the fugitives had last been seen. How far could one small girl get in a single morning? Not far, was their assumption. Even with the so-called help (more a hindrance) of a goblin.

Eryl sniffed the air. 'Gobshite's that way,' she said, referring to Muggins, using their favourite slur for goblin folk. 'We think they're staying together.' That last part wasn't a question, more a statement of fact.

Yes, they agreed, without speaking on it further or even looking each other in the eye. The girl and the goblin were together. Unquestionably so. Big as the girl child was in proportion to a fairy, she was still a child, no less than any other. And children got frightened. And children looked to grownups for support. And the gobshite, waste of flesh and bones as he may have been, was still more a grownup than the child. Ergo-

'The others will be leaving soon.' Mae interrupted Eryl's thought process. She knew she had. She did it on purpose most times. Her sister's easy annoyance tickled her. 'We should be gone a good distance before they set off. We need to be ahead, some.'

The sisters knew full well that Mae's disability put them at a disadvantage. It didn't need to be said out loud. To do so would hurt them both, but for different reasons.

They moved quickly, each step accompanied by a gentle clink. As was the case with many of the Faretheewell native fairies, the Skylark sisters chose not to adopt the new-fangled weapons of war introduced by the hummers of the north, preferring instead the hand-crafted bows and arrows and coal-forged swords of their ancestors. Intimacy over utility, you might say.

Low hanging clouds tinted orange by the burnings gave the sky a late evening appearance. It was nowhere near dusk, but still the sisters walked through the brush with a sense of urgency. If they didn't find the girl soon it would be nighttime and nighttime meant other dangers, some worse than the captain, hard as that was to imagine having only that morning seen their friend and colleague sliced in two and tossed into a shallow grave.

'Recon?' Eryl said without needing to elaborate.

'Okay, but quickly.' Mae no sooner wanted to be alone in the woodland after dark than she wanted to be here at all, but what choice did they have?

The winged sister took to the air. 'I'll meet you at the shrine,' she called down to her wingless other half.

'The shrine, yes. Go, now.'

Mae watched Eryl flit off ahead, effortlessly, toward the trees in search of a girl and a goblin. At that moment, she felt as if a rock were stuck in her gullet. It caught her that way sometimes, when she remembered that she could no longer leave the ground on a whim.

She swallowed, forcing the rock away to join all the other rocks that filled her chest and that weighed her down on this wretched land.

She blamed the people.

People were the reason things had changed, the reason the hummers had arrived, the reason her wings were ripped from her body.

Mae sometimes dreamed they were still a part of her. She'd skim the treetops and soar and swoop above the snow capped hills, only to wake and crash to the ground each morning. When they took her wings they might as well have torn out her beating fairy heart at the same time. Her soul, too. That alone was reason enough to find the girl and drag her by the hair to Borealis.

Perhaps then she'd be allowed a wish, Mae thought. As a reward or a bonus or as payback, she didn't care which. Might the captain look kindly on her for once? She wasn't asking for the whole of Diamond wrapped and ribboned on a plate. Just one little coin to drop down the well, to get back what was rightfully hers.

If the price of that was the life of a no good trespasser and an off the leash gobshite then so be it.

Hail to the goddamn King.

12. VOICES

'Take it back!' Marie booted some poor rock that'd done nothing to her that the goblin could tell. 'Take it back, right now!'

Alas, of all the things he was guilty or capable of, the goblin wasn't the sort to rescind a truth after he'd told it. Fact was, he was at a loss to pinpoint exactly what he'd said that so upset the girl. Was it the 'pretend-friend' thing? he wondered. Which, in the goblin's mind, was as far from a falsehood as the North gate was from the South.

These woods were empty of people and had been for an age, so this Dale fella she kept wimbling on about wasn't a real, existing sort of chap. Least not in the sense that you could see him or hear him or smell him or anything. He'd either gone with the last of them or she'd made him up. And if the girl couldn't parse such a fathoming? Well, that was just fine as rainshine. Goblins weren't made of the stuff to judge. Only she'd best not expect him to play along or to rally behind those daydreams of hers. He'd had enough of that game from those fluttering shitterbugs.

No, sir. Not anymore.

He pondered the tactic of apologising. Might that get him the information he required? Perhaps. But he stopped short on account of the fact that the girl struck him like she needed a bit of truth for a change. He was fast approaching the conclusion that this particular piece of West gate trash, however vital in the scheme of it, was a funny plum, with fictions doing circles in that big person's head of hers. More than he bargained for by a ways.

Cut the child some slack–an expression the goblin remembered a biggun he once knew saying. *Girl's got her reasons.*

Another voice chimed in, then: *And, besides, we're not done with her yet.* Within the words a diabolical rage clenched behind rows of sharpened teeth.

The goblin quietly huffed. 'Yes, yes. I know. Stick with her a while longer, find out what she knows, else she blunders into more trouble. Better two of us when the troops return, I suppose.' Which they would, he reckoned. Soon as likely as ever.

Meanwhile, Marie had seemingly given up waiting for the goblin to admit his wrongdoing and was busy shuffling her shoes in the ashes of the cottage, as if searching. For what, Muggins hadn't the faintest notion.

It annoyed him to admit that this small, deranged person might be useful to him. He thought he was done with all that. But then the situation did come with the added benefit that the hummers–heck, even the lesser woodland recruits–would be drawn to a biggun such as her, more than they would to a lowly goblin.

More than to a regular-day goblin, anyhow. Not, perhaps, a goblin who knew their secrets, could bring them down given the most perfect set of circumstances.

A goblin, as chance had it, like him.

13. DALE THE DISAPPEARED

Dale was gone in more ways than one. To Marie's relief, there didn't look to be any sign of him in the remnants of the fire. She felt confident there would be a scrap of him left if he'd been inside when the cottage was set alight.

What worried her more, though, than how her friend was gone from his home, worried her more than the fire itself, was how Dale was also gone from her memories. As if scrubbed out. Like the school cleaning lady might take a bristle brush to a dried splodge of paint on the classroom floor.

She tried to picture him as she kicked through the coals, to no avail. She could imagine a person, sure enough, a generic person with arms, legs, and so on, if she set her mind to it. That was as far as it went. No detail or character to speak of. No specifics. Just a blur where a face ought to be.

Barbara would always tell the other mums what a good imagination her daughter had. 'Got that from her father,' she'd say. 'He liked his stories, that one.' And it would irk the girl how her mother would give it a negative slant, implying that this was a bad trait to inherit, as if imagination and lies were interchangeable concepts.

So when Muggins accused her of making Dale up it hit a nerve. He wasn't make-believe. He wasn't a lie, either. Mind you, that didn't quell the creeping doubt that something was off about all this.

Marie realised she may have shouted a teensy bit too loudly when she told the goblin to take it back about her friend being imaginary (he'd gone awfully quiet after that, apart from mumbling to himself about something, the details of which she didn't catch).

'Right,' the girl said, all of a sudden, swinging her backpack up onto one shoulder. 'How long before it gets dark, would you say?'

Muggins looked up, then around. He popped a finger in his mouth then held it up in the breeze. 'More than a bit. Less than a lot,' he said, after a moment.

'Okay, then.' Marie headed toward the path. 'Guess I'd better hurry. You coming?'

And after checking the way ahead for shitterbugs, the goblin followed.

14. DANNY BOY

Danny reached the foss just as the clouds cleared. The moon, not quite full but almost, lit up the bubbling falls and the silver pond they flowed into. He put the torch back in his pocket.

The cave entrance gaped, maw-like, in the rock face that flanked the far side of the escaping stream. It dripped steadily (or was that salivated?) fed by oceans of rainwater from the saturated hills and fields above.

The boy pictured himself as a raindrop, enveloped high in steely clouds, drifting, roiling, then falling free, blown the breadth of the county. Then landing with a soft splat on a remote peak, chasing a path through moss and limestone, searching for a river to carry him far, far away. Until, finally, joining all the other raindrops in the vast open water of the sea. Only to start over again.

Danny knew well enough that this was an oversimplification. Sometimes water would become other things, like pancakes, or grass, or animal pee, and sometimes it might go underground and stay there a really long time, or freeze and never, ever thaw out.

The thought of being a raindrop was his most favourite, though. It seemed like a nice way to spend your days: simple, reliable, rhythmic. He liked the science of it. Raindrops, after all, didn't have to worry about a drunk parent forgetting you needed new shoes or not liking the way you looked at them. They just cycled around the globe for an eternity, exploring the heavens with the other raindrops.

It wasn't the easy scramble up to the cave he'd often thought it would be when he used to walk this way with his father. He scuffed his knees good, tobogganing back down the slippery riverbank a couple of times. When he reached the opening and climbed over the rocks and into the dark hole, Danny felt the shaky, desperate hunger that had become more familiar to him than was right for a boy of his young age.

Inside was dry, thank goodness. Danny nestled in as far back as he could and used his jacket as a makeshift cushion. He thought it best to save the torch batteries, so dug in the bag for a candle he'd kept for just such an occasion. It was the one he'd stolen from church the last time he went with Grandma and had hidden it in a drawer under his socks figuring God would let him off this once.

His father would likely miss the cigarette lighter before he missed him, Danny thought, striking the flint wheel with a shivering thumb. A warm glow filled the space. It was cold and damp, alright, but the light somehow made it more bearable, a bit less bleak.

He got his first good look at the inside of the cave and saw things scratched onto the rocks, words he couldn't read, images that meant nothing to him. He wondered how many other people had been there over the years. Perhaps even boys like him, seeking sanctuary from a harsh world.

Most folks would've had a hard time trying to imagine a damp cave being anyone's preferred choice, but for Danny it wasn't much of a stretch. He ran his fingers over some of the words on the wall beside him. Short, uncomplicated words. He was able to sound them out: *We Are Here,* they read. Danny didn't know who wrote those words or why, but they seemed to resonate with some part of him. Beneath the words was the outline of a small, green and somewhat rudimentary skull.

He reached into the bag again and opened a tin foil parcel in which he'd wrapped up a handful of leftover roast potatoes that morning and one by one shovelled them into his mouth. They were cold and kind of greasy, but so good.

He read the words again: *We Are Here.*

It didn't matter who the *We* in the statement was. To Danny, it was an affirmation, proof of life and hope in the face of overwhelming odds, a scream of defiance in the night.

We Are Here.

Yes, the little boy thought, gulping down another cold but delicious roast potato. Yes, we most definitely are.

Outside the cave, a swarm gathered. Small fluttering someones, biding their time, listening for the right moment to enter.

'Let the child eat,' whispered one.

'Nearly, nearly,' said another.

'What are we waiting for?' growled a third.

Their leader raised a hand to silence the subordinates, who backed away, heads bowed out of either reverence or fear depending on the individual. She hovered closer to the open mouth of the cave and slowly tapped her sharp fingertips on the wet rock: *tip-tap-tip-tap*, walking them ever closer to the child.

The others quietly watched on.

How heavy the boy's eyes had become. The flickering light and the trickling water lulled him, so much so that he could've easily nodded off where he sat.

Tip-tap-tip-tap.

Not the rain, he thought through a haze of almost-sleep. Not the waterfall either.

Tip-tap-tip-tap.

An adrenaline surge pulled Danny awake and he knew in his pounding heart that he wasn't alone. He looked out toward the circle of darkness that was the outside, noting subtle movement in the night air.

He saw it in the light of the candle, the little flying person, no bigger than his palm. And the boy, Danny, decided in an instant that he was still asleep and that this was a dream and he was flat-out dreaming, because what he was looking at wasn't real. It couldn't possibly be. He was tired and hungry and his brain was making stuff up to help him feel better, or at least different.

He was dreaming. No doubt about it.

'Hello, young Daniel Evers,' the flying person said (Danny avoided the word 'fairy', even if it was just a dream, as that would've been silly. No such thing, he thought. *Nuh-uh*).

At first, he didn't notice how the thing that wasn't a fairy knew his name. He was too transfixed by the sound of its wings. Like hearing his grandma through the floorboards whipping up a cake batter with her electric whisk. A deep, gentle, buzz. One you felt in your chest.

No, he stopped himself. That wasn't quite right. Not a buzz. More of a-

He craned his neck, listened closer.

It was actually more of a hum.

15. GHOST TOWN

The air was thick in Must. You didn't breathe so much as tolerate it one rasping breath at a time. Plumes of vapour carried untold poisons into the atmosphere where it swirled and expanded and drifted about on what almost passed for a breeze. With no-one to stop them, the machines continued their work, unabated, such was the legacy of mankind.

The people had long since abandoned the city. Having spectacularly fucked it up with their choices, the final choice–of those who still lived, at least–was to start afresh somewhere new, where new choices would no doubt lead to scores of brand new fuck-ups as was the way of their sort. Creative in their endeavours to the last.

Only shadows remained. Beneath the dirty, towering monuments to the West Gate vermin, alleyways creaked and groaned with a lingering sense of regret, of resentment. But into the vacuum others crept. The unseen, as dark and empty as the city itself. They curled up in the festering ruins and found themselves quite at home.

Such destruction. Such, dare they say, evil? The two-legged roaches would get their well-deserved pudding, and a hefty portion at that, but not from these new city-dwellers. After all, it would serve little purpose for those who thrived in darkness to punish those who extinguished the light. Defence, however, was a different matter.

There had been no green in the capital for a thousand moons. From the vantage point of Centre Square, as far as could be seen in any direction, buildings like gravestones crowded the sky, a mouth full of too many teeth. It would surely be the most unnatural sight for the wretched green-lovers. Not a single tree anywhere. How suffocating for the softlings, poor dears.

Ha ha ha.

Not so for the hidden, whose skins itched at the mere mention of grass.

One day, they knew, a few stray seeds shitted down by a sparrow blown off course (for why else might any right-knowing creature make their way to such a metal nether world?) would find a corner to settle into where, swelled by the humidity, encouraged by the suggestion of light filtering through the grey, they'd cast roots into the remnants of the dead.

But not if the dark ones could help it.

From their lairs they monitored the levels, burned or pissed on what looked like promise. Green was life, after all. Green was hope and future and growth, none of which would do in the South. And this was resolutely South land now. Challengers would be met with claw and blade. String 'em up by the gizzards, they would. Take great pleasure watching the pink-fleshed thing fade yellow, before pulling the cured carcass down days later for a feast.

They weren't so naïve as to wager the green never someday returning to Must. They knew full well it was a case of when, not if. If only the when wasn't so hard to calculate. Going by the state of the landscape, another hundred moons could pass or another thousand before the towers crumbled into a carpet of moist leaves, wrenched from the heights by curling tendrils persistent in their slow upward march. At which point it would be over, the battle lost, and the South Gate would call the unseen back.

Until then, they scuttled about the city, laid low in the wreckage of what the men had built and plotted ways to extend their residency, cuckoos in abandoned nests. For in the absence of any biggers or bolders, they ruled the city now.

16. MIDWOOD: HERE BE TROLLS

The deeper into the forest they walked, the less defined the path became. The edges of it blurred and Marie wondered on occasion if she hadn't in fact taken a turn from it some ways back and was now recklessly meandering to goodness knew where. But then the path would form again, peeking through the moss and overgrown weeds, and she'd feel relief at the solidness of it underfoot.

Her steps never faltered either way. 'Front it out,' was what her father would've said. So she did.

She wasn't sure if the goblin knew any better than she did which direction to take, or even if he'd alert her if she did stray from the path. For all Marie could tell he was about as clueless as she was when it came to the right way or wrong way to get where they were going. Besides, they hadn't formally decided where to go, only that they should keep going forward. Though even that might just have been Marie choosing to do that, and the goblin following along behind. He did, for the most part, come across as the agreeable type.

That was until the last fork in the path.

The goblin had signalled to go right, whereas Marie, pulled by some indescribable knowing, had wanted to go left. Left was darker and more foreboding. But still, it was where she felt she had to go.

'Ain't no ways for us,' Muggins said, shaking his head. 'Down there be the troll graveyard. Give you bad dreams, that will. Right is right. Come on, biggun,' and he turned toward the right hand fork as if the decision was made.

'Fine,' the girl said. 'You go your way and I'll go mine. Maybe we'll meet again further down the road. Maybe we won't. All the same it was nice to meet you, Muggins.' And off she went to the left, backpack bobbing from side to side with her steps.

The goblin, apparently weighing the pros and cons of the matter, paused. He might have known something Marie didn't–talk of troll graveyards was indeed worrisome–but the girl continued on just the same, only glancing back once. Front it out, she thought. Front it out. Before she rounded the next corner she heard the fast *pat-pat-pat* of small goblin feet as Muggins begrudgingly raced to catch up.

'Fogglin buzzocks,' he grumbled. 'You is one stubbornly person, does you Ma and Pa tell you that?'

'My Daddy's dead.' The girl spoke without a hint of emotion.

'Oh,' Muggins said. 'Sorry an' all that.'

'S'alright.'

'And your Ma?'

'She watches too much television.' As if that covered it. And the way the goblin didn't enquire further, just gave a solemn nod as they walked on, side by side, it seemed it did.

***

A short while later, the pair arrived at what Muggins had euphemistically called a graveyard. But it was no such thing. There were no graves or headstones or crosses, no wilted bouquets or angels carved out of granite, just the twisted stumps of felled trees dotted between the non-felled ones, contorting to give the appearance of faces that at a pinch might be taken for trolls.

Marie slowed her walk by half. She was no longer in a hurry to get anywhere. At that moment she was more taken with the numerous strange wooden effigies and cast her eyes back and forth as she went, not quite able to get past the feeling that the tree stumps saw her as easily as she did them.

Muggins, however, kept going at a pace. For the first time on this jaunt of theirs he was ahead of the girl, his legs powering him along the path with a clear sense of purpose. He didn't stop to look at the trolls, not so much as a sideways peek.

'The girly wants left, so we goes left,' Marie heard him mutter. Then he raised his voice only slightly and said over his shoulder, 'Best hurry, biggun. Dead trolls don't like dawdling folks in their resting place.'

That seemed to Marie, who had heard a fair number of ridiculous things already that day, to be possibly the most ridiculous. Dead trolls? Angry trees? To prove a point she stopped and rapped a handful of knuckles against the nearest stump, which triggered the goblin to spin on the spot and dash back down the path toward her, arms raised, palms pushing through the air ahead of him.

'Stop!' he said in a forced hush. 'Wake 'em, you will. And piss 'em off while you're at it.'

The girl went to lower her fist again, to rap on the stump a second time. 'Don't be silly,' she said. 'They're made of-'

She stopped, yanked her hand back, when a pair of large glassy eyes that most definitely hadn't been there before stared up at her from the tree stump and blinked.

'Dang it,' the goblin said.

Marie stumbled away from the grass verge where the stump with eyes was rooted. And not just eyes. When she looked closer she saw it had a little button nose in the middle of that bark-encrusted face, ears poking out through the sphagnum and ferns that made a bed for themselves on its head.

The fern-haired, glass-eyed, wood troll opened its mouth and let out a lazy yawn that Marie reckoned it must've held in for a really long time. It didn't look scary. At least not enough to warrant the way the goblin now cowered behind her legs. She could feel him quivering against her skirt.

'I thought you said they were dead?'

Muggins kept himself out of the tree stump's line of sight and stayed quiet.

The tree troll slapped its lips as if warming them up. 'Dead?' it said, then let out what could've been a chuckle. 'Whoever made up such a thing? Believe the fools, do we, child? Careful, now. Not all who talk do so kindly. Depending upon which way the wind blows, I suppose.'

The tree troll rolled its eyes upward and repeated the phrase back to itself, accentuating the various elements differently each time: Blows I suppose. Blows, I suppose. Blows. I. Suppose.

Marie waited for it to finish.

'My friend and I are looking for someone,' She said, impressed at herself for saying 'my friend and I,' not 'me and my friend.' Her father had often stopped her mid-sentence if her grammar was off, and that phrase was one of his favourites to correct. Annoying as she had found it when he did that, it was like he'd given her a gift, a part of himself she took with her everywhere she went, the gift of his voice in her head.

'Friend?' the tree troll echoed back. 'Don't see any friend about these parts.' Another yawn. 'F-r-i-e-n-d,' it said again, sounding the word out on ancient lips of ridged bark, followed by another gruff chuckle.

Marie didn't get the joke.

'Yes,' she said. 'His name's Dale. Have you seen him? Somebody burned his house down and I really would like to know he's safe.'

The tree troll thought about this for a moment. 'Dale, hmmm?' it said.

'Yes. Dale.'

'House burned down, you say?'

'Yes. Completely. Back that way.' She jabbed a thumb in the direction of Faretheewell. 'Other houses, too. At least five that we've seen.'

'Why might that be, do you think?' the troll said.

Funny, Marie had been wondering this whole time about the who not the why. But the more thought she gave to it, the more she had to admit that the troll's question was probably the better of the two.

'Why?' the troll said again. 'And to what end?'

'I- I don't know,' she said. 'Dale was nice, and made cakes. He was my friend, and my daddy's friend. If I were to burn a house down it wouldn't be his. Do you have any idea how I can find him?'

The tree stump yawned again, blinked more slowly now as if running out of juice. 'Maybe. Maybe not,' it said. 'Been here so long. Only here. Nowhere else. Hard to see what's going on in the world if you're in one place the whole time.'

Marie looked around. It was then she noticed the scale of this so-called troll graveyard. There were dozens, if not hundreds of wooden stumps along this section of path, stretching back through the forest. From what she could tell the others were all still asleep.

'Have you always been here?' she said, turning back to the first troll.

It looked to have nodded off. But before Marie could ask again, perhaps a little louder to wake it up, the troll opened its eyes and drew in a deep breath through its nostrils, which were nothing more than cracks in its bark. 'Oh no, child,' it said. 'This is where we ended, but it's a long way from where we began. Not a bad place. Just a place like any other.'

The troll's eyes slowly closed a final time. 'Hope you find your friend,' it said, practically in its sleep. 'Don't pay heed to the tricksters.' One last exhale and the troll settled back into itself. 'Especially those that think themselves trickier than you.'

After a moment, Marie knew she would get nothing else from the sleeping tree troll.

Muggins, however, wasn't convinced. He waited a few beats more after the troll fell back into its deep slumber before he stepped out from behind the girl. 'We gots to go now,' he whispered. 'No more to be done here. On we trot, before we gets 'em angry.'

That one hadn't sounded very angry, Marie thought. Weary, yes. But angry? Where had Muggins gotten the idea that the troll was a threat?

The goblin set off walking. It wasn't until they'd left the graveyard far behind and reached an area of the forest where the sunlight held more purchase on the ground below that he spoke again. 'Midwood ain't no place for us. Takes my word, biggun.'

Marie kept her eyes forward as she walked. 'What do you suppose he meant by *tricksters*?'

The goblin grumbled something to himself that Marie didn't catch, then said,' You gotta watch them fellas, girly. Bitter, they are. Bitter, bitter, bitter. Picked the wrong side when picking time came. Now they don't likes where it landed 'em.'

Marie said nothing. Evidently there was history there that she had no knowledge of. Still, she stored it away for later. The conversation as she saw it wasn't done.

The light filtered through the forest canopy more freely now than when they'd first gone down the left hand fork, though it had taken on the low-slung copper tinge of late afternoon. If Marie had been on a walk in the hills with her father, they ought to have been making their way back to the car about now or else risk being caught out in the dark.

But this wasn't the hills of Yorkshire, this was Diamond, and it felt like there was more at stake than getting home for dinner before nightfall. All the same, Marie did a quick mental sum of roughly how long it had taken them to get this far and therefore how long it would take to get back to the gate.

While she wasn't afraid of the dark–not that she'd admit to anyway–Marie knew that Barbara would at some point drag herself away from the quiz shows and notice her daughter gone. Better she was home before then. The last thing she wanted was half the local police force searching for her, finding the gate, and piling through the hedgerow into Diamond.

Before he fell to his stupid death, her father wrote that this place was special and was to be protected at all costs. From what Marie could tell, even Barbara didn't know it existed. Not that she'd care. She hadn't cared about much as far back as the girl could remember. Her father used to say that they should *cut Mummy some slack*, whatever that meant. Like Barbara was poorly or something. Although she hadn't seemed poorly at all.

It occurred to Marie that she could no longer smell the burning buildings. The air was heavy with something else, now, a familiar scent rather than the stink that had bothered her nose up until then.

All of a sudden the goblin stopped. 'Shhh,' he said. 'Waits here while I check for shitterbugs.' He went on ahead, crept as if hunted. Or perhaps he was the one hunting, it was hard to say. He kept low, scanning the woods as he went.

Honeysuckle! Marie thought. She'd know the scent anywhere, given that it framed the front door and wove around the windows of her house wherever the bright summer sunshine touched it, back in Marble Falls. She studied the goblin as the distance grew between them; odd little fellow. He turned the corner and padded out of sight. A flag waved somewhere in the recesses of her mind. But before she could figure out the meaning of it, Muggins reappeared further down the path and gestured with a clawed hand for her to follow.

Safety was relative, the girl decided. And whatever scheme this universe had going on she'd likely be safer in the company of a dubious goblin than alone.

17. A SIMPLE CASE OF GOOD VS. EVIL

(PART 1)

Danny felt a surge of panic riffle through his bladder. Not because of the tiny flying person (definitely not a fairy) per se, who was at that time still hovering at the entrance to the cave. No, this panic was about what the unexpected appearance of the tiny flying person might represent. He realised his jaw had fallen slack so snapped his mouth shut, not wanting to gawp.

'Hello, young Daniel Evers.' The words, the cadence, set his scalp hairs on end.

The tiny flying person practically glowed in the candlelight. Danny watched as they dipped their small head then looked up and smiled at him, a strange combination of shy and bold. He couldn't make out if they were a boy or a girl. Not even by their voice.

'Oh, sweet boy,' the tiny person said. 'You need not fear us. We're here to help you.'

The use of plurals in that sentence alarmed him. He could only see one, but he knew us and we meant there were more. Perhaps a lot more.

If Danny had to bet on it, he'd say the tiny flying person was a girl given how pretty they were even from across the dimly lit cave. And something in the way they carried and moved their body, which was small enough to sit in his hand.

Their delicate silver-edged wings twinkled in the flickering shadows, catching the light here and there.

As often happened, a picture came into the boy's mind of his mother dressed in the most beautiful white silk and lace, candlelit and peaceful, and laying perfectly, too perfectly, still.

'How on earth has a darling thing like you ended up in a damp old cave all alone?' the tiny person said.

Danny didn't reply. He wouldn't know where to start. What does someone say to an impossible person? Fairies, as he reminded himself, most definitely didn't exist. Only in stories. And yet here he was looking straight at one.

Somewhere on the fringe of the boy's consciousness it registered that the can't-be-a-fairy had inched slowly forward. They were still quite some distance away, but the cave wasn't deep from mouth to rear and if the tiny flying person kept moving as they were they'd reach him in no time.

The hum of the surely-not-a-fairy's self-powered flight made for an oddly soothing white noise as it reverberated in gentle waves within the cave's stoney hollows. It reminded Danny of the large summer dragonflies that danced and congregated by lazy river bends, and settled on blooms of cow parsley to warm their glassy wings. He liked insects. They were simple to understand, uncomplicated in their wants and needs. Though it was a leap to imagine the same of the tiny winged person several yards away.

'Do you have a voice, biggun?' the might-be-a-fairy said. 'We don't bite. You can speak without fear.'

The boy felt a sting in his throat. He gulped it down. 'Did my Daddy send you?' was as much as he could think to say.

'Daddy? No, he didn't send us. Nobody sent us.'

A pause.

The closer the tiny person hovered, the easier it became for Danny to make out her delicate, almost translucent features. He felt certain that she was a she. He also had to concede that she was a fairy, however impossible that might have been. The panic gave way to a sense of grim resignation that he knew all too well.

'Hey-' The fairy reached into a small pouch dangling from her waist. 'You look hungry. I have just the thing.'

Danny's heart nearly jumped up his throat as the fairy darted across the full length of the cave in half a second. The boy's feet bicycled in an involuntary bid for escape.

The fairy saw this and backed off a little on its humming silver wings. She held up a hand to the child as if to say, It's okay. Hush. You're safe. She pointed to a shelf of rock, nodded, then drifted down a foot or so until she was level with it.

Danny watched.

The fairy sprinkled the shelf with powder she'd taken from the pouch then clicked her fingers. In an instant, the rock shelf housed an array of cakes and biscuits and puddings and a jug of steaming warm milk. Then she hovered back, arms outstretched as if playing the role of a maître d' showing Danny to his seat in a fine restaurant.

He wasn't sure at first. Was magic food okay to eat? Might it poison him or turn him into a toad? Such things weren't uncommon in stories involving fairy folk. But hunger overtook common sense and a moment later he scrambled from the back wall of the cave to the shelf of sweet treats. And a moment after that he tucked in.

***

With his belly full, Danny was willing to overlook the impossible nature of the fairy's existence. The cakes and desserts sure did feel real on his tongue, and sliding down his oesophagus (a word he'd learned from a science programme on the telly only a few days earlier. He enjoyed how the syllables bounced around in his mouth). He noticed with some relief that he wasn't poisoned, though time had yet to tell if he would at some point transform into a toad.

Still, he allowed the fairy nearer and no longer flinched when she moved or gently fluttered her wings. Funny how quickly you can acclimatise to even the strangest of things, Danny thought. He brushed cake crumbs from his lap, downed the last of the milk, now tepid, still creamy and delicious. The waterfall trickled and whooshed relentlessly outside. If he were home now he'd want nothing more than to climb into bed and go to sleep.

The fairy introduced herself to the boy as Two. He wasn't sure if it was spelled like the number or any other variation of the word, but in his mind's eye he saw it written as '2'. Without thought he said, 'Are you a fairy?'

'Yes,' Two replied. If she was surprised by the question it didn't show.

'What are you doing here?'

'Helping you, Daniel,' the fairy smiled. 'Don't you think the world would be a much happier place if we all just helped each other? A sprinkle of kindness goes a long way, you know.' She rubbed together her fingertips that had pinched the magic powder from the pouch and created the feast he'd just eaten, and the friction of it produced soft wisps of twinkling light.

Danny nodded. He was all for kindness, familiar as he was with the alternative.

Two sighed and sat back against a lichen covered rock. She looked around with a wistful gaze. 'Not everyone sees it the way we do, Daniel.'

'How do you mean?' Danny said, leaning in. The fairy looked sad, and he didn't want her to be sad. She was so beautiful and had the kindest smile. He wished he could look at her, talk with her, make her smile at him for always. He felt sure he was falling in love with her a little bit.

Two adjusted her wings. 'Nothing for you to worry about, my friend,' she said.

Friend, Danny thought. A swell of what he remembered as joy filled his chest. 'No, tell me,' he said. 'Is someone being mean to you?'

'Well, yes,' Two said. 'Not to me, exactly. But someone is being very mean indeed.'

If there was one thing Danny couldn't stand it was injustice. He felt it in his bones when those who had power wielded it with impunity, which in his small sphere of experience was often. 'Anything I can do?' he said.

The fairy's eyes glowed at the boy's words.

'Now you mention it, Daniel, maybe there is,' she said, before pulling back, shaking her head. 'No, no. I can't ask you to do that. Forget I said anything. Would you like another glass of warm milk?' She went to stand, reached in the pouch for more powder.

'Tell me. I want to help. Please, let me help.'

The fairy studied the child's eager face. These people, she thought. These stupid, stupid people. How easy the young and the damaged were to bend.

For the next hour, seven-year-old Danny Evers listened in fascination to tales of things he didn't fully understand, stories of corruption and destruction, set in a world he'd never heard of.

And with the boy hanging on her every word, the young and cunning Two Borealis unveiled the next phase of her master plan in a way that only a child could grasp.

18. EVERY QUEEN NEEDS HER SECRETS

Were you to ask those who remember long ago, they'd tell you Queen Janet ruled with the evenest of hands. Never did her people know her to make a bad judgement or reckless call on their behalf, at least not on purpose. Which, frankly, was no mean feat in Diamond.

It was said she inherited from her elders the desire to foster a world patterned with differences, rather than some great grey fortress designed to keep any perceived 'other' out. Welcome were those, she declared, who came from beyond the four border gates. If it was their true dream to live a life of community, acceptance, and peace, then all of Diamond was theirs to enjoy.

This wasn't just the future Janet wished for her Kingdom, it was the future she wished for herself. And for the most part the two aligned. It wouldn't be overstating things to describe her as the most beloved of her noble line. But in the end that wasn't enough.

She was known to walk the land and fly the skies far beyond the royal citadel and could often be sighted attending social events meant only for commoners, or turning up unannounced at places where a member of the royal household had no business being. Throughout her reign, and afterward, she became known to all as Queen of Diamonds. Mention this to any Diamond inhabitant, even all these years later, and they would still know exactly who you meant.

'Ah, yes,' they'd say. 'She was a lovely one, alright.' Then they'd sigh and move on with their day, a little sadder having remembered that she was no longer around.

Oftentimes, Janet would arrive bearing gifts of food or wine for the people of whichever region she was of a mind to visit. They delighted in it and would welcome her with warm hugs and cheek kisses, and cater to her with fresh bakes and teas and whatever else they had to offer, just as they might for any traveller passing through.

For all the hidden doorways and myriad worlds within her reach, the land beyond the West was the place that filled her soul the most. It had parts that were reminiscent of the woodlands of Faretheewell and parts that might've easily been stolen from beyond the other gates. How varied! How vast! If it weren't for the burden of responsibility she carried at home she would've spent all her days there, exploring the spherical world's furthest reaches and mingling unseen with the bigguns until her end days.

During her later travels, it didn't escape the queen's attention how factions had begun to form, some of whom had other, less cosmopolitan ideals. As she wandered and met with the people–native and migratory alike–she'd listen more than talk so as to honestly hear their concerns and share in their hopes for all the worlds.

In time, fear overshadowed most other chatter.

'The city,' they'd say in alarm. 'It's becoming quite monstrous, don't you think?'

And, 'Their machines, Highness. What's to be done to prevent further industry engulfing the whole of Diamond?'

Or some variation of, 'How can we hope for equity, my queen, when they take so much more than they give?'

Over and over again she had this conversation, up and down the Kingdom.

'Yes,' she'd nod. 'I'm fully aware. I shall set aside time to speak with the people, discuss ways to shore up the safety and wellbeing of our land. Leave it with me, dear ones. And thank-you for bringing this to my attention. Diamond is nothing without your voices.'

She truly meant what she said, each and every time she said it. But there were many facets to the problem, the politics of which the average Diamonder would not have the wherewithal to wrangle.

It was while out on one such exploration of the kingdom's westernmost region that Janet discovered the slip. She left her guards at the gathering. Protocol dictated that they follow her at a discrete distance on all such trips outside the citadel, but she instructed them to allow her a few moments of alone time, *real alone time,* to enjoy the woodland air.

Ordinarily they might've reminded the queen, with respect, that it was more than their wings worth to leave the monarch unprotected. Or they might perhaps have pretended to agree, then shadowed her without her knowledge. But this was spring festival day and the folk of Faretheewell put on quite a spread. So, accepting the Queen's guarantee to be no longer than a sun's blink, the guards stayed at the round table with the locals and ate their fill of the best stew and greens the woodland could provide.

It wasn't a new part of the forest or undiscovered, unmapped land. She'd flown that way on occasion before, albeit at height. She enjoyed the air there. It felt lighter, although that may have been due to the fact that she had no guardsmen tailing her. (She'd know if they were. Security detail believed themselves discrete when they were anything but). No, to spend time in this place was another kind of existence, a freer one where she found her breath came more deeply and her wings flitted with greater ease.

The queen flew in figures of eight around the trees at full pelt, faster than she ever might were she being observed. It was unbecoming of a monarch to live so wildly and exert such energy, so she pushed herself harder and harder until the rush of it made her head burst with stars, and she whooped and laughed then rested against a decrepit silver birch that was fit to crash to the ground any day now.

A wisp of smoke caught Janet's eye. At first she assumed it to be a campfire–the people had been known to forage this deep in the forest, although usually they kept within a reasonable number of heifer's lengths from the village, and she'd already flown further than most people would dare to stray. As open as Diamond was to visitors, there were still wild parts with wild things in them that didn't adhere to niceties.

She darted between the trees, nearing the smoke. If her guardsmen could see what a risk she was taking they'd have squealed in wide-eyed horror. But she wanted to smell it up close, to feel it on her wings, in her hair. Her grandmother would be smiling from the clouds at all this, of course. Grammy was a wild one, too.

Janet came to an abrupt halt. There was no campsite, no people toasting corn on sticks in the flames, no fire that she could see. Just light and curling tendrils of something else. Not smoke. Oh no, not smoke at all.

Beneath the–what was it, vapour?–a glowing hole the size of the citadel's great round window gaped in the forest floor. Janet drifted closer, closer, barely noticing that she was out in the open and at risk of capture, attack, or worse.

She was lucky that the nastiest predators kept to the darkest corners, far beyond Midwood and to the south. Strong as she was, as fleet of wing, if a number of them cornered her without backup she'd be carved up and skewered quick as spit. It wasn't spoken of how some still considered fairy flesh a delicacy. To do so would be to admit that outers didn't always play kindly, however welcoming you may be.

Not here, though. Even they wouldn't dare tread on Faretheewell or its bordering territories to hunt the winged–especially the royal winged–and risk the kind of backlash that would inevitably ensue.

Janet eased closer still. From there she realised that the vapour emanating from the hole in the ground was not vapour either, but a pure and powerful magic, drifting up and tossed about in ripples of its own radiating force.

At that moment the queen cared not about predators, be they the four or two-legged kind. This was bigger than that: a spontaneous rift. A slip. She'd heard tell of them but always as legend. Nobody in living memory had ever heard of one springing forth in the real world.

'Fuuuck.' The word escaped her lips as she forgot her upbringing.

This was no fire, she knew. This, like the four corner gates, was a doorway to somewhere else. And Janet had a fair idea where it led.

19. SHRINE

The Skylark sisters crouched behind the enormous stone monolith. The girl child would be along any moment now and they'd be here with their traps and magics to steal her away as per the plan.

Seemed their idea to get a head start on A Troop and the others was as smart an imagining as any city folk could muster. The rest of the hummer crews, along with the woodland recruits (recruits–like they had a choice!) were well beyond snatching range and would likely be a thousand brown heifers away by the time the girl trod the nearby section of path.

She was with the goblin, alright. They'd seen him, or rather they'd smelled him. This might actually work.

Mae didn't speak of magic coins or wishing wells or wings, but Eryl knew what lay at the foot of her sister's wants. Didn't have to be a seer to see the obvious. She didn't blame her either. The thought of having her own wings torn off, to be grounded for all time, to have to walk everywhere, brimmed a vomitous anger in her chest.

That wasn't to say Eryl didn't have motives of her own. Any Diamonder would agree: get the opportunity to make things right and, by fuck, you take it. Take it and ram it where the boss least expects it to go.

Mae reached in the pockets of her gown and pulled out a grouping of nettle flowers bound with vole-hair cord. She laid it on the shrine with the other offerings. It wasn't honeysuckle, as was the custom. Difficult to come by those without trekking beyond the borders and into the outer West. But it was the gesture that mattered. We remember you, it said. We remember you fondly and with love.

Eryl smiled at her wingless sister.

The twin fairies waited for the outer girl and goblin to arrive.

***

Marie caught up with Muggins as they rounded the last corner, by which time the air was syrupy thick with the scent of honeysuckle. It was then she saw the flowers, piled high and scattered all about what seemed to be a stone monument tucked into a narrow crescent of trees.

'Look!' she said, not even considering that her pudgy companion might already know full well about this place.

'Queen's Table,' came the goblin's flat reply. He'd have kept walking had the girl not stopped.

'Queen?' Marie said. 'Like an actual queen?' She noticed symbols carved into the stone that reminded her of things she'd seen when visiting her father at St Bart's. 'Is she...dead?'

'Dunno,' Muggins said. 'Not for definitely, anyways. Goes missing, like, out of the blue. One night: woof, she's gone.' Muggins looked up. The girl appeared startled. 'Oh, she's not in there, biggun. No, no. Empty, that is. Just a table.'

'They didn't find her?'

'Not as I knows about.'

Marie stepped cautiously off the path. The table, as Muggins called it, looked so weatherworn, decades old, that she wondered how it could be sat in the forest that long and yet still be adorned with flowers as if it were put there only yesterday.

'Lots of flowers for just a table,' Marie said. 'Looks like someone believes it's more than that.'

She wanted to feel the rough stone against her fingertips and to lower her face to the honeysuckle blooms and breathe them in. They smelled like a garden in summertime–a memory she closely associated with her father, before he upped and died.

'Nope,' the goblin said. 'Just a hunking slab of stone. They likes to put bits on it. Suppose they be hoping it'll bring her back or something. Boggled if I know. You'd reckon by now they'd sees it as a bad lot, but nah. Shitterbugs be like that, persistent little gerps.'

Marie wasn't listening. She was too busy crunching across dead twigs and leaf mould and was nearly at the shrine.

The goblin spoke louder, almost too loud to be talking to Marie, who wasn't so far away. 'Whatever you be thinking of doing,' he called out, 'I'll tell you, it ain't be smart. You hear me? Muggins knows better. Listen or else bad things happen. Clear?'

A pause. Marie stopped then, as if taking notice of him for the first time. She turned to look back.

'Bad things,' he said again, reiterating for effect.

Thinking better of what she guessed now might be a fool's folly, Marie took a step back toward the path, when her foot met with something on the ground. It made a sound like a gentle clink. She looked down to see a small metal object glinting through the leaves. The grass and weeds had grown about it such that it must've been there, unseen, for a long while. She reached to pick it up and turned it this way and that. It was most definitely a coin, but a strange one.

The coin had a loop at the top, as if it belonged on a necklace or on a pin to be mounted on a breast pocket, more medal than coin. It was similar in feel and weight to the medals her old grandad left in a box in the attic of the house at Marble Falls.

Muggins craned to look. 'Whatcha gots there, girly?'

Marie slipped the coin into the side pocket of her backpack thinking such a pretty object should not be left to fester on the ground. 'Nothing,' she said. 'Dropped my key is all.'

* * *

From behind the stone altar, Mae almost exploded out of her own skin. She would've rushed the child and snatched the damn coin from her grubby fingers had her sister not reached a swift arm about her neck and clamped a firm hand over her mouth.

'No!' Eryl said in a harsh whisper. 'You heard him: bad things.' And when she was sure Mae could be trusted not to dash after the girl, who was by then back on the path and walking away, she slowly loosened her grip.

'But, the token–'

'Yes,' Eryl said. 'Dumb stupid luck a biggun would stumble on it. But we can't allow ourselves to lose sight of the end. I know how much you need this, Mae. Really I do. And I'll help you all I can just as soon as we've done what has to be done. Please try, Mae. For me? For all of us? This is more than one pair of wings.' She raised a hand to her sister's cheek to caress away tears. 'You see that, don't you?'

Easy for you to say, Mae thought.

Hidden deep within the wingless fairy's broken mind, her master's words tickled at the edges of what she knew to be true: *Do as I ask and all will be returned to you, fourfold.*

Mae nodded. Perhaps at her sister, perhaps at the echoed words of her master. Taking the child to Borealis to curry favour with the captain was one thing, but the girl had a token now–a silver fucking token!–so despite the face she presented to Eryl, or anyone else for that matter, the rules of this war had changed.

20. A SIMPLE CASE OF GOOD VS. EVIL

(PART 2)

Danny knew how it felt to be on the underside of someone else's thumb. He'd never been a hero. Nor did it serve his interests to stand up to his father. Running away and hiding in the cave at the foss was about the bravest thing he'd ever done.

He looked at the glass jar the fairy had manifested and given him, thought about what she'd asked him to do, not *directly* in return for her kindness (nothing so crass as that). Still it felt to the boy like a debt was being called in.

It wasn't a big ask. Heck, he'd chased fireflies before, caught them and housed them in a beer glass and played with them in his room. Watched them hop and flutter about, their tummies flashing up a storm. Then, when they lay flat on their backs, legs wriggling, he'd jiggle them until they no longer did much of anything. What was one more?

But this wasn't a game. For the first time in his life his actions would be of great consequence. It was, as Two had eloquently and tearfully explained, important to her home world that he helped her.

Important. What a wonderful word. Didn't it then follow that he was important? Two had certainly seemed to think so.

Danny pictured the slow and steady destruction of a previously untouched and magical land. It wasn't difficult to imagine people doing as they always did, moving in and building their greedy machines, chopping down forests, stealing from the kingdom the fairy had told him the name of (and which he promptly forgot).

Two described how the queen of this other place was blind to the wants and needs of her people. That she had allowed, maybe even invited, the industrialisation of their world while sitting back on her throne of gold to enjoy the spoils as her subjects suffered in squalor. (Of course the fairy didn't put it quite like that. She phrased it to make sense to the boy, dumbed it down some, not wishing to lose her young audience).

'I should warn you-' Two glanced toward the cave opening, then back, conspiratorially. 'She plans to do the same here. There's another way through, Daniel. A back door, if you will. She uses it as her own private corridor between here and there.'

Danny thought for a moment. 'The foss?'

'The foss,' Two nodded.

The boy and the fairy talked and talked. After a while, Two felt sure that Danny believed he'd come up with the idea himself. He was after all a very clever boy, as she reminded him often, whose actions would go on to save worlds. It was the darkest of night when she finally hummed away to join the others outside.

'Come live with us,' she said on her way out, almost as if she'd just thought of it there and then. 'With the queen defeated, my land will need a brave new leader.'

The fairy had spoken earlier of a castle high on a hill with a view that looked out over the entire kingdom. 'It's yours if you want it, Daniel. Would you like your own castle? My people will be so grateful. You'll never want for anything again.'

So it was agreed. The boy would feign illness or distress to draw the queen away, while Two and her friends (who Danny never met, hidden as they stayed in the undergrowth outside) would distract the guards somehow.

He'd take his chance when it came.

He'd be important.

Danny blew out the candle and felt his way to the mouth of the cave, clutching the jar with its tight fitting lid close to his body. It was no ordinary jar. Patterns roiled under the glass. Two said it had been impregnated with a special magic which formed a barrier that not even an evil queen could break through.

Hold tight, he told himself. One shot at this. One shot to save her world.

The constant rush of the falls guided Danny to where his attention should focus. Then another sound layered in with the rest. Not Two and her group, this was a gentler sound, a soft fluttering rather than a hum. And Danny knew that Two was right about the secret doorway, that the fairy queen and her entourage were at that moment making their way through a tunnel behind the foss.

The boy thought of the castle in the hills–*his castle*–how far away it sounded and how exciting the prospect of being far away was. He felt for the first time in forever the satisfaction of not just a full belly but a full heart, and he liked it. Wanted more of it. He pictured Two, beautiful and kind in ways that made his head swim and his imagination run wild.

Tiny specks of light twinkled over the pool.

Danny Evers felt the cold of the jar in his hands and slowly, quietly, unscrewed the lid.

The queen was near.

He reminded himself that under no circumstances was he to fall for her lies.

21. A TROOP 2.0

There was no scenario in which Squad Leader Rickett would allow A Troop to fuck this up again. Fair enough, they'd made the mistake of being too recruit-heavy, utilised too many Faretheewell civvies to make it work last time around. Local knowledge, she told the group as they cruised in formation, was all well and good until the fighting started. Then what you needed was firepower and the willingness to use it.

This was a hummer squad now, she said, first and foremost. And hummers didn't put up with the kind of West gate crap the forest flutterers did. Magic or no magic it was time for action. They'd be as well not to forget who they were.

There was zero chance of that. And no point bringing Green 5 into it either. Rickett knew the image of their last squad leader's decapitation had been permanently branded on the eyes of her team, as it had on her own. And while it was true that a healthy dose of fear proved a good motivator, pure white-knuckle terror did not.

Hummers were tough but not without feeling.

'Faij. Varla.'

'Boss?'

'Check around the well at ground level. I want to be damned sure nobody snuck in or out. Got it? Nobody.'

'Aye, Boss.' The young gunwings dropped out of line and disappeared through the canopy.

'Bomber. Klick. You too. That's a lot of ground to cover. You see the biggun, plus or minus the gobshite, hang back. Await my word.'

'Boss.' The second pair zipped downward toward the forest floor, following the first.

'Free?' Rickett turned to face the young hummer who'd been angling all season to be her second in command. She made a point of not softening her voice. There could be no favourites out in the field.

'Boss?'

'Get to Janet's Table,' Rickett said. 'That's where they were headed. At least we learned that much from the last recon. If they're still there, stay low. We'll catch you up after a sweep around what's left of the village.'

'Boss.' Gunwing Free tapped her feet together and darted away, but not before curling up the side of her mouth in a secretive half-smile that told Rickett their encounter the night before was still at the forefront of her mind.

Rickett didn't reciprocate. She didn't much fancy her head taken off.

***

A shout came from the direction of the shrine just as the sun tipped the hills, casting shadows through the treetops, darkening the woodland below. The girl and the goblin had indeed been there, yes, but they'd moved on. Where they'd moved on to was anyone's guess as the path split off in any number of combinations from there. Something like a vascular system were you to view it from above, which at this time of year, with the trees still laden with leaves, you could not.

'Fuck's sake.' Rickett made the drop from cruise height to ground level in a flit, stopping just short of the ferns then humming carefully down to her feet. There were some skills that came with being partial West-blooded, at least, so as the only member of the troop with a lick of green to her name it fell upon her to pick up the scent from there.

It vexed the hardened soldier to have to rely on her repressed woodland traits. She would scrub them from her insides if she could, lest she be mistaken for one of those softling shitters. She was so sick of their run-and-hide attitude to what was going on in their own lands. So you dropped your guard, opened the doors and let them in and now you wonder why you got what you got? Boo-hoo. Pick up a weapon and fight, you dumb fucks. (It was no accident that Borealis had chosen Rickett for squad leader, given how they shared a common view on that).

'How long, Boss?' Free asked, from a safe enough length away to ensure any possible retaliatory sparks from the squad leader wouldn't reach her.

Rickett pulled a fern frond from its stalk and sniffed it. She looked about the clearing at the floral offerings. Resting against the stone table, tucked between the sprawling mix of pink and yellow honeysuckle, she spied a humble bunch of nettle flowers. 'Not long enough,' she said.

She felt it, then, the subtlest of waves in the air, rippling trails left by a recent disturbance. 'That way,' she said. 'Find them and bring her to me.'

Free didn't need telling twice. 'Yes, Boss.'

The young gunwing called to the others, rallying them together and guiding them away through the trees with all the leadership of a worthy second in command. There was no mistaking her aspiration or how much she enjoyed her work. She was destined for greatness, that one, if she could only get a handle on whatever it was inside of her that fed her hunger for war.

When Rickett was quite sure A Troop was out of sight, she turned back to the shrine. 'You can come out now, ladies,' she said, shaking her head.

Slowly, Eryl and Mae Skylark crept out from behind a large outcrop of knapwort where they'd been hiding since the girl and the goblin left some several blinks earlier. The sisters met the soldier with heads bowed. They fully expected the worst.

Squad leader Rickett reached out and placed a firm hand on each of their shoulders and the rogue forest fairies, eyes closed, held their quivering breaths.

Rickett was intimidating beyond measure. Armoured up in full combat gear and weaponry, she could blow a jumping flea out of the air from twenty black heifers away and you simply didn't argue with that.

We're done, Eryl thought.

Agreed, Mae though back.

Rickett paused for a moment to gather herself. 'Don't do that again,' she said.

22. RICKETT

Leddy Rickett was an infant when she moved to the North with her parents. It wouldn't have done for her father to take his wife and young child back to Faretheewell. Remember, these were the days before such things were accepted as ordinary. Before the new ways had been fully ushered in.

Back then, you stayed true to your world, mixed with your own, and you sure as shoot didn't breed outside of your same kind. The North and the West had many shared attributes, that's as maybe. Virtues and magics were not among them.

But love doesn't always follow the rule of Diamond law any more than wings follow a breeze and along came Leddy in all her messy, fluttering glory and oh, how her parents adored her. She was the best of each of them in every imaginable way.

Despite this, Boon and Flora Rickett felt the pull of their respective homelands: Boon, to Faretheewell, and Flora, to the floating islands of the North. Different as they'd been raised from one another, neither was meant for such ostracism, however self-imposed it may have been.

In any other place or time, a coin toss might've been enough to decide. The draw of a straw. Going their separate ways was out of the question, regardless of the consequences, now they had a child to care for. Had they been around to see all the changes that were to come, they might have considered themselves early pioneers in that respect. But things were rarely as simple as all that, certainly when it came to a choosing of such magnitude. Careful thought had to be given to the future that presented itself in either world. Theirs and Leddy's lives depended on it.

Where to go?

Hummer, Flora was too strong for the woodland life and would never fit within that silhouette of fairyhood. She wasn't a stallholder, a grower, a seamstress, or a maker of tinctures. She was lean and strong, built for long-haul flight, and her lungs were of a higher function having lived a life at altitude, commuting from one rock to another, one island to another, training her entire adolescence and young adulthood.

Even if none of that mattered, she didn't have the born skills of a Westerner. What was one to do when surrounded by those who lived each day according to their innate magicalness if you yourself had none?

Besides, Faretheewell at that time was fiercely protective of their unspoiled lands. So while the natives would likely have tried to welcome her into the fold– they were more open to such things than her Northern kin–that would only happen if (a big if) they first let her through the quarantine.

Boon Rickett, however, was a green to the core. To go north would mean either death or weakness, neither of which was desirable in a society that deemed him a homemaker. (It should be noted that the North's idea of a homemaker is that of an axe-wielding, log-lugging, quite literal, home maker, *a maker of homes*, while with few exceptions the mothers and sisters, nieces and aunts go off to train).

Boon would be expected to pull his weight. A challenging prospect given his lesser woodland wings and his lower stamina in comparison to his Northern counterparts. He simply wasn't designed for sustained hovering in the thin air. To not have the facility to rest on a branch now and then? To have to self-propel across vast distances? The thought of it made his back cramp.

By way of compromise, they lived the first few months of Leddy's life on the outskirts of Must in an unnamed and rundown suburb known to those who were aware of it as The Scratt, where folk didn't ask questions and made it their business not to know yours.

This worked for a while and the Ricketts kept to themselves, until changes in policy allowed people to transfer across from the West gate sphere in greater numbers, and the bigguns built upon the native Diamonders' low-level structures with their high shining workplaces and belching smoke towers.

Flora would whisper to Leddy bedtime stories about strings of unclaimed rocky islands at the end of the world, in the far archipelagos of the North, on which they could land and settle and make a place of their own. She said some of these islands even held freshwater lakes, which fed the green that she knew Boon pined for in his sleep. If they could make it that far, if they could be left to prosper and not dragged into conflicts not of their making, might it be worth a shot?

But of course Boon would have to suppress his gifts. Dead giveaway, those.

For the longest time it felt like an unattainable dream. So the Ricketts tolerated the steady increase in the biggun population. They were far enough from Must that they rarely came into contact with the people anyway. Waste from the discharging stacks was another matter, but even that wasn't what eventually drove them out.

When the Southern creepers first began showing their nasty faces, squatting in corners, masked by shadow, casting their eyes about and searching for things of others they could take, Boon and Flora knew time was short.

There weren't many at first, which is how it always went with their kind: creep, creep, creep. Nothing so as you'd notice if you weren't paying attention. The South-gaters hadn't strayed from their own lands since the last recorded moonfall. For them to cross the border into Diamond now meant something was most surely up.

The people had no clue about the relevance of all this. 'Heads up their own fat arses,' Boon said. But then only those who'd lived their lives in Diamond, heard the tales passed on from elder to elder, from troll to troll, had the wisdom not to linger south of the capital if those hungry bleeders came a-wandering.

And as much noise and mess as the bigguns made, they'd been around Diamond mere blinks, comparatively speaking. They weren't to know.

Little Leddy had just started to find her wings when the words appeared, scratched deep into the wood panels lining the outside of their small home, one grey morning in a small corner of The Scratt: DRAFT DODGER CUNT. And: YUM YUM, LITTLE ONE. Claw marks ragged about the edges of the words like twisted frames. Next to that: two dots above a curled line, meant as a smiling face.

Flora wasn't one for crying, but she sobbed that day. Angry, broken tears lurched out of her for hours as Boon held her and little Leddy napped by the fire. Had it been one of the neighbours, one of the creeping South gate shadows, or someone sent from the North to pass on a very clear message? You defect, you pay, draft dodger. One way or another.

No matter. The impact it had was the same.

Perhaps it was imagined. Perhaps it felt worse than it was. Still, Flora feared for her child's safety. By then, it was a matter of when not if they'd leave. And before season's end, they packed up their things, gathered Leddy's few beloved toys, and headed north.

There were guards posted at the North gate. This was nothing new and Flora had warned her husband that they might need to answer questions on the purpose of their trip, the nature of their relationship, and so on. Boon wondered if they'd overestimated their chances of safe passage, even with a child in tow. She was half hummer. That had to count for something, right?

This argument appeared to hold at least some water and they were granted entry, but only after Flora was made to sign paperwork regarding her North citizen status and her willingness to rejoin the military if required.

This hardly seemed important at the time. They figured if the hummers were to come looking for them they'd be long-disappeared, ensconced on their island in the furthest archipelago. Firstly, how would they find them? And, secondly, why would they bother?

At last, it looked as if freedom, a life worth living, was within reach for Boon, Flora, and their beautiful, blossoming child. This wasn't to be, however. No sooner had they entered the Northern skies than a council crew, backed up by a hummer squad, rounded the Ricketts up and took them in.

An example needed to be made.

Not that she could remember it–or if she could remember, that she would ever talk about it–but that was to be the last time Leddy Rickett saw her parents alive.

23. THE CORPSE

The goblin was searching for something, Marie felt sure of it. She'd been watching him a while now and had noticed how at every turn and upon entering every new stretch of path he'd scan the section of forest around them. He kept on and on about the fairies, or 'shitterbugs' as he called them, despite not seeing any this entire time, to the point where the girl had begun to doubt they existed at all, except in the goblin's funny little head.

Marie didn't much like his foul mouth, but kept quiet about it. She realised early on that the poor creature probably hadn't been around children much, or else he'd do what all grownups did and default to child-speak. She'd far sooner hear cusses than be patronised.

There was no sign of Dale anywhere and there hadn't been any more buildings, burning ones or otherwise, for a long while. Marie was about ready to call it quits and head home when Muggins let out a triumphant, 'Ah-ha!' and veered off into the woods. She was right, she thought, he had been on the lookout.

Marie followed the goblin's line of sight and noticed a pyramid of felled tree trunks heaped up on top of one another in a clearing off to the side of the path. She wondered briefly if the logs were in fact the bodies of the tree trolls she'd met earlier. The thought gave her shivers, so she pushed it out of her mind.

'Have you found something?' she called to the newly animated Muggins, as she followed on some ways behind him.

'Not for you to be worrying about,' the goblin said. He used language that sounded more succinct, more like the words a person might use than his usual garbled style. 'Go find your friend now, girl. Off you pop.'

There it was again: *girl*, not *girly*.

'Can I help?' Marie said.

Rather than be grateful for the offer, Muggins looked back at her, somewhat irritated. 'Shoo, biggun! Shoo!' He flapped his little goblin hands as if to waft her away then returned to kicking through the leaves. After a moment he wasn't ignoring Marie so much as not registering her presence at all.

How rude, Marie thought to herself. She didn't need the goblin–she didn't need anyone–but she'd gotten used to him being around. 'Okay then,' she said. 'I'll get back to the gate. Be dark soon. Guess I'll come back another day.'

'Right you are,' Muggins said, not bothering to look up.

Marie turned and shuffled back toward the path. 'Right you are,' she repeated quietly.

But before she reached the edge of the clearing, halfway between the pyramid of logs and the path, she stopped and let out an involuntary cry. On the ground, nestled in the shadow of a large rock, was a skeleton, a tiny lifeless skeleton, with wings.

***

It took Marie shrieking to grab the attention of the goblin, but grab it she did. Muggins dashed over to see what all the fuss was about. When he saw the skeleton he let out a tut of disappointment. 'Ugh,' he said. 'Is that it?'

'Look at the poor thing. What do you think happened to it?' Marie reached a hand down, whether to touch it or pick it up she didn't know.

'Don't!' Muggins barked.

Then, 'Don't be touching it, biggun. Cants say as where it's been. Here, I gots it.' His demeanour and vocabulary had returned to that of the hapless goblin Marie had come to know.

Pulling a handkerchief from about his person, Muggins carefully wrapped up the skeleton along with the few remaining shreds of desiccated flesh that hung from it like Spanish moss. He took extra special care of its tiny fragile wings, as if they might crumble away to nothing on contact.

Marie was taken with how gentle he was in his handling of the dead fairy (there was no doubting that's what it was: a dead fairy) considering how disinterested he'd been in it a moment ago. Not even disinterested, more like disdainful, as if it were a smear of cow dung that needed scraping off his foot. She wondered what these fairies had done to him. It must've been something awfully bad for him to hate them quite so much.

He was a strange one alright. Marie couldn't get the measure of him. One minute he was this, the next that. Might these have been standard goblin characteristics where he was from? Were each of them odd little, mood-swinging chaps, changing personality as easily as the wind?

She decided to study him more closely before rushing to a conclusion. It occurred to her that even people were rarely just one thing, easily pushed and swayed by forces outside of their control. They'd respond accordingly, behave accordingly. Hard to imagine why goblins should be any different.

Muggins wandered away with the fairy corpse wrapped in the bundle of cloth. 'I'll finds it a nice place to sleep,' he said, disappearing behind the log pile. When he returned a few minutes later he no longer held the package and Marie guessed he'd dug a hole for it somewhere.

Part of her had wanted to hold the fairy, to examine it, to figure out what happened to it. But she knew it would've been disrespectful to poke around at a dead body like that, so it was as well they buried it safe and sound.

As the goblin ambled back, Marie noticed he was smiling as if he could barely contain his delight. He had a bag slung across his squat body, a leather satchel with a long leather strap that'd been shortened so as to prevent it dragging on the ground.

This clearly wasn't a goblin bag. It was a person bag. And Marie knew it well, had seen it before, could practically smell the cowhide it was sewn out of even from this distance. Her heart skipped.

Muggins paid her no attention and instead tucked the flap of the bag over, latching it shut with the buckle.

In the brief moment before the bag's insides disappeared, Marie just about made out the spine of a book. No, not just any book: a journal. Her eyes widened. She'd seen that before, too.

24. HERE WE GO

The goblin had a fearsome want to see what the girl kept hidden in the pocket of her backpack. He wasn't so great at subtle. He dropped clumsy hints, sought to draw it out of her, get her to tell him what he already assumed to be the case: that she'd found a coin on the ground near Janet's Table. He could feel it burning a hole in there. Damnit, why didn't he spy it first?

The small biggun had no vision for her find or else she'd have long since high-tailed it to the well, with or without his goblin self in tow. Still, this girl was savvy. She dodged his queries like a hummer ducking the swift swipe of the back of his hand. He wondered if he'd given her enough credit. Not quite so slow as her old man, it would appear.

It was obvious that she wanted to get her grubby fingers on the treasure he'd salvaged from the log pile. Hardly surprising. He'd taken care to whet her appetite, having allowed the girl just enough opportunity to sneaky-peek an eyeful of the tattered book. What wasn't clear was why she hadn't straight up asked him for it.

Maybe she had an instinct, or maybe his recent lapse of personality had led her to feel uncomfortable doing the asking. Whatever. He'd keep the book in his metaphorical back pocket for later, a bargaining chip. The girl wasn't to know it would be destroyed like the others either way. He'd dangle that juicy carrot a while longer.

But after a few more bends of the path the girl informed him she planned to turn around at the next junction. She wasn't sure she could remember the way back as it was, and if they took too many more turns she'd be truly lost. She didn't seem to know that the gate was prone to wandering after dark. Not always, but sometimes. And were that to be the case, even if she sprinted the rest of the way home, navigated every last fork correctly, didn't encounter any shitterbugs, she'd likely be stuck in the woods regardless. But he didn't tell her that. It thrilled him to think of it, though.

The goblin knew he was all out of time and ideas. When he at last caved into the inevitable, that waiting and fishing wouldn't get him the coin, he decided upon stealing the thing. He knew outrunning a biggun on the flat was a no-go, but through the woods he felt confident he had the better skills.

He'd have done that in the first place had he not believed her curly head to be rattling with information he could use. Things the window scrubber might've shared with her, anecdotes loaded with truths, cloaked in story.

But, as she had evidently forgotten the most of it, she was of little use to him now. Still, it was best not to let her rot in the woods like the dead fairy, as the people had a habit of searching for the likes of her.

Grab and go, he thought. Grab and go.

'What's that?' Muggins stopped and jabbed a clawed finger at a shadowy patch some way off in the middle distance.

Marie followed the goblin's gaze. 'What are we looking at?' she said.

Before Muggins could curl a finger inside the pocket of her backpack, the girl set off for the area of woodland he'd gestured toward.

Curious little-

Muggins interrupted himself and went after her. There was something in the woods he hadn't planned for. From the path, he'd pointed at nothing. Absolutely nothing. It was a distraction to make the girl look away and allow him to do his thieving. And yet, there was most definitely a change in the air.

'Wait up, biggun!' he called after her.

'I don't see anything,' Marie said, turning on the spot in the dark patch of ground. There were brambles and ferns and saplings all fighting for their place on the forest floor, but little else of note.

Suddenly, a loud crack rang out. Marie covered her ears.

Immediately after came a girlish yelp, which it took the goblin half a blink to realise came from him.

***

Marie turned just in time to see Muggins get his legs pulled out from under him and his view spun wrong-side up, right-side down. He was left dangling and flailing from the trees, trapped inside a mess of hemp netting. Each time he moved, a tiny bell jingled. A sound not unlike Christmas.

'Chuffin shitterbugs!' he raged. 'Get me down! Get me out of here right now!'

Marie walked a few paces until she stood beneath the furious goblin. But before she could figure out how to get him down–if such a thing were possible; he was higher than her arms reached–she noticed the journal he'd taken from the log pile clearing earlier. It had dropped from the leather bag onto the ground and fallen open. Straight away, she recognised the writing as her father's.

Muggins saw the girl looking at the book. He stopped flailing, then, watched as the realisations played out on her face one by one.

'Leave that,' he said, forcing a smile. 'Help old Muggins down, girly. There's a nice biggun.'

Marie wasn't listening. She reached for the book, picked it up. Some of the pages were torn out, but that didn't matter. She stroked the words as she read them.

A sound pulled her back to the forest, a vibration growing in strength, far off but closing fast. She felt it as much as heard it.

The goblin shook his net cage, suddenly and violently. 'They be coming, biggun. No time to reads. Down! Down! Gets me down!'

Marie saw the humming cloud swirl and weave through the trees toward them. She didn't know much about fairies, only that the goblin was afraid of them and that there was an unpleasant backstory she wasn't a party to. There was no time for her to do anything but try to escape. She looked at Muggins and he looked back. They both knew how this was going to play out.

'I'm sorry.'

The goblin's eyes widened. 'No, no, no-' He tried to grab at her, but she was too far and his stubby hands caught on the netting.

Marie stumbled backwards and then turned around to face the path, moving away from the gathering noise. She tucked the book under her arm and ran. She didn't look back, as sure as she was of anything that even a momentary pause would mean certain capture for her as well, and what good would that do?

So it was that she didn't see A Troop swarm the place where she'd been standing a few seconds ago. Nor did she see the true and hideous face of the goblin, his veil of stolen magic wearing off, as he screamed and screamed for her to come back.

25. FLY

The Skylarks followed behind as Rickett caught up with A Troop. They were entering an area of the forest previously laid with traps and mines, so if the girl and the goblin were anywhere nearby they'd soon know about it, be it by bell or boom. Rickett wanted the girl in one piece, preferably breathing, but the others weren't fussy. Borealis could work with it either way.

To Eryl's immense relief, Rickett had at some point picked up on the fact that her grounded sister wasn't functioning at full capacity, and not just because her wings were gone. Much as it bothered her to speak negatively of her twin, she could no longer hide the fact that Mae was a liability both to herself and others. The front line of battle was not a safe place for her to be. For anyone.

So the squad leader went ahead, told the sisters to hang back. 'We've got this,' she said, in a way quite apart from the usual North army tone.

And when a bell jingled in the distance–a sign that a trap had been sprung–Rickett and her crew darted away as a singular swirling mass through the trees, leaving the Skylarks alone once again.

***

'Talk to me, Mae.'

They were sat cross-legged on the ground, sheltered by a lightly bobbing fern frond. Eryl waited, but Mae was looking past her as she often did nowadays, her head slightly cocked to the side as if she were listening intently to someone speak.

Since forever they'd heard each other's thoughts. Now when Eryl listened in she was often met with words she didn't understand, voices she didn't know, many more than ought to have been there, engaged in nonsensical talk. Sometimes these voices were whispers, sometimes shouts, sometimes laughter. But always, always wails of despair.

'Mae?'

Still nothing. Eryl took to her feet in frustration.

'He says you're here to save me, sister,' Mae said after a while, a hint of good humour now pulling at her lips. Still she didn't make eye contact, the effect of which Eryl found quite disconcerting. 'He says you were given to me to serve a purpose. From the womb, Eryl. Isn't that wonderful?'

'What are you on about? Who's *he*?' While Eryl was glad her sister was at last speaking aloud again, this was not the conversation she'd hoped to have. 'Mae, please. You're worrying me.'

The wingless Mae, half a blink younger than her twin, looked up and stared Eryl squarely in the eyes. 'Don't be afraid,' she said. 'He's chosen you. Don't you see?'

'I want you to get better, Mae. How can we do that?'

Mae smiled warmly, then, and lifted her gaze to the forest canopy. 'Take me there.' She pointed up. 'Fly with me? I do miss it, so.'

'Of course!' Eryl helped Mae to stand and pulled her close, rocking her gently. 'You only needed to ask. I didn't want to be the one to say in case it upset you further. But of course I'll take you up. You must know I love you, sister. Here.' She took Mae's arms and wrapped them around her own shoulders. 'Hold on tight.'

No sooner had she spoken the words than the Skylarks shot upwards into the branches above. Mae let out a joyous squeal. This was her first time airborne since the day of her punishment. Though her wounds had healed, in some ways they never would. Yet here she was flying again.

'Higher!' she said, tipping her head back and pulling on Eryl's neck, steering her into a spiral as she flew up and up and up.

As the sisters crested the treetops, Mae gasped at the beauty of the golden sky, the sun dwindling over the hills ahead of its inevitable descent. It would turn dark soon. But for now Diamond was as glorious as could be.

They hovered there in silence a while, Eryl keeping them effortlessly aloft on translucent wings, Mae dangling like a doll from her sister. It was everything, this moment. Everything the wingless woodland fairy had hoped it would be.

'I'm sorry,' Mae said, in a fragile, almost child-like voice. She sounded like she did when they were small.

Eryl was reminded of how she'd always stood up for her sister, offering protection even when she might've done well to let the younger (dare she say weaker?) sibling fend for herself. 'Don't apologise,' she said. 'There's really no need.'

Mae looked up with the most curious expression. 'Thank-you for your sacrifice,' she said, before slicing Eryl's throat with the sharpened blade she had hidden in her bodice. 'You will not be forgotten, I promise.'

Eryl clutched at the wound that opened around her neck, that pulsed blood out over the both of them. No words came–no air travelled far enough from her lungs to where the words were made–just gurgles and wheezing and gulping sounds. Shortly after that her skin began turning a distinct shade of blue. Her arms flopped to her sides.

'I love you.' Mae kissed her dying sister on the cheek and carefully stroked away stray hairs from her face. She licked at the blood that trickled down her own fingers then placed her lips about the wound on her sister's throat and drank.

A moment later, Eryl Skylark's eyes rolled back in their sockets, her wings abruptly failed, and they both fell crashing into the canopy and down, catching branches as they went, sending the sisters tumbling away from each other until they eventually hit the forest floor with a crunch.

It took the wingless fairy a few blinks to shake the wind out of herself, then a few blinks more to locate the body of her sister some several beige heifers distance. But find her, she did, and the wings came off easily after that.

She thought of what she'd be able to do, where she'd be able to go. She considered the pact she had made with her master and how she must fulfil her duty else lose her wings again.

Her wings.

They lay there as still as her dead sister. Mae took the small pouch of dust and sprinkled it onto the freshly severed raw wing edges.

Her wings.

They twitched on the ground, glistening, suddenly alive again, stunning in their vitality. Mae turned, raised her arms to the trees above and allowed herself to fall backwards. It surged through her body like lightning as the wings connected themselves to her scars. In an intense, orgasmic rush, they tore into the flesh in search of muscles and nerves to attach to, blood vessels to feed from.

Her beloved wings.

Once they had rooted and she was able to flit and angle them at will, Mae felt a power like nothing she'd known, not even before the punishment. She, like the others of green heritage, always had magic to a degree, but this was something else, something darker.

'I'm ready,' she said to the voice most prominent.

'Good,' the voice replied.

She stood, then, and gave Eryl's flightless, lifeless body a sympathetic glance before taking to the air. It was worth it, she thought. And she'd do it again in a heartbeat.

26. WHAT WE LEAVE BEHIND

George Fisher was no more than a lad when he found the gateway to Diamond. That summer in Marble Falls had crawled along at a mind-numbingly slow pace. He counted the remaining days until he would at long last swap the quiet Yorkshire town for the bright lights of Birmingham, having scraped together enough marks to get into the university third on his list. He planned to study English and creative writing. After which, he felt sure, he would henceforth be known to one and all as a literary genius.

His choice of subject was in no small part due to a conversation he'd overheard in school, years earlier, between a group of older boys who said that girls were statistically more likely to shag you if you got your name on the cover of a book. George didn't know then (or now) if this was true. But if his awkward attempts at asking Selina Boyd to the leavers' dance were a clue to his current chances, it couldn't do him any harm to stack the deck a little.

He had yet to meet Barbara.

At eighteen, George, like most if not all of his peers, had no understanding of the kind of love that didn't require tricks or gimmicks to lure a woman into bed. That would come after graduation, during a chance encounter on the side of an office block (him on a cleaning gurney, her at a secretarial desk, inside).

Meanwhile, he helped his ageing parents around the house and garden for a bit of extra cash. They liked having him there as much as he enjoyed spending time with them, each quietly knowing that their remaining time together would be limited by life expectancy and, soon, distance. Far from George's mind was the fact that in a handful of years the cottage would become his.

The hedgerow at the end of the garden had grown wild for as long as he could remember. It was while cutting it back one afternoon (a job his father hadn't flagged but that George had taken upon himself to do) that he saw the tunnel winding back through the brambles and branches. It was narrow enough to remain hidden from prying eyes, but just about wide enough for him to clamber through if he went on his belly, commando-style.

He wasn't able to explore the tunnel that day. Before he got the chance, his mother called him back to the house with what George came to realise was a ruse. It occurred to him much later that his parents had been all too aware of the tunnel, and likely the gate and Diamond, too, but had steered him away from it, allowed it to disappear and be forgotten, encouraging the weeds to grow out of hand so nobody would think to look there.

George fully intended to go back. He set a mental reminder to wait until such a time that his parents were busy so he could return to explore the tunnel and where it led.

But life had a way of going by.

George left for university, and the longer he lived away from the cottage, known to locals as Darkwood, the less he thought about the hedgerow and what it might contain. After six months, maybe a year, it was the furthest thing from his mind, school and girls having erased the bulk of what came before.

He read, he wrote, he drank, he smoked, given half a chance he played the deeply troubled artist card and pulled himself a psych student. Oh, how they loved a project! In truth he was neither deep nor troubled, but no matter. That was the game they played back then, and it was reasonable to say that all parties knew the score.

George kept a journal. It was a habit he'd developed in his early teens as a way of navigating the testosterone trials of youth. To write his thoughts down meant no longer needing to hold them inside or carry them on his back. To George, the act of swirling a pen across paper was profoundly meditative. He found it to be the most satisfying and productive when using a fountain pen, the type with a reservoir you filled from a bottle of ink. He liked the ritual of it, which tended to act as a trigger for the words to flow.

Each evening he'd capture the day's highlights. It was unusual for him to skip a day, so it might have seemed strange that were one to read his earlier journals (he had filled many a hardback A5 over the years) there would be no mention of the tunnel he found in the hedgerow that day. Not a word. Maybe it was a mere oversight, or maybe he decided it was too unimportant a detail to record, who knows?

It wasn't until several years later, shortly after George learned of his inheritance, the cottage he'd loved so much as a child, that he and his then-pregnant wife, Barbara, moved their meagre belongings in and memories of that day began calling to him from the end of the garden.

It might be of use to know that the work of George Fisher could be discerned by a number of literary quirks, affectations that he enlisted in order to make his writing, both fiction and non, stand out. Though ordinary in practically every other way, George-the-writer endeavoured to be extraordinary on the page, with varying levels of success.

One such affectation was how he began each entry in his journals with the words, 'On this day'. He liked how it sounded as if the events of his life were of great value and therefore demanded to be documented. You might argue that this was an act of self-prophecy: make your days sound grand and they shall become so. Fake it 'till you make it, as the saying goes. And that certainly was true of poor George.

Grand, that is, until they weren't.

An unfortunate irony was that on the day of his death he didn't have his trusted journal at hand, having departed Diamond in such haste that morning and leaving behind his current volume on a felled tree. He'd thought to go back for it, knowing what it contained, but had seen how the kingdom was changing and how the people had grown afraid. He witnessed something atrocious that day which made his swift exit essential, and return not wise. He fully expected that to be the last time he set foot through the gate. And how right he was.

To have noted the circumstances leading up to the fall that killed him would have proved useful to those that followed in his footsteps, and most useful of all to his young daughter, Marie, especially when she took off in search of adventure through the hedgerow, the gate, the woods of Faretheewell and beyond.

Still, even without such details George Fisher's last journal would turn out to be his most important work, albeit posthumously, and forever one 'On this day' too short.

27. STRANGE ALLIES

Marie thought she could still hear the goblin screaming after her, *come back, come back, come back!* Over and over again. It might've just been that the horrible sound of it was imprinted on her eardrums somehow like the music imprinted onto her father's old vinyl records. Sooner or later, a noise like that was bound to carve a permanent groove.

She'd wanted to help Muggins get down from the trap. But the roaring, humming murmuration that swept through the trees after her had filled Marie with an awful fear the likes of which she hadn't felt since the day she found out she would never again walk the hills or go exploring with her father.

Wait-

She couldn't hear the humming things anymore. Or maybe she could, but only if she turned her head to listen more closely. Yes, there it was: quiet, low-key, barely there, blended into the forest soundscape.

Marie slowed to a brisk walk and risked a glance around. The swarm that she had been so sure would engulf her at any moment was hanging back, seeming to avoid the tree stumps that punctuated this section of forest.

She was back at the troll graveyard.

Muggins had been afraid of the tree trolls, Marie remembered. Was it possible that the fairies were, too? It certainly looked that way. She stopped to catch her breath and leaned against a nearby stump, waking the troll inside.

'Excuse me?' the tree troll said with a disgruntled yawn, as one very well might upon being woken from a long and satisfying dream, to find a human child treating one's head as a perch. 'Would you please not do that?'

This wasn't the same troll Marie had spoken to earlier, she realised, but it had the same rasping tone that put her in mind of a dying branch splitting from its parent bough. She also realised that at some point since their last encounter she'd stopped thinking of the trolls as its so much as thems.

'I'm sorry,' she said.

'Yes, yes. I dare say you are.' The troll sighed. 'Always sorry. Never not doing the thing to be sorry for.'

'I didn't mean to sit on you. It's just that I was being followed, you see, and then I wasn't, and then I needed to stop a minute to think, and then there you were.'

'There I was,' the troll echoed. He sounded as if he'd been through this a thousand times and was thoroughly over it. 'Just because something's there doesn't mean it's yours to do with however you please. Don't they teach you that where you're from? Stupid question. Course they don't. Else you wouldn't be here now, am I right?'

This troll was rather a lot grumpier than the one Marie had spoken to earlier. But then, she thought, she hadn't tried to sit on that last fella.

'I really am sorry.' The fight left her voice, the adrenaline surge wearing off. Marie felt she might for the first time that day shed a tear. Only out of exhaustion, mind you. Not sadness or anything like it.

The troll's face softened and he gave the girl a moment before speaking again. 'They won't get you in here, child,' he said. 'Wouldn't dare. All fight, that lot, no stomach for reckoning. And believe me when I tell you, we're ready to reckon with those that planted us here. Overdue, that chat is. Long overdue.'

Marie fumbled with the journal she'd taken from the goblin. The sun was setting. Long shadows merged to usher in the evening dark. *The gloaming,* Marie thought. That's what her father would've called this time of day. The word always conjured in her something between sadness and dread.

But the feel of the book brought her some small measure of comfort. To know her father had held the same leather binding in his own broad, soft hands. That the words inside were his. It felt to Marie like the book was her very own shield and the words contained inside bristled with magic.

The troll lowered his voice to a whisper. 'Calm yourself, little one. We'll get you back safe,' he said.

'You can't make promises like that. You don't know.'

'Oh, I can. And I do.'

'How? How do you know?' This happened to be something Marie had a considerable amount of experience with. At some point, she'd stopped allowing herself to be tricked by lies. And that's what unmet promises were: cleverly packaged lies.

'Because you have a token.'

From the blank look on the girl's face, it was clear to the troll that she didn't know about such things. He raised his brows and, in a peculiar move that would've sounded impossible had Marie not witnessed it firsthand, tilted his tree trunk head off to one side. 'The coin? In your bag?'

Marie drew a defensive elbow up to the side pocket of her backpack.

'The roots speak, child. We see even what we aren't there to see. Don't worry. The token is yours to use as you see fit. We have no cause to take it from you. Others, however, most certainly do. Guard it as you would your heart.'

'By use,' Marie said. 'You mean spend?'

'In a fashion.' A wry smile crunched across the bark of the tree troll's face. 'If you would think of it that way. But know that wish tokens can only be spent once. Careful what you choose to spend it on. There's powerful magic in those small coins. Queen's magic.'

Marie thought of the arcades at Whitby and Scarborough and about the tokens her father would buy in rolls the size of a Smarties tube to drop in the slots and make the machines whir to life. She'd kept a few of them after their last visit to the seaside. Hidden them in a sock in her drawer. Every once in a while she'd jangle them to summon the memory.

But a token with no place to use it was a pointless thing. Was one of these supposed wish tokens any different? Might she end up keeping it in her sock drawer with the other useless tat?

The troll seemed to be waiting for the girl to finish working through her thoughts. 'The well,' he said at last. 'If you're wondering where it belongs, it's in the well. The one near the gate. You passed it once already, yes?'

'I think so.' She remembered seeing something like that.

'Good. We can only get you as far as the furthest of us. Beyond that keep your eyes up and your feet forward. Those Northern warmongers will no doubt be waiting for you somewhere along the path. The days of them letting folk leave of their own free will have gone, I'm afraid.'

Marie rubbed her eye with the heel of her palm. Ordinarily, she'd be sitting down to supper about this time in the evening, her mother running a bath upstairs, folding her bedsheets back ready for her to climb in and go to sleep. Barbara would surely have noticed she was gone by now, Marie thought. Then again, maybe not.

'Through there,' the tree troll said, tipping his eyes to the side to indicate the woods behind. 'You'll find a place where those nasty little bugs didn't burn. Take a while, read your book if you like, get your strength back before you head on. Follow my friends. They'll show you the way.'

Marie noticed, then, that a number of the other troll stumps had woken up and were blinking, yawning, some of them smiling. One troll had the remnants of a sapling branch attached just below where the rest of the tree had been sawn off. He was waving the branch at her like an arm, ushering her over to him.

'Thank-you,' Marie said, to the troll with whom she'd been speaking. 'I'm really grateful for your help.

'Anytime, biggun.'

'And sorry again for sitting on you.'

But the troll only mumbled what could've been, *don't worry about it*, and closed his eyes.

These trolls sure did like their sleep, Marie thought, as she left the path and headed for the arm-waving tree stump.

28. JULY–SEPT '93

Among the woodland shadows, nestled between powerful oaks and twisted yews, stood a small cottage not unlike the one belonging to her friend, Dale, before it was reduced to cinders. It was quiet here, no birdsong or hum. Just the gentle snores of several dozen sleeping trolls.

Marie opened her father's journal and began to read.

***

On this day July 9th 1993

I have decided that in this volume and all those that follow my entries shall relate only to my trips through the gate. From this point on, I think it best to separate the extraordinary from my other, everyday entries. It's becoming clear as the months pass that the two can not mix, despite what my new friend might think. I suspect he would abandon this place in a heartbeat given the option.

He does seem rather enamoured with Marble Falls and the greater Yorkshire area. Each time he asks to come to watch me at the windows of one of the many churches and cathedrals I'm contracted to clean, he says he would sit happily for hours on the guttering. I imagine it would take some convincing for me to get him to return home.

I have to admit he is good company, jolly little fellow that he is, and always in such good spirits, even if his never-ending questions do grate on my nerves on occasion, so I'm loath to talk him out of it. It seems a fair trade that as I spend time in his adopted homeland, he should spend time in mine.

That said, were the council to find out I'd smuggled him through, there'd be hell to pay!

***

On this day July 31st 1993

Marie has been asking about her forest friends again. I can tell she would greatly like to return to Diamond. She did, after all, have such a wonderful visit the last time. Unsurprising that the mind of a child sees only the best and not the worst of a place and its people. She needs it to be true, more so than I, I think.

By way of placating her, I took pictures on a small disposable camera left over from the birthday party she went to the other week, that of one of her playschool friends. The little girl, who turned 6, is obviously blessed with a mother far more able to engage and organise than my dear Barbara. They put on quite the do.

I snapped a few shots of the village folk in Faretheewell proper, who were kind enough to pose despite thinking me quite mad. 'So we'll be inside this box?' Manny asked, incredulous at the notion of his image being transferred to little squares of paper.

I did my best to explain. Perhaps I shall take the pictures to show them when I get them developed. I know young Dale especially would get a kick out of it.

I would've stayed longer but for the fact we were interrupted by odd noises coming from the southerly end of the forest, where the woods join the land that leads to the city. I was ushered back to the gate quick-smart by the Harrows, who had just gotten through warning me of possible repercussions of the industrial developments in Must. And who I had just gotten through telling not to be so alarmist.

Right on cue, it began: a wailing noise. We were all disturbed by it. Connie Harrow, may her own god love her, looked as if all the blood had left her face and drained down into her boots.

I've decided it's probably a good idea to listen more closely to the residents from now on. I sometimes forget I am merely passing through Diamond and therefore have less claim on an opinion.

***

On this day August 17th 1993

If only I could remind Barbara about this place. I believe with all my heart that it would help her, that she would find comfort in the magical properties of who and what resides in these woods. I feel sure she could heal and recover here. Alas, I doubt I could find the words to encourage her out of her stupor in order to make the journey. Words are all I have, and even those fail me when it comes to her. Besides, there's a chill in the air I can not describe.

What to do?

***

On this day August 21st 1993

Another day in Faretheewell. I spent the afternoon helping Dale clear his path of debris left by the rioters. Such a mess!

We swept and piled up a fair amount. But with each barrowful shifted, another ten seemed to appear. We joked that it was magic rubbish and that the fairy folk had cursed us to forever have to clear our paths, as they are forever cursed to clear the air of man's foul blight. Wouldn't blame them, frankly. Karma's a bitch, as the saying goes.

Dale is giving thought to moving away from his cottage in the forest. I can see he's becoming twitchy following the latest round of protests. There's only so many times you can rebuild, so many times you can tell yourself it'll settle, before you have to take a long hard look at the situation and decide if this is the best place for you to be.

I told him I'd support him whatever he chooses to do and that his safety and that of his son should be his priority. Faretheewell is delightful, but it isn't the most important thing. He can find another place if it comes down to it. And I would, of course, help him in any way I can.

For now, though, he's staying where he is. He knows the armies are building in strength. The North have influence and are doing their best to sway the will of the cunning but inherently non-violent woodland fae. And it seems from the amount of crap we're having to clear that their tactics are working. He says this is his home and he'll leave only when he chooses, or in a box.

Let's hope it doesn't come to that.

***

On this day September 2nd 1993

I spoke with a troll today. He told me his name was Johan. I shared with him the sandwiches I'd brought, and he was kind enough to share his interesting perspective on the cultural shift the people of Diamond have felt of late. I sat for the longest time listening to him speak. Trolls, I've come to realise, are the historians of Diamond and are the most fascinating of sorts.

Johan told me that this wasn't the first time such a shift had occurred, that this happens periodically. Cyclical, he said. I'm of a mind to believe him as he and the other trolls know things the rest of us can only imagine.

I stopped short of asking how it might end, and instead thanked him for his time before going on my way. I wondered afterwards, if I had asked the question would he have told me the truth even if the answer wasn't in my favour? Either way–if he'd lied to save my feelings or given me the honest, unvarnished truth–I suspect he'd have done so with the best intentions. He seemed that way inclined.

I hope to one day cross paths with him again, but I fear other forces are at play, and the people here are growing increasingly nervous. Better I don't draw attention to the kindly ones by seeking them out. I fear by doing so I'd risk their safety as well as my own.

***

On this day September 24th 1993

This place is changing. The last time I visited, I was welcomed with open arms and treated like one might treat a family member. But today, I entered the woods to the sound of cries. I followed the sound and discovered a young couple with their newborn, hiding in a ditch. 'Go back!' they said. 'We're not safe here anymore.'

Naturally, I was shaken by this. But still, I went on. I know the village and this part of the woods. These are the kindest, most welcoming folks I know. I wanted to hold onto the belief that even in these unsettled times what real danger could there possibly be?

I would later come to discover that the young family I had just encountered had good reason for fleeing Faretheewell. I saw them again on my return, only this time they were in no position to talk, their mouths and ears stuffed as they were with moss and twigs, their eyes staring blindly at the sky. I pray that by stopping to talk to them on their way out I didn't in some way bring about this hideous end.

Even the baby.

That beautiful innocent baby.

I cannot bring my darling girl back here again. The image of her like that-

***

Marie closed the journal. She didn't want to read anymore.

121

29. WISH

By the time she arrived at the well, Marie's feet burned. The walk had taken far longer than she'd anticipated. She didn't remember there being quite so many twists and turns going in the other direction and found she had to stop a few times just to give her toes a wiggle.

The trolls had kindly offered to open an underground corridor through the roots for her to walk along, to keep her out of sight for at least part of the journey back. But she hadn't felt the need to take them up on it, given that the fairy swarm hadn't made even the tiniest bit of effort to enter the troll graveyard for as long as she'd been off the main path.

Despite warnings from the trolls to the contrary, she thought perhaps the fairy army had given up. They had certainly gone very quiet. Besides, she wanted to avoid further delay so said her goodbyes at the edge of troll territory, thanked as many of them as she could, those that were awake anyway, and set off.

Small creatures rustled and scurried in the forest around her, but thankfully nothing fairy-like. Still, she kept low and walked quickly and quietly, eyes up, feet forward, doing what she could to not attract any unwanted attention.

The backpack pulled on her shoulders under the additional weight of the journal, not to mention the fact that she'd been lugging it around all day. The coin, too, felt oddly heavy. She wanted so much to get through her front door and drop the wretched bag down next to the shoe rack, toss it in amongst all the boots and sandals and busted brollies.

Nearly there, she thought as she passed the smoking ash footprint of Dale's cottage, and again as she recognised the patch of trees and flattened ground where she'd shared a picnic with the goblin. Ever so nearly there.

Then, around the next bend, there it was: the low circular stone wall of the well. In the darkened forest it was unmissable, a glow emanating from it that Marie hadn't noticed the last time she'd passed by. Maybe it was more noticeable in the dark, she thought. Yes, maybe that was it.

She reached around into the side pocket of her backpack and fished out the silver token. It was the darndest thing, the coin didn't move and yet it tickled the palm of her hand as if vibrating at a frequency she could only feel.

There was something strange about the well, too. Something stranger than its new-onset sparkly glow. No sooner had she exposed the coin to the air than the curling wisps of light over the well's gaping mouth began to dance. Did they see each other? Feel each other? Were the well and the coin in some way connected?

Marie thought about her wish and about exactly how it ought to be worded. She could only spend the token once, the tree troll had said, so she reminded herself of how important it was to get it right.

She wanted to help both Dale and the goblin so decided she would wish them both to a place of safety. It didn't strike her as being necessary to wish herself to safety. She was so close to the gate, after all, practically home free. Besides, the woods were silent, give or take a few owl hoots and the occasional mournful screech from what Marie hoped with all her might was just a fox.

The closer she got to the well, the brighter the light above it became and the greater the tingling sensation inside her fist from the token. The tingling began to feel more like a pull, until her arm involuntarily lifted up. It was as if she were being towed to the light, dragged along by the metal object in her hand. She imagined if she opened her fingers the coin might fly out like a ball bearing drawn to a powerful magnet. She wondered, if that happened would she still get her wish?

Dale and Muggins, she repeated in her thoughts. A place of safety.

The coin tugged and tugged the girl through the forest. She was no longer in charge of her own feet.

'Careful what you choose to spend it on,' the tree troll had said. 'Powerful magic...Queen's magic.'

From nowhere, the image of Barbara entered Marie's mind. She pictured her on the sofa at home, crying over a game show or some other tosh, and for no particular reason the girl hoped for better things for her mother. Or to be more specific, she hoped for her mother to be happy.

In that instant, the token jerked out of the girl's hand almost causing her to lose her balance. It flew through the air and briefly hovered over the well, before seemingly giving in to gravity all at once and plopping down into the darkness below.

'No!' But it was too late. The token was gone and Marie had no idea what, if any, wish had been made.

Meanwhile, deep inside the well the silver coin swirled and whirled down and around until it exited below, landing with a clink on a heap of a hundred other spent coins. It laid, unnoticed by anyone, in the empty inky blackness of the tunnel which, were Marie to find herself there, were she to walk along it a ways and not stumble or crack her biggun head on the rocky ceiling, would lead her out through the falling waters of the foss and home.

30. THE WEST GATE

Marie thundered through the forest, closely followed by the swarm of fairy soldiers that found her at the well just seconds after the coin flew from her hand. They must've sensed magic in the air, honed in on it and on her.

She ran with everything she had, sometimes on a clear stretch of the path, sometimes launching herself over logs, around trees, stumbling then righting herself again. Each time she nearly fell, the squadron above guffawed and let out a unified, 'Wa-heyy!'

Marie didn't much like their sense of humour.

She thought she spied a glistening light through the branches off in the distance and for one terrible moment Marie panicked that she'd run in a complete circle, that the light ahead was just her arriving back at the well. But, no. This light was different from the one before.

She prayed with every pounding step that what she saw was the gate and not just another burning cottage or her imagination playing tricks. A mirage, like those she'd learned about in school.

Her teacher, Miss Bramley, did a whole lesson on mirages once, reading to the class about a boy who took a wrong turn on holiday and got lost out in the sand dunes of Tunisia. Which, when Marie thought about it, conjured up horrifying images and had been quite the departure from their usual story time of Narnia or Roald Dahl. Some of the mothers complained.

She told the class how, if you're in the desert and get thirsty enough that you might actually die, your brain makes stuff up and you see things. You buy into the lie because it might be (and you so badly want it to be) true.

But, Miss Bramley explained, the closer you get to a mirage the further it moves away. That's what gets you, she said. Not the thirst, but the desire. It teases you deeper into the sand. And you follow the shimmering palm trees, the promise of fresh spring water, forever chasing the dream (of rescue, of salvation) when all the while what you're really doing is walking further away from those things. And so you die never having found what you were looking for. (The teacher didn't say that last part, but the kids worked it out for themselves. The smart ones did, at least).

Miss Bramley left not long after that.

The hum grew louder. Marie wasn't about to risk even a quick look around, but there was no doubt in her mind they were gaining on her.

Just keep go-ing.

Just keep go-ing.

Just keep go-ing.

The words fell into a loop matching her footfalls and it helped. She forgot all about deserts and mirages and most other things besides. She focused only on the act of running and dodging obstacles in her way: one step, then another, then another.

But as the flying horde closed in, their shrieking cries broke Marie's protective mantra.

'Girl!' they called. 'Hey, girl! We see you, there!' And, 'Oh, gir-rl. We're coming for yooou,' which was met with a disturbing volume of delighted squeals from certain elements within the swarm.

'Go away,' Marie said, no more energy to shout than she did to cry or lash out at her winged attackers. 'I just want to go home.' The words caught in her throat and threatened to steal her breath. Breath she needed for her legs to work. She thought it best not to give them the satisfaction.

Just. Keep. Go. Ing.

Eventually, the light that had until then blinked in and out of view steadied itself into a tall rectangle. It no longer escaped her gaze or threatened to pull her in the wrong direction. Not a mirage after all, but a doorway within a sturdy wrought iron frame. Strange that she hadn't noticed how beautiful the gate was when she'd entered Diamond through it earlier that same day. But then, she couldn't recall turning around to look at it, too busy as she was going forward.

The inner gate twinkled like liquid glitter. Not solid, not still, but in constant motion. Marie thought she might like to swim in it and wondered how it would feel floating in a warm, calm sea, with all the galaxies in a clear night's sky reflected in the water around her. How nice it would be to slip below the surface and drift among the stars. Who needed air when you had the universe?

She noticed, then, that the twittering voices behind her had stopped. No humming, no taunts. Still she ran. The gate was close enough that she could hear it crackling like popping candy and the sound of it tingled on the insides of her ears.

She ducked under a branch and suddenly felt something wrap around her face, as if she'd run through a huge sheet of cobweb. She tried to brush it off, but her fingers stuck in the thing and her vision blurred.

A cheer went up from the trees above.

Marie focused her eyes in closer, close enough that she could see the tip of her nose, and what was over her face and head: a cloth of the finest muslin, with stone beads dotted around the edges. The scheming little buggers had dropped a net! This one was much smaller and stickier than the one that had trapped the goblin, but it was a trap nonetheless.

She fumbled with the cloth, which had thoroughly entangled itself in her hair and under her chin. The only saving grace was that it wasn't big enough to interfere with her ability to run, however blindly.

Another word she'd heard recently in school: serendipity. As it happened, Marie had stopped biting her nails that summer at the behest of the local vicar, who'd offered to treat her to a large box of Maltesers if she went cold turkey. This now proved an extremely worthwhile endeavour as, using her new nails, she tore a hole in the sheer fabric, freeing herself from the net.

Marie's heart thudded in her chest. The path straightened out ahead and the gate was suddenly in front of her, a short enough distance away that she could've tossed a tennis ball in there and sent it swirling back to Marble Falls.

It was then the real fear came, the undeniable sense that the swarm might descend to block her way out, that they were playing with her, letting her think she was about to escape before dashing her hopes and stealing her back. But their previous whoops and chitters of amusement had turned to urgent barks of, 'Get her!' and, 'She's getting away!'

Some of them shouted words at each other the likes of which Marie had never heard: gonewing or gunwin or gunwig. What did that even mean?

No time. Just move.

She hit the door running, didn't stop to question the ripping apart of every cell in her body, or why that felt no worse than a nasty case of pins and needles. And a finger snap later she was on the other side.

31. HIS PRISON, A SONG

This time of year, the king was reminded of a far away place. It was the light, he decided, how it formed golden halos around things and magnified the crisping edges of the leaves as they clung hopelessly on. The sun never got quite high enough to warm him through.

He took a sip of berry wine. That warmed him, at least. 'I shall walk the grounds,' he said to a startled fairy maid. 'Fetch me my cloak.'

'Your cloak, Lord?' the maid said. She looked around for backup. She was new and had forgotten the words she'd been taught only that morning by the cook. If she lost him, she'd be made an example of and likely lose a wing or an ear or some other such indignity. Then what good would she be to her sweet Mama?

'Yes, imbecile,' the king said. 'What part of *my cloak* is so difficult for you to understand? I would like to take in the air and think. Can I do that? Can I?' He didn't know when he last went outside. A week? A month? Maybe longer. He couldn't for the life of him remember why.

Perhaps he'd been unwell. Yes, probably. He was recuperating, of course. No wonder it all felt so vague and intangible. One cannot expect to be in full command of one's faculties after an illness. He gulped down the last of the berry wine.

The maid hovered, mid-room, alternately glancing with nervous, blinking eyes at the door and at the king, who was hauling himself out of the gilded throne as if going to leave.

'For crying out loud. I'll get it myself,' he said, batting the maid out of his way.

'Lord! Lord!' the maid called out louder than necessary, aiming her voice toward the door rather than at the unwieldy monarch, in the hope of alerting another maid or, better still, one of the guards. 'Please, Your Highness. I will find your cloak. I do believe it's in the kitchen vestibule. Now, sit, sit. I shall get it and bring it at once.' She fluttered forward at speed to put herself between the man and his exit. But it was obvious to them both that if he wanted to leave, magic or not, there was little she could do to stop him.

The king paused, then, so that he and the fairy were eye to eye, inches from the solid oak door.

'Lord?'

'Move,' he at least had the decency to say. Although it hadn't been a request so much as a warning.

The fairy did as she was told.

The full-grown human man, resplendent in robes of the finest silk, woven and stitched by the artisan makers of Diamond, gold crown atop his equally golden locks, clacked the handle down and yanked the door open with a frustrated grunt.

Instead of the open hallway, he was met by a bank of tiny faces, courtiers hovering at chest-height to the king, their wings humming gently, echoes of which were muffled by the plush carpets and fabrics that adorned the castle floors and walls.

'Good morning, Sire,' a well-dressed fairy guardsman said in soothing tones. 'How wonderful to see you up and about. Can I bring you anything? Breakfast, perhaps? Or more berry wine? I would say, Sire, if you would allow me the impertinence, seeing as how you're-'

'Get on with it, boy,' the king said. 'Before we all die of a waiting disease.'

'Yes, Sire.' The guardsman was not a boy, nor even a man, but a fairy, some seventy-odd years old. Middle-aged in fairy terms. But he let that slide. Not worth biting at such small bait when you've other rats to catch.

'What I was going to say, Sire, is that the staff and I have been preparing something for you. If we could only have a moment of your precious time?'

The king rolled his eyes: fine. He backed into the room a few steps, allowing the courtiers to manoeuvre themselves through the door. The guard doing the talking gave the maid an *I'll-deal-with-you-later* glance, but she was less concerned with that than she was relieved to be keeping both her wings.

'Thank you, Sire,' the guard said.

The king perched his ample bottom on the headrest of a purple velvet chaise lounge and crossed his arms impatiently across his chest. 'Well?' he said.

The guard ushered the others to form a ring about the king, a biggun arm span or so distance from the man's frowning face. The guard raised his hands like a conductor. In a brief moment of stillness, some of the fairies gave gentle coughs, clearing their throats in readiness. And with a nod of his head, a twitch of his fingertips, the guard rallied them into song.

The words-

The king knew them.

The tune-

His head whirled, a sudden kaleidoscope of memories. No, no, no, he thought. Not again. Never again.

'Oh, Danny Boy,' the courtier fairies trilled in beautiful harmony, the sweetest voices in the kingdom.

'Stop. Please, stop-' The king waved his arms about his head as if fighting off wasps. But there was just too much air between himself and the offending mouths, and the flitting things dipped back each time he reached out.

'The pipes, the pipes are calling...'

The king slid down to the floor. The choir lowered themselves as one to follow him there, all the while singing, all the while their humming wings acting as yet one more layer to the music.

'But come ye back when summer's in the meadow...'

He became small, curled himself into a tight ball, arms held up to cradle and protect his head. His crown tumbled to the ground where it rolled across the rug, past the throne stand, and came to a stop against the door, which the maid had eased shut as the singing began.

The maid fluttered down. She picked the crown up despite its monumental size and used her skirts to dust off the fuzz it had gathered on its journey across the room.

'Oh Danny Boy, Oh Danny Boy, I love you so...'

The man's cries turned to whimpers. No words, only sounds and rocking.

Then silence.

The guard-cum-conductor held up a palm to the others. Were they done? It seemed like they might be done. 'My Lord?' he said.

The king made no effort to respond either in voice or gesture.

'Would you like to go back to your bed, Sire? You look tired.'

After a moment, the man lowered his arms. His expression was one of bewilderment. 'Yes,' he muttered. 'Yes, I rather think I will.

32. BETTER OFF DEAD

Within the castle was a room.

And within this room was a cell.

And within this cell was a cupboard.

And within this cupboard was a dust-covered shelf.

And on this shelf were jars, dozens and dozens of jars.

And in one of those jars, tucked away as if no more important than any other, was a fairy once known to all in the kingdom as Queen, subsequently known only as Janet, now known only as her, or it. If, that is, she was referred to at all.

And the fairy tore at the cursed glass that contained her, just as she had every hour of every day for many a year, since her capture long ago. She fought until her fingernails were gone, then until her voice was gone. Her sanity would follow and someday, too, her life.

All the while, they milked her of her magic, twice a day, every day, without fail. They didn't ask, they took. They stole. They raped her of what little of herself the fairy had left.

Between times, they returned her in the jar to the dark and dusty shelf in the cupboard in the cell in the room in the castle, to be alone with her tortured thoughts. And she would scream and wail and wish for the day when she could finally, mercifully, be allowed to die.

33. HOME

Night had fallen hard across Yorkshire as it had across Diamond and any visibility at Darkwood was long gone. Times like this, the cottage and adjoining farmland stayed true to its name.

Marie dragged herself out of the hedgerow and onto the dew-damp grass that sloped up to the house. She looked for any sign of Barbara in the windows, but there was none. All was still.

Behind her she could hear faint sounds of soldier fairies rattling and shrieking their annoyance, and if she squinted her eyes she could just make out the iron surround of the gate, the galaxy of stars within it, albethey camouflaged with magic. A further effort to keep unwanted intruders out.

Had those nasty little winged devils also made it through, she wondered? Could they get through? Or was the gate an escape route only people (West-gaters, bigguns) were able to take advantage of? Marie had no desire to ponder this further so got to her feet, ran the gamut of pitch black garden in her best time yet, and burst into the cottage through the back door, which had thankfully been left unlocked.

She dumped her backpack on the floor in the living room, a space dimly lit by a flickering television and a dying fire, which her mother enjoyed whatever the season. The falling bag knocked fire tools that hung on a rack by the wood burner, and a clatter ensued. This in turn woke Barbara, who looked up, bleary-eyed, over the arm of the sofa.

'Back, then?' the woman said. 'What time is it?'

Marie didn't answer. But, by God, she was glad to be in familiar surroundings. The cottage, for all its faults and isolation, felt safe for once. Just try getting in here, you mean fairies, she thought (stopping short of calling them shitterbugs even in the privacy of her own mind). Just try.

Marie's bravado kicked in now she was no longer alone, and had a trusted solid door and wall between her and the garden. Yes, her mother was as useful as a polystyrene hammer, but she was a grown-up, and grown-ups fixed things. That's what they were supposed to do, anyway. Even the rubbish ones.

'Where have you been?' Barbara said, wiping dribble from her chin. 'I was worried about you.'

Sure you were.

The girl didn't bother to explain and apparently didn't need to. A warm bath and a jam sandwich later, she climbed into her cosy white-framed bed, with just a strip of light from the hallway to guide her. Barbara came upstairs a short while later to say goodnight.

Marie wanted to tell someone, anyone, about the fantastical day she'd had, about the strange characters she'd met–some nice and some not so nice–and about her narrow escape from the humming fairy folk. She wanted to talk it out, to ask her mother if it was okay that she ran away. If it was the right thing to do, leaving the trapped goblin behind. Most of all, she wanted to know if, by allowing him to be taken in order to save herself, was she a horrible person? That last one was bothering her quite a bit.

But the girl had no confidence that Barbara would have answers to any of those questions, or that her mother was even capable of finding the right words to make her feel better about the choices she'd made. In fact, there was a good chance she might make her feel worse and an even better chance that she wouldn't believe her, anyhow.

So Marie said nothing, instead keeping it to herself as was often the case. Besides, she was awfully tired and, as her mother stroked her cheek with a gentle shhhh, she couldn't help herself but drift off to sleep.

*****

Through the night, Marie saw her father. The two of them walked across the hills and her slumbering heart swelled to be reminded, if only within a dream, of their shared love of the Yorkshire Dales.

Or maybe it was that she loved him enough that being almost anywhere was wonderful, so long as they were together. She wasn't sure. And it didn't feel like it mattered anymore.

In the dream, George Fisher looked just as Marie remembered him: shoulders broad for sitting on, a week-old scraggly beard, twinkling eyes that made you feel certain he was seeing you and listening to you, fully. He wore the same battered hiking boots he always did and the orange anorak with pockets for just about anything you could imagine. His trusty compass dangled on its loop.

He walked in front, always slightly too fast, slightly too far away for them to hold hands, making Marie need to skip a few steps every now and again. Even if she could've kept pace she was forced to dodge the places he'd walked as wherever his feet touched the ground the rocky soil crumbled and disappeared. At some point it fell through altogether, and he floated away leaving Marie behind on a newly formed cliff edge.

'Help me with these,' George Fisher said, hovering in the cloudy air.

Marie noticed a pile of journals beneath him, also hovering. So many books, each beautifully bound and tied shut with a length of leather twine.

'They're too heavy,' she said. 'And too far away. If I try, I'll fall.'

'Great,' her father said, only half serious. 'Guess old Muggins here's got to do everything as usual.'

He rolled his eyes in jest, and Marie remembered how that was one of his favourite phrases to say around the house when Barbara wasn't feeling up to doing the dishes, or went off to watch one of her shopping channels for hours at a time.

How had she forgotten that?

Old Muggins. The Dales. The clear plastic compass. Something connected in her dream, dots separated by time and comprehension.

Her father stopped laughing, then. A look of terror replaced his smile and coins vomited from his mouth like a waterfall of silver. When at last the coins stopped flowing, he drifted down to where an island had formed beneath him. He leaned forward to pick up the pile of books but couldn't.

Marie watched from afar as he lurched his torso forward a number of times, his lower body unable to follow. She saw his feet had grown into the dirt like roots, firmly planting his legs into the ground and anchoring him in place. His arms became branches tipped with sprouting leaves and his face, to Marie's horror, had at some point crusted over with bark.

'What a silly...girly...you...are,' he said, slowly and deeply, as the last of his mouth sealed shut.

***

The next morning came swiftly. Marie was woken by a scream. She threw off the covers and practically skidded down the stairs on her heels and by the time she reached the hallway she'd all but forgotten her dream, as is the rightful way of these things.

In the living room, Barbara was spinning around, babbling on about numbers, shaking her head, clearly having an episode of some kind.

Marie's first thought was that something or someone from the place through the hedgerow (what was it called, again?) had followed her and cast a terrible spell to send her mother out of her mind. But then she saw the smile on the woman's face and gladly ruled that out as a possibility.

When Barbara spotted her daughter in the doorway, she rushed over to pick her up and spun her around several times, which made Marie dizzy but also made her laugh.

'We won!' Barbara said when she finally put the girl down, restraining her hysterics long enough to form actual words. 'We're rich, Marie. Can you believe it? Rich!'

Marie noticed her mother was holding the paper tickets she always purchased when she went for the big shop on a Friday. The ones she stuck on the fridge and, week in, week out, tore up and threw away.

Oh, wait just a minute.

'We won the lottery?' Marie said, after a moment.

But Barbara was back in manic mode and rushed off to make a call on the phone in the kitchen. Marie heard her mother try as best she could to maintain a calm voice as she answered questions to someone on the other end of the line: 'Barbara Fisher. All six. Yes, yes, I'm sure. I have it here. Now? Okay, they're 4, 5, 7, 21, 44, 48.'

Marie recognised some of the numbers as corresponding to her birthday (fourth of May), and it surprised her a little that her mother might think to use them. A coincidence, Marie thought. Knowing her mother, it had to be. All the same, she wondered what relevance the other numbers had.

For a minute or three there wasn't much of anything for Marie to do except look around the room blankly. She saw the backpack by the fireplace. The wood burner next to it still glowed with the embers of the fire from the night before.

It occurred to her that she wanted to read more of her father's journal. The place from yesterday had begun to seem like a dream, everything about it slipping away, and she wanted to remind herself, or rather prove to herself, that she hadn't made it up.

Before Marie even got to the bag, she saw that it was open, that the flap with the little metal poppers had been flipped back, the bag's innards exposed. She rushed over to the backpack and fumbled a frantic hand around inside it. All that was left were scrunched up bits of tin foil from the cake she'd shared with the goblin, a handful of coins–ten and twenty pences, mainly; certainly nothing over a quid–and some dry leaves and bits of brambles.

She looked at the empty bag, then at the smouldering fire. No, no, no!

Barbara got off the phone and walked back to the living room, still grinning from ear to ear, to where Marie was sitting in a slump on the floor, the bag open in her lap.

'Tell me you didn't,' the girl said.

'Didn't what?' The woman's expression shifted from joy to confusion.

Marie wondered how a person could get so good at hiding the truth when they did nothing all day long. 'Daddy's book. Where is it?'

The smile dropped from Barbara's face.

'The journal. It was right here.'

'It's not for you.'

'Liar!'

'It isn't,' the woman said. 'And even if it was-'

'He wanted me to have it. He told me.' Marie made a conscious choice not to say, *in my dream.* Even at her age she knew that wouldn't strengthen her argument any.

Barbara inhaled deeply and let out a long, carefully controlled sigh. 'And even if it was,' she started again, 'I wouldn't want you to have it yet. Not until you're old enough to understand.' She lowered herself to sit on the edge of the sofa. 'What you don't know, darling, because I didn't want to spoil your memories, is that Daddy was a bit too fond of telling stories.'

Marie couldn't believe the words coming from Barbara's mouth. She felt sure that any second now her mother would say something that couldn't be unheard. By way of a preemptive strike, she jumped to her feet and fought back the tears that made everything go blurry, gulped down the sting in her throat that threatened to make her sound like a child. 'You had NO RIGHT!' she shouted. 'I hate you. I hate you.'

She threw the bag down and ran from the living room, up the stairs, and into her bedroom, slamming each and every door behind her, unaware that things had been irrevocably changed.

Nothing would be the same again.

34. THE KEYS TO DARKWOOD COTTAGE

(24 Years Later)

The warning barrier flashed and dinged in the cool summer night, echoing across the countryside and lighting up the hedgerow-flanked road in pulsing bursts. In the air hung the musk of sweet hay and hoof-trodden fields, the last lingering heat of the day expelled by a flash storm, the kind your body longs for.

Marie sat alone in the car, her eyes heavy. She could so easily have rested her head on the wheel and slept. So what if I did? she thought. Let all the other drivers peep their stupid horns. Let them huff their inconvenience at having to go around me. Let them slow down and glare at me through their stupid windows.

But there were no other cars. No people. No life but that which scurries away and hides from the din and drama of a railway crossing. There was only Marie in her car on a dark and lonely road, waiting for the train to pass.

She stifled a yawn. Nearly there, she thought. Stay with it.

The storm from earlier had moved on. Tiny rain specks settled quietly on the windscreen, sparkling grains of amber refracting the flashing lights from the barrier. But Marie stared blankly through them, thinking only of home. Funny really, she hadn't considered it home for a long time and yet here she was. And to think, all it took was for her mother to die.

By rights, the engine should have stalled by now, and her decision not to stop at the last service station on the motorway could yet prove foolish. She told herself it was only another mile or so, glancing at the empty fuel gauge, knowing deep down it was probably closer to five.

The lies we choose to believe will be our undoing, she mused, the irony resonating.

The engine idled. Only the occasional phut of a misfire interrupted its otherwise rhythmic purr, presumably in indignation at being run down to the fumes. In a moment of what Shaun would've called 'girl-thinking' Marie wondered if taking her foot off the pedal on the downhill parts of the journey might help. 'Stupid,' she muttered. Firstly for being an idiot and secondly for bringing Shaun into things. She cast her eyes upward, determined not to crack.

Previously, she would have navigated the roads up from London with all the ease of slipping one's arms into a familiar cardigan. More often than not, she would find herself coasting along on instinct, blinking and missing towns, entire counties going by in a blur. Every junction, every turn, every gnarled tree along the route had long since been saved to her inner sat-nav. The scenery around Marble Falls was reassuringly fixed, changing only according to the time of year.

But today was different. August or not, the drive had all the warmth and familiarity of a lunar expedition.

As she sat waiting for the train, Marie knew the hardest was yet to come.

She couldn't bear the thought of always feeling like an empty, broken version of herself. Although it was true that she and Barbara's relationship had never been the greatest or closest when it came to mother-daughter bonds, to imagine herself as an orphan left Marie feeling like a damaged compass, needle spinning, no sense of true north.

Her hand quivered as she lifted it off the steering wheel. She wondered if this was what it felt like to have a nervous breakdown, but quickly reminded herself she hadn't eaten since breakfast and even then only coffee and one slice of toast. Though food was the furthest thing from her mind she knew she would have to eat something when she got to the cottage. Olive had probably left something for her, something ready to eat and easily digestible. The old dear was good like that.

Suddenly, the car was too small. She needed to breathe, to escape. As the panic rose in her chest, she reached for the window. But something stopped her, something she couldn't quite explain. Instead, she cranked up the air con (a poor second to freedom, but the safer option at least).

Stupid, she thought again, shaking her head. A grown woman afraid of the dark? Somewhere inside, a voice, whispering and child-like, reminded her it wasn't the dark she needed to fear. Before she could make sense of it, the thought was cut short and the road ahead disappeared.

Marie's heart lurched as the train raged past in a flurry of windows and wheels, forcing her back to the here and now. She gazed up at the flashing carriages as they clackety-clacked at speed across the road. It seemed to be mostly empty, a ghost train in the middle of nowhere. But it was late and probably the last of the day to run.

It seemed to Marie that most people would be tucked up safe and warm with their families on a night like this. Then, as if to drive the point home, the train was gone, leaving her alone in the dark once again. The silence was something else.

Almost immediately, the lights stopped flashing and the barrier lifted. Marie flipped the wipers once to clear the windscreen. At the same time she grudgingly wiped away a single tear that made a break for her cheek. 'Don't you dare,' she told herself. 'Don't you bloody dare.'

And with that, she put the car into gear and headed off on the last leg of the journey toward Darkwood.

***

The headlights streaked across the garden and through the wooden slatted fence into an adjacent field. Several rabbits took umbrage at this sudden shift in the nighttime status quo and skittered away in search of shadows. The porch light was already on. It cast a glow some twenty feet down the garden path and something about that made Marie momentarily curl up and die inside. She pulled on the handbrake.

Of course, she knew in her rational mind that Olive, having gotten the heads up about Marie arriving late, would've gone in to turn it on. Even so, the need to run in through the door was overwhelming. To call out to Barbara or find her mother standing in the hallway, arms outstretched, ready to give her best approximation of a hug.

But the cottage was empty, no fire would be lit, no dinner would be bubbling on the hob, so instead Marie sat in the car unable to move.

Throughout her younger years, she'd played in this garden and in these fields exploring every inch of the place like a wild thing. The imagination that now fuelled her art was undoubtedly born out of a childhood spent climbing and hiding, splashing and conquering, hunting and building. Where every stick was a weapon, every boulder a mountain, every pile of logs a fortress.

Though never in the dark.

It was then that the engine decided its own fate and grumbled to a halt. The sudden quiet changed the atmosphere within the car, and outside of it, making the house seem like the smart choice. Marie switched off the headlights. If it weren't for the porch light everything would've been in darkness. There was no moon or stars to take the edge off the gloom as the last of the storm clouds had yet to vacate the sky.

She pulled the keys from the ignition then counted to three before summoning the courage to grab her bag from the passenger seat and step outside.

One foot after the other.

Halfway to the house, fear took hold and Marie's pace quickened and by the time she got to the front door she was almost at a sprint. She reached out with the key, but low blood sugar and panic meant it took a number of scratching attempts to infiltrate the lock. She was beyond relieved when it finally clicked into place. No sooner was the door open than she flew inside. She swung round to shut it behind her, pulse racing, eyes now tightly shut as if this was the greatest defence against all bad things known to womankind.

Meanwhile, on the passenger seat of the car where it had been overlooked in all this, the silent ring of Marie's phone went unnoticed.

***

From a secluded corner of the garden at the back of the cottage, a whispering chatter began to build. A thicket of wild climbing roses, hawthorns, and sweet-scented honeysuckle, neglected and overgrown, disguised the elaborate whorls of the wrought-iron gate through which the noise gently drifted.

At first, it was just a hint of voices lost on the faintest breeze. But soon, whispers became murmurs, murmurs gave way to mutterings, and as the kitchen window came alive with light, the anticipation was such that frenzied squeals of unbridled delight rang out.

Those who made such noises were instantly silenced by authoritative shushes from others. But before long, the whispers and giggles returned to a low-level rabble as the voices struggled to contain their excitement.

A hundred pairs of glinting eyes watched eagerly as Marie made her way slowly across the kitchen. They tracked her as she went to explore the fridge and lifted the lid on the big orange pot she found there. From beyond the gate, they studied her closely as she replaced the lid, shut the fridge and left the kitchen, switching the light off on the way out.

Audible disappointment followed, a cacophony of hushed voices punctuated with impatient tuts and sighs. They frantically scanned the darkened windows at the rear of the house, each of them desperate to spy a glimpse of the woman. Then, there she was in an upstairs window, a bedroom, perhaps.

The hundred pairs of glinting eyes tilted upward and watched as Marie wearily moved towards the window, a hush descending amongst them. Collectively, they held their breath as she approached the glass and reached up, drawing the curtains for the night.

'She's staying', the voices seemed to say, almost as one. 'The Fisher girl's staying.'

PART TWO

1. SCOUT

The man adjusted his diving helmet to check seal integrity, and squeezed his eyelids shut a few times, clearing the salty sting. No leak, just a trickle of sweat murking up his vision. He tried to shake off the nagging possibility of this becoming his last time. Nah, he thought. He had more missions left in him and more work to do. He wasn't done with this place yet. Too many unanswered questions he wasn't prepared to leave behind for the younger ones to figure out. And the clues were right there.

It was obvious that the core world was dying. Each visit, things grew incrementally and catastrophically worse; the sky became darker, signs of life fewer and farther between. It was easy to see a decline when you witnessed it across intervals, the differences rendered as steps rather than a gradual, imperceptible downward slide. And that's how it was for the scouts. They went only every few weeks now, rotating shifts so as to minimise the risk to any one individual. There wasn't much point in going more often than that, especially given the airborne hummers' propensity for taking down intruders, as brutal as they were swift. Risk versus benefit, et cetera.

With that thought, the man glanced up: nothing but smoke. He went back to taking his samples, making his notes. He'd become hardened to the grey as one does to that which you cannot change, that which might rip your soul in half if you allowed it in, let it affect you. There was a job to finish and to get emotionally attached to any chosen outcome would be a massive failure of self-control.

Some scouts managed better than others to follow their training, to keep hope quelled, to not waste energy wishing for the impossible. Lapses led to errors and errors led to worse. They all agreed fantasies of recovery were mere bedtime stories for the youngsters, though even the children knew to keep their expectations low when it came to the state of Diamond. There was no evidence to suggest this thing could be turned around now or a hundred years from now. It was absurd to believe otherwise.

Rock, so named for his strong build and lack of sway, had an eye for the important. He was known by those at base to push himself to the edges of what was safe, time-wise and distance-wise, to get what he needed from a mission. He'd been warned before by the higher-ups about risking his life and advised to curb his reckless ways, though deep down he suspected the dive kit was worth more to them than a single scout, even a veteran like him.

'If the hummers catch up to you,' they said, 'you're on your own. You'll be good as gone. There will be no rescue, Rock. No rescue. Understand?'

And he did.

Depending on tank size, the average scout might have a couple of hours, three at the outside, which was long enough even for the toughest among them, those that remembered the world as it had been before the city trashed everything around it. The younger ones never witnessed with their own eyes the core lands as a living place. They were the luckiest of all–hard to miss what you never had–and while these exploratory missions didn't impact them in quite the same visceral way, they lacked the dogged determination of those that it did.

Between them, the scouts had charted a good number of isolated pockets of green in the years since the project began. They knew from word of mouth how the last colonies of Faretheewell hid themselves as best they could, secreted away to delay the inevitable desecration that would someday swallow them up, too.

On the rare occasion that both breeds of fugitive crossed paths, they would pause to acknowledge a shared history, scouts honouring beleaguered locals with a nod in recognition of all they'd lost, fairies gazing back briefly with an expression not a million miles away from blame, before darting off into the haze. Such encounters were almost unheard of, nowadays.

Lately, Rock came to notice more of the curious inscriptions carved into dead trees dotted through the forest, made using what he surmised were sharp blades or points of chiselled flint. The words were big enough for him to see and read, but were made up of thousands of tiny scratches, by hands significantly smaller than his own. Not that it was clear when observing them in the forest shadows, but back at base he could zoom all the way in, study the detail up close, and the craft and skill and dedication that must've gone into completing them was mind-blowing.

He tried to imagine the effort it took someone small enough to fit in his breast pocket to carve lettering large enough and deep enough to ensure it be seen by someone of his size. That in itself created an odd paradox in Rock's mind, as those he assumed to have written the words so often went to the greatest of lengths to remain hidden from view.

They led somewhere, these messages, he felt sure of it. According to the charts on which he recorded each such marking, the carved words, which were essentially graffiti, formed a huge arrow toward the old city of Must. Any idiot could see the pattern, the clear trail pointing south, inviting (begging?) him to follow. And, damnit, if he didn't want to see it through.

'Open to interpretation,' is what the higher-ups said when he'd raised it as a point of interest and requested additional scout time to investigate. 'Old data, probably.

Could've been put there decades ago. Not relevant to the project. Might be a trap. Thanks, but move on.'

Arseholes.

He did a quick mental sum and decided begrudgingly that today was not the day. It was no good chasing ghosts if the air got you first, and he needed a fifth of a tank just for the last leg of the journey home or nothing else he did would matter after that. Maybe next time.

He marked the new find on his chart with an 'x' and made a note of the corresponding grid reference then checked the dial on his wrist: a quarter tank. It wasn't so much the oxygen he needed as the filtration; particulates were a bitch on the lungs. He toyed with dropping to eighteen per cent and breathing shallow, then thought better of it. Time to go.

First he snapped a few last images of the nearest scorched tree stump. Not for the higher-ups but for his own collection. The others might dismiss this as a so-called 'passion project', a waste of good scouting time, and warn him off using communal supplies in such a glutinous manner, but that didn't mean he couldn't work on it off the clock.

He checked the etching had captured at a high enough resolution that when he pulled the images up on the screen on his personal machine back home it would replicate well. The outline of the familiar green skull was gouged into the wood and daubed in what he took to be a natural chlorophyll dye. It wasn't as clear against the blackened background as he'd have hoped, but he had many more similar images to compare it to, so wasn't overly concerned. The words, however, were as crisp and readable as any typed script. Always the same phrase, over and over across the dead woodland. How badly he wanted to know their mission goals.

WE ARE HERE.

Defiant motherfuckers, Rock thought, giving the inscription one last hard stare, in a bid to wrestle the meaning from it. Then it really was time to head back.

2. THE HOLLOWS

Inside the cavernous body of a dead tree troll, keepers of the green ways privately thrived. Some among them watched through a rotted knot as the biggun tramped the blackened ground outside. He was no threat. They didn't fear this lumbering steel-suited oaf, but still, they monitored his whereabouts. With so few of them left, they could ill afford to be complacent about wanderers in their midst.

When the man was gone, a calm returned to the hollow. Until a short while later, when a contingent of gate watchers arrived just as the babies were being put to bed and the olders were settling down for an evening with their dearest, and fairies of all ages poked their heads out of hidey holes and fluttered themselves upward and closer to get a better look.

For gate watchers to return early was highly irregular. It sent a flurry of interest throughout the timber confines of the structure, from roots to rings. Only the tiny ones slept through, unaware of the excitement, not yet old enough to recognise an aberration when they saw one.

The gate watchers flew in single file via the upper broken branch entrance of the trunk. Most hung back allowing the head of their small group, an experienced volunteer called Broadleaf, to proceed.

'Where's Cerulean?' she said to anyone who might answer, looking from her mid-height position around the lamplit interior of the tree troll fort. 'I have to speak with her.'

'Out on her walking meditation,' one villager said. 'Shouldn't be gone much longer.'

'She told us she'd be back for supper,' another chimed in.

'Here.' Hoff Skylark emerged from his tent with a stack of wooden bowls and spoons. 'Help yourselves to stew. You lot must be starved. Warm yourselves.'

The other gate watchers turned to Broadleaf for confirmation, which she gave with a look, and they all lowered themselves to where Hoff–or Pappy Skylark as he was more commonly known–handed each of them a bowl. He directed them toward Miss Milda, the self-appointed cook and jolly old dear, who stirred a large cauldron as it bubbled gently over an oil stove nearby.

'Where's the gate sitting lately, my friend?' Pappy said, sitting carefully back on his hammock as Broadleaf returned from the cauldron, bowl in hand. 'You ladies had far to travel this time?'

'Near the Southern border,' Broadleaf said. She blew on a spoonful of stew and took a tentative slurp. 'Hey, this is really good.'

'Milda's finest.' His smile was fleeting. 'South, you say? Air's gotta be mighty thick with smoke down there. Never mind gates. You watchers wanna watch yourselves, ya know. No good to us coughing up ribs.'

Perched on a ledge above, legs dangling, the more junior gate watchers were getting rowdy amongst themselves, bickering and howling with laughter at whispered jokes, emboldened from being home before the planned switchover and with bellies full of warm, delicious food. Broadleaf scooped up a palm of gravel and hurled it toward the unruly fairies, which shut them up, if only momentarily.

'Seen worse,' she said, returning to her conversation with the older Pappy. 'Stacks kick out a hell of a stink, though. Few thousand spotted heifers away and still coats the back of your throat like goddam roof tar.'

'No sign of a let-up?' Pappy said.

'Wish I could tell you different.' Broadleaf looked at the life going on around her, the community, the society that refused to collapse in the face of such overwhelm. 'Still churning as always. If there's one thing can be said about those biggun city engineers, it's that they built a place to last.'

Broadleaf knew what was coming next, a question she'd come to dread, but one she knew Pappy Skylark couldn't help himself but ask. She didn't blame him. It was heartbreaking, was all.

'And any sign of my girls?'

'Not this time, Sir. We'll keep looking, though. You have my word.' She briefly considered breaking her own personal protocol, putting her hand on his by way of reassurance. But the moment passed.

Pappy sighed the sigh of an old man not quite ready to quit but sensing it on the horizon. He pushed himself forward out of the creaking hammock and with a stretch and a yawn and a, 'Righty-ho, then,' he took himself off to bed.

Broadleaf leaned back against the spongy inner of the trunk wall. This place wouldn't last forever, not when the termites took to feasting, but it was a safe enough haven for now. Tomorrow's worries were for her tomorrow self to be worrying about.

This tree, she thought. This beautiful, wise old tree. At one time it had been a troll known to her as Oskar, before he turned from flesh to oak then lost what was left of himself in the burnings. She stroked the inside of the great supporting outer shell with a kindly hand. There was warmth there, still. And a deep and lasting sorrow. Even in their passing, the trolls of these woods were a gift to the folks of Faretheewell, protecting them to the last with their lifeless bodies.

'I'm sorry, my love,' she spoke quietly to the wall. 'Know we are grateful to you, always.'

With the woodland outside cooling from the oncoming night, and the inside hollow warming from lamplight and a host of small crackling fires, the tree trunk shell creaked and groaned, shrinking in places and swelling in others, settling into itself.

Broadleaf chose to believe these shifting sounds were Oskar making himself heard. That he was saying in his own sweet way, 'You're welcome, little one.' And she knew she would never not miss him.

3. COLOUR ME BLUE

Halfway to open ground, the scout paused. His diving helmet muffled the sounds around him, all but the steady, quiet hiss of air, the crunch of his feet. And yet, outside of the steel goldfish bowl that sat heavily weighted on his shoulders, he heard something. For a heart-stopping couple of seconds, he thought it was a hum.

He scanned the gaps between the trees at head height and above, spun a little faster on the spot than he might otherwise have, his breathing pace doubled, his senses stepped up to high alert. He tried to convince himself it had only been his imagination. Tried and failed.

The walk back was often the worst for seeing and hearing things that either weren't anything to worry about or simply weren't there. Jitters were understandable; good people lost their minds and their lives with less warning so it paid to listen to what your gut was telling you around here.

The winged armies of the North had a penchant for letting you think you'd made it out safely, encouraging you to drop your guard before swooping down to finish it, and to finish you. It would be an understatement to say they got a kick out of such tactics. Little shits.

He'd seen it himself, witnessed fully grown men snatched up by the hair on their scalps and carried away in what was nothing short of a flailing, screaming horror show. That was back when on clearer afternoons a helmet was optional, landside, and you could feel the breeze on your skin. Strange to think there was a time when scouts went on missions in pairs. Then, if one got taken the other could report back to Liaison for debrief. It was nobody's idea of an enviable task.

Swarm took him up fifty feet, Sir, dropped him on the spike of a dead pine. Swear I couldn't help him. Only just made it out myself.

Or: *Ripped his hands and feet away and tossed his middle in a pool of sludge for the city dogs. No, don't reckon they took him for processing this time, Sir. Not that I noticed, anyhow.*

Or the one they feared the most: *Carried the geezer off to the city, they did, Sir. Last I heard of him was going off into the clouds. Still alive? I believe so. Poor bastard.*

Things changed as the seasons passed, with the worsening air, the shrinking footprint of the forests and the decreasing numbers of those willing and able to do the legwork required. For the longest time, missions had been solo ventures and those back at base were left to ruminate over what might've happened to a lost colleague in their desperate final moments. Or, the preferred option, to not let themselves think about it at all.

Rock was set to head on, continuing toward where he knew the forest thinned and dispersed into the central plains, when he saw a small glowing light emerge from behind a teepee of dead branches some ten or fifteen yards back. It might've been an ember or a will-o-the-wisp, but for the fact it moved–walked– across the forest floor. He knew the colour of wing, recognised the calm gait of the small figure. The scout checked his wrist dial before making his way back.

'Ahoy there, traveller,' the winged one said, as she and the scout neared each other.

Rock saw how the fairy smiled, having coined the greeting as something of a joke on one of their many previous encounters. 'You do know I'm a diver, not a sailor, right?' he said. 'We've talked about this, little 'un.'

The fairy shrugged: *Meh. Whatever. All the same to me.*

She gave her glowing wings a last stretch and a brief flutter before folding them down and wrapping them under her cloak. The forest dimmed a little after that.

'Still not told them, huh?' Rock said.

'Not yet. I don't imagine it'll go down well when I do. Last thing they need right now is to feel lied to. They've had enough betrayal to last them ten lifetimes.' The fairy sat on a low branch and twirled her feet in circles, having never truly grown accustomed to the strain that walking wrought on her calves.

Rock joined her, taking a seat on a fallen log, still dwarfing his small companion.

'How about you?' the fairy said. 'Good mission? Scout out anything of note?'

She was taking the piss when using that word–*scout* –they both knew it, but Rock quite enjoyed her teasing. He took it as a sign she hadn't been completely broken by her fall from the heights of hummer leadership.

'Just more tags,' he said, referring to the carvings he'd photographed earlier. 'Walked right past your place, actually. Quiet as a tomb. If I hadn't known different, I'd have taken it to be as empty as the next. Not sure they even noticed me.'

'Oh, they noticed. You think a great stomping biggun like you gets past a Faretheewell colony without the whole place knowing about it? Shush, now.' Another smile, this time giving the scout flutters of his own.

Rock's mood darkened when he considered the implications of his mission and the reason for him being there in the first place. How many more times would they meet like this before even these last remaining patches of forest were gone the way of the rest? The loss of green was one thing, the loss of the colonies another, but the loss of this winged one in particular felt to him like the worst of all evils that the South could inflict upon him, personally.

The fairy noticed the saddening on the man's face and in his eyes. 'What aren't you telling me?' she said.

Rock didn't want to have this conversation, least of all with someone who'd already had everything that held any kind of meaning to them stolen away. He didn't want to be the person to say it. But still, it needed to be said.

'The South will mobilise once they reach minimum viability.'

'Okay.' She paused. Then, when the man didn't go on, 'Rock? You know something, and you're terrible at hiding it. Please stop trying to protect me. If you have information, you owe it to us to let us help ourselves.'

This hit where it counted and the scout knew the fairy was right. 'The levels are up, Cerulean,' he said. 'Like, way up. Like, a minute to midnight up. You get what I'm saying?'

'Yes,' the fairy said, calmly.

'If we can't stop it, or at the very least get you all out, you will die.'

The fairy looked away as if considering her reply. After a moment, she turned her eyes back toward the giant man in the tin can suit. 'We're not divers, like you, biggun. I thank you for your concern, and the continued intelligence, but we stay until the end.'

She got to her feet. It was a sign for them both to be on their way.

'And you can, if you wish, call me by my given name. It feels right that you do, seeing as we are friends of a sort.' She took a breath. 'Leddy. You may call me Leddy.'

'Well, Leddy,' the scout said with a bow. 'As always, I'm pleased to see you. And tell your people, our gate is open for any of you that choose to use it.'

'I shall. Until next time, Mister Rock.'

The scout watched as she made her way on foot through the trees in the direction of the hollows. It didn't seem to matter how many times they spoke, he was never not in awe of these tiny magical beings. He knew her true name, of course, had all along, and had merely been waiting for the proud fairy to feel safe enough in his presence, maybe respect him enough (like him enough?) to open up and tell him herself.

It was interesting to Rock how the former hummer had chosen to hide behind a name that so represented the sky-blue of her Northern homeland–*Cerulean*–and he often wondered if she wasn't in fact hoping to get found out, a form of self-flagellation, as punishment for crimes she'd committed against the Diamonders in a previous life. To date, he hadn't seen anything to suggest that the Faretheewell residents knew, however, and he wouldn't be the one to break it to them, now or ever. Not that much of an arsehole, he thought. Regardless of any reputation he might've formed back at base.

'Until next time, Squad Leader Rickett,' he said, quietly and to himself within the confines of his diving helmet, before setting off for the far side of the central plains.

***

Crossing the wilds of Middle Diamond, the scout could if he wanted to make out the silhouette of skyscrapers and stacks to his right, could trace a finger along the skyline of the city of Must scorched into the heavens some thirty miles south. He didn't stop to look, having seen it a hundred times before in progressively darker shades of grey. To spend another moment studying it, to give the smoke clouds spewing high into the atmosphere a single ounce of his attention, would trigger a fury in him so great he would likely be unable to control it.

How the scientists did their jobs was a mystery to him. He'd be inclined to rip the screens from the wall if he had to do what they did all day long, which was monitor and categorise and record the city's outflow and calculate the damage being done. He knew he was incapable of such restraint.

So, on he went, eyes forward, periodically checking only that his dial wasn't tipping into the red. And when the home gate came into view he moved a little faster, glanced up a little more often to check for hummers, before finally, blessedly, falling back into his own world.

***

In the penthouse of the highest tower in Must, the crystal eye of a powerful telescope focused in on the man as he approached the shimmering gate. From this distance he appeared as if the same size as the one watching him.

No, smaller.

From here he was pick-up-able, crush-in-your-hand-able. A weak and tiny man trespassing in a big world where he didn't belong.

'Has he gone?' Master of all the South said.

'Yes.'

'How long until they return?'

The hummer stepped away from the window to face the intercom. 'Long enough, Sire.'

'Good. Ready your troops. And, Borealis?'

'Sire?'

'Be sure to leave none behind.'

4. SHE SEES

Synapses fire as chemical, electrical, and magical combine. At one time, a powerful charge unmatched by another. Now, a perfect pulsing storm of all she is and was, a final plea in the vacuum of perpetual death, a grab for what little airtime is left, a transmission from here to anywhere.

Far and near, now and ever after, she sees what she sees without judgement, hate, or expectation. Just sees what she sees and knows what she knows, none of it within her control.

That which she emanates was once hers to say and share, now just is, existing within her, a part of her not to be steered, just released, in the hope of a hearing ear, an open mind, a willing receiver, to connect...to connect. And maybe change the unchangeable?

She sees all, knows all, knows what will be, what could be, what in no uncertain terms cannot be. That is what she is now. That is all she is.

In the city she sees a woman, as fierce as any. Sees her as plainly as her own reflection on the curved glass. One more knowing joins the infinite number of other knowings, as if it were there all along: 'Tis she.

She cannot think, cannot decide, cannot action. These things are lost to her, a fingertip away, out of reach. And yet, from somewhere strength is given, lent, enough for a single coherent choice.

Call to her, now, with all you have. Cry out until she too knows what she must. And the knowing of what can be and will be and has to be done will make it so.

'Tis she.

The woman.

The girl.

In all of time and place.

'Tis she.

5. GREEN SKULLS

By the time Leddy arrived on foot at the meeting tree, the others were already there. How she wanted to fly. How much easier that would be. But then they'd know and it would cause a lot more problems than it solved. Like being banished or tried for war crimes, or being shipped off North where she'd be dealt with accordingly.

The group shifted in such a way as to make room for her to sidle through and she took her seat next to a warm, glowing oil lamp and waited for the mutterings to subside.

'I've spoken with the scout,' she said, once attention had turned to the business at hand. 'Things are happening as we suspected they might. He says time is short.'

One among the group cleared his throat. Fig was a lithe looking young 'un, green under his fingernails from a day spent scratching tags into bark.

Leddy signalled for him to speak.

'Did the scout get our messages?' he said.

'Yes. He saw the carvings and knows where they lead. However, he doesn't yet understand what it is he needs to do, nor was he able to follow the trail on this occasion.'

A ripple of groans and tuts went through the group.

'I know, I know. He can't help but need air. Would you rather we get him to the city and he dies before he can complete the task?'

Some appeared to consider the question.

Leddy sighed and rolled her head back. 'No,' she reminded them. 'We wouldn't. If he's able to help us, then we must first help him, yes?'

This at least was met by mumbles and nods of resignation.

Many in the hollow couldn't recall the vibrant hub that was Diamond in the days of Queen Janet. When you could barely hop from one tree to the next without stumbling across a West gate person making their way to or from Must. All they knew was what came after. They had no affinity with the people and certainly no loyalty to them. This notion of accommodating the biggun to achieve their aims was hard to swallow, but they were coming to understand that one thing wasn't to be without the other.

'We cannot do this without a person,' Leddy continued. 'One we can trust, or at the very least believe has similar interests to our own. And he, whether you like it or not, is probably our best and last shot. The South is coming, and soon. We'd better hope the scout returns before they do.'

Pappy Skylark leaned forward through the others from where he'd been quietly listening. Leddy hadn't even realised he was there until he spoke.

'What is this man to us, then, Cerulean?' he said. 'If he can't survive when the air is thick, then what good is he? What if he gives us away before he does his part? Surely we haven't time to babysit the vulnerable, big as he may be?'

'Speaking of which,' said another. 'What of the king?'

'What of him?' Leddy said.

'He has to be held accountable. Or are you proposing an amnesty for all bigguns, regardless of guilt?'

This was followed by a rousing chorus of cheers and nods, and Aye, that's rights, from certain elements within the crowd. Not all joined in, but enough to make Leddy nervous. Their commitment was waning. She could feel it.

Some were struggling to hold onto the vision that togetherness was the solution. They were leaning more towards vengeance, which Leddy knew from bitter experience was no kind of way out. On the contrary, it would almost certainly drive what was left of the Faretheewell folks to their deaths. And fast. She was about to counter the uproar, though how she didnt know, when Pappy came to her defence.

'Pipe down, the lot a ya,' he said.

The hollow quietened and Leddy was grateful. She hid her weariness, but had nothing left to battle those supposedly on the same side.

'Look,' Pappy said, as all eyes turned to face him. 'I hear your anxieties and I know you're worried for yourselves and your young 'uns. Believe me, I understand. You'll be aware–well most of you, anyways–that I lost my girls to the hummer campaigns before some here were even born.'

Quiet turned to breath-held silence.

'I know how it feels when the worst happens. Ain't much more them buzzards can do to me than what they already did. So I got nothin' to lose.'

'What's your point, old 'un?' a young recruit with an inflated sense of self-importance piped up.

'My point is this, child,' Pappy said. 'They only win if we let 'em. They can come for us, might even kill every last one of us.'

There came gasps from mothers whose little 'uns looked suddenly horrified.

'I'm sorry, not gonna shine yer shit. They might. But we don't make it easy. Ya hear? We catch in their teeth, make 'em choke on our bones. We give those filthy scumlickers bellyache. We tell 'em, Hey! If you want our bodies, our magic, you gotta come get 'em. But what they don't get is this.'

Pappy tapped his chest.

'Don't know about you, but I'll be ready. And I sure as stink won't be laying down on a platter for 'em, a berry for a garnish. No, sir. And if our friend Cerulean here reckons this biggun fella can help, then I'll be gosh-darned if I ain't gonna do everything in my power to see he gets what he needs to finish it. Try at least. We fight together, child, or not at all. Because if we don't, they win.'

Pappy slowly sat himself back down. 'That,' he said, his eyes seeming to pierce clean through the young recruit, 'is my point.'

Leddy suppressed a smile.

It was then that a sudden flicker, a bothering of the light from an oil lamp in the doorway, made the group look to see who or what had cast this new shadow. Hovering there was the gate watcher, Broadleaf. She dropped herself down and in through the gaping arch of the tree trunk, and by the furrow of her brow, she was none too impressed by what she saw.

Leddy stood, ready to do damage control.

'What happened to keeping together?' Broadleaf said. 'And no secrets among hollows? How long, Cerulean?'

'It's not-' Pappy tried to intervene.

'Don't FUCKING lie to me.' Broadleaf pointed a sharp finger on an outstretched arm at the older fairy to her side, while not taking her eyes from those of Leddy Rickett.

Mothers covered little ears at the language.

'Now, listen to me, young 'un,' Pappy said.

'It's okay,' Leddy interrupted. 'She has a right to be angry. Let her say her piece.'

Broadleaf lowered her arm, but the snarl on her lips that masqueraded as a smile, the slow shake of her head, captured her rage quite clearly for all to see.

Leddy waited. She wasn't about to tell the Faretheewell native how to feel or what to think, having seen, and in many cases partaken in, the ruin of hollows such as hers. Only she, Leddy, an ex-hummer, could possibly understand the devastation this poor fairy had observed and to what length such trauma had affected her.

'You promised me, Cerulean. When you took me in, dragged me a hundred damned heifer's lengths from my burning home, from my dead fucking family, Cerulean, you promised I would never again see the likes of what they did.'

Enough was enough for the mothers, who, without saying a word, agreed among themselves that it was time to take the children home to bed. They slipped out into the night with the little ones in crooks of arms or snoozing over shoulders. Some older babies wanted to stay, preferring this unexpected hullabaloo to the duller alternative. But their protestations went unheeded and they were carried away, nonetheless.

'I know what you're up to,' Broadleaf said, once the bustle of movement settled, leaving only eight or ten of them standing inside the tree. She hadn't taken her gaze from Leddy the whole time.

Leddy felt a wave of fear at those words: *I know what you're up to*. She chose not to jump in. Let the fairy speak, she thought. See where this is going. It was a rare situation that could be made worse by keeping your mouth shut.

'I get it. You want to lead. To take over old Skylark here's position?'

Pappy didn't respond. He too wanted to know where this rant was headed.

'So you play up the whole wingless angle like you don't know that'll remind him of his dead daughter. How stupid do you think we are?'

One of the gatherers attempted to step in to defend against the accusations, but Pappy held him back.

'You're dragging us into a fight,' Broadleaf went on. 'That ends up with us dangling by our feet from hooks, drying over coals for jerky, with our magic stripped and harvested and used against us. The whole damn colony. Is that what you want?

'Do you know why I'm here, Cerulean? I followed Pappy so I could report back to you about developments at the gate. But I don't suppose that matters, does it? Did it ever? Or did you only send us there to get us out of the way, so you could hold your little meetings and plot your little plots, while the rest of us flutter about doing as we're told?

'Well, you know what? Fuck you, Cerulean. In fact, no. I take that back. Fuck all of you. You want to kill off the last of Faretheewell? Guide us to the doors of our enemies? Go ahead. Just don't expect me to be there when you do.'

Broadleaf took to the air. 'Oh, and just so I've played my part in this charade,' she said. 'The girl's back.'

'The girl?' Leddy said.

'Yes. She's back and she doesn't appear to be going anywhere. Now I'm done.'

A moment later, the furious gate watcher zipped away into the night. The recruit named Fig was about to follow, to make her answer for her disrespectful words, no doubt. But Pappy stopped him, told him he'd deal with it later.

'Let her go,' Leddy said, mirroring the sentiment. 'Give her a night to come around. By morning, I dare say she'll feel better for getting that out.'

One by one, the gatherers went back to their beds until only Leddy and the old fairy remained. Together, they rearranged the twig benches and chairs and bundled up drink shells into waste bags so as to make it appear like there hadn't been a meeting. It wouldn't do to let the others know that the notorious Green Skulls existed so close to home. The risk to them would be too great. Leddy banked on Broadleaf, however angry, understanding that and keeping her mouth shut.

'Is she right?' Pappy said when they were finishing up. 'Do you think I'm treating you as some sort of replacement daughter?'

'Of course not.' Leddy hoped her answer came across more convincing than it felt. 'Besides, even if you were, and anyone would understand why you might, I'd be honoured. Any daughter of yours must be pretty special.'

'My Mae had her problems, can't pretend otherwise. But she was my girl and I loved her. Loved 'em both.'

Leddy stroked her hand across the old fairy's arm, gave his shoulder a squeeze.

'I just wish,' he said. 'I just wish-'

Leddy pulled him in close, then, and held him until his words trailed off.

'I know, Pappy,' she said. 'I do too.'

6. NEST

Smoke and ash billowed around the abomination that had formerly been Mae Skylark. It gave her no cause to cough or retch. She was used to it now. She and her sister thought nothing of the darkening skies.

Here atop one of many perches across the city she had build for herself out of twigs and branches and nettles and moss scavenged while raiding the West, a watch post from where she could not only spy on the shadows below, but also intercept the messages with greater ease, she perhaps didn't realise the comfort these nests of green brought her. A home away from home, one might say, if one dared.

Her master called to her shortly after nightfall. His voice was fearsome and deep, as a bear or a lion, yet he whispered. His words cut through all others. 'Green blood,' he said. 'Oh, green blood.'

'I am here,' the fairy said, her own voice carried away across the rooftops. 'How may I serve?'

'A man, green blood, a filthy trespassing man met with a shitterbug in the West. Such treachery cannot be allowed. Find them and bring them to me.'

'I shall, Sire.'

'Good. Use your skills, green blood. Show me why you continue to be my most prized asset. Deliver the traitor to the gate and I shall be sure to reward your loyalty.'

Her wings twitched–a reflex. 'Thank-you, Sire. You are generous as always.'

The quiet roar of her master faded and the other chatter returned.

'The wings,' Eryl said, in a voice closer and clearer than most. 'Get him to revive our wings. Look at the state of them, sister. They fade and crumble like the dead relics they are.'

'The wings,' Mae said. 'Always the wings. Must we have this every time?'

'You stole them from me so, yes, I'm afraid we do. You know they won't carry our weight much longer. Then where will we be? Grounded again, that's where. And killing me will have been for nothing.'

Mae smacked her own forehead. 'Shut up!' she said.

Eryl didn't shut up, her voice was swallowed by the others, which at least gave her sister some semblance of respite.

Mae stood, her toes curled in amongst the woven twigs, then gently hovered upward to check her own strength and that of the wings. It was enough for now. When she was quite sure they would hold for the flight to Faretheewell, she left the safety of her nest and flitted over the city in the direction of what little remained of the forest.

***

The darkness didn't phase Broadleaf. She was too enraged to notice any risk to herself. She would eventually have to go back and face Cerulean and the old 'un in a more civilised fashion, but for now she needed to fly, to burn off the energy that hung like a clenched fist in her gut, the feeling of being tricked, insulted, of being the last to know.

The hummers would come for them at this hollow just like they had at her own. They'd take the gifted, the strong, those with something worth stealing, and burn the rest. This much she knew having seen it up close in intimate detail. The smell would never leave her as long as she lived.

After a while she reached a pocket of open ground between two clusters of scorched and splintered trees in the middle of which was a stone monument of some kind. Broadleaf hovered down to get a better look, her anger momentarily taking a back seat to curiosity. She slowed and lowered and came to a standing halt on top of the thing.

At first she didn't recognise it, blackened by flame, no adornments of flowers, out here in the open like a stray tooth.

Janet's Table.

Broadleaf read the inscription: We await your return, always. Our beloved queen.

She slumped down onto the stone slab that formed the top of the shrine. She'd been so young when Janet was taken, but she remembered how the air had changed as if the disappearance were a catalyst for all the changes that came after. Like the rest of Faretheewell and many from further afield, across

Diamond and beyond, she had travelled here with her parents to leave gifts of flowers as a mark of respect. This had been a place where they could share their grief and join as one, where they set aside perceived differences.

Broadleaf realised she was crying.

'I'm so sorry,' she said to none but the memory of a fallen monarch.

Behind her, the sound of a light breeze picked up, a fluttering of dead leaves, a rush of air through the branches. By the time it grew close enough for Broadleaf to register that it wasn't the wind, it was already upon her. As she turned to look, a cloth sack was thrust down over her head and pulled tightly around her throat, her arms were yanked around her back and lashed together, crushing her wings in place.

First she was blindly pulled up to stand, then her feet left the stone table behind altogether. She was airborne, though not under her own power. She tried to call out, but, just as one of her assailant's arms was looped under her elbows to drag her along, so too was a hand firmly clamped over the sack cloth and over her mouth. It was all she could do to breathe.

They'll save me, she tried desperately to believe. The others will come. They'll follow. They'll save me. Then she remembered that the others didn't even see where she'd gone, so quickly had she flown off in her hot-headedness. As far as anyone at the hollow knew she'd gone back to her bed to sleep off the argument. They likely wouldn't even check on her until morning.

She thought of Janet and wondered, if a queen could vanish without trace then what hope was there for a commoner like her? No hope, was the answer. None at all. And she knew it was her day to die.

7. THERE ONCE WAS A BOY

The boy, Danny, grew. When at first he arrived in the strange and beautiful world beyond the foss, so many moons ago, he knew not what it meant to lead other than the fact he answered to no-one. That he kept losing moments of time was by the by. A few grains of sand in the hourglass. Was he happy? Not entirely. He still missed his mother, of course, though that diminished with the years. Not having to duck the swoop of his father's hand helped balance out the scoresheet of regrets.

The Diamonders feigned a welcome. Too stunned were they (though not yet afraid; that would come later) to be anything other than swept up in the parades and coronation events that sprung up alarmingly soon in the wake of the queen's disappearance.

A void must be filled. Not least a void at the top.

They weren't to know that the boy was the cause of their sadness. That he'd tricked the queen into a cursed jar, slammed on the lid, screwed it down tight.

'Such apathy will pass,' the courtiers told him, their tiny hands stroking his cheek when he questioned why the citizens didn't love him unconditionally as was promised. 'They'll come to know you as we do, Your Highness. Just wait. You'll see.'

But what cannot be achieved fairly and graciously in one way, they said, must be strong armed in another. If nice didn't gain the loyalty and worship of one's subjects? Well, the King's winged forces knew what had to be done. And they did it with the clarity of thought reserved for those who knew their end play before they began.

Danny, alas, was late to the party. Too late even to save himself.

As he grew, they whispered in his ears what to say, how to say it, stole his will along with his days, tied him up in invisible strings, drugged him with everything he could ever possibly desire. And he danced for them like a good boy, all the while unaware that this was their game from the start: control of a different kind.

He didn't know it then, but the boy was a prisoner no less than the queen herself. A tranquilised puppet rolled out when needed and boxed up and kept out of sight when not.

There once was a boy named Danny, who grew to be a man as blank and angry and crammed full of resentments as his father was before him.

And that boy believed himself king.

8. WHEN WE ARE GROWN

The week of the funeral went by in a strange haze. People Marie vaguely remembered from childhood, or whom she knew only in passing from times she'd run into them at the village shop, stopped her in the street to pay their respects or knocked on the door as they passed by. There were more quiches and lasagnas clogging up the fridge than any reasonable person could eat in a month, let alone someone who'd lost their appetite, as Marie had. Each time, she politely took their offerings, though she was finding it increasingly difficult to disguise her irritation at not having a single goddamn minute alone.

The service itself fell on a Friday. A modest crowd showed up to mourn despite hard rain that bounced off the tarmac and soaked even those with umbrellas, whipping up at them from below.

Inside the small church, the people sat, quietly spoken and uncomfortably damp. The warmth from creaking pipes thick with a century of repaints brought out that dusty whiff of oak and parchment, of stale wine and candlewax. It would impregnate their hair and the fabric of their clothes, making them smell like Sunday until they washed them next.

Father Colin's eulogy seemed to be about someone else, and Marie, who read a poem about how flowers weren't meant to last forever, wondered if he'd even met Barbara. He was new and looked too fresh-faced to be a full-fledged vicar. But wasn't that the way? Marie guessed that the phenomenon of too-young-to-be-a doctor/vicar/teacher/et cetera would only get more noticeable from here on out.

She cried a little (not an exorbitant amount, but enough that others wouldn't think her cold and unfeeling) and she held it together for another hour and a half at the hall, directing people to a trestle table of sausage rolls and triangle sandwiches and mini Scotch eggs, and several Tupperware bowls of 'fancy crisps', as her mother would've called them, had she somehow been at her own wake.

There came the inevitable time when Marie had nothing more to say. Like the fall of an iron portcullis, her mood dropped almost from one moment to the next. She quite simply ran out of words.

Fortunately, Olive, who'd been watching Marie throughout, clocked the change and gave Hubert a nudge, who then did an admirable job as the de facto responsible adult and gently eased people on their way.

Marie tried to help the church volunteers clear tables, collect glasses, and so on, but they wouldn't hear of it.

'Let us do this for Barbara,' they said, with a touch of a hand on her forearm, which Marie found bizarrely hilarious in the murk of the day. As far as she knew, her mother saw the volunteer group as a bunch of old busy-bodies hell-bent on mothering this vicar or any other into submission. So she left them to it. Far be it from her, she thought, to muscle in on their roles as the runners and keepers of all things church.

Hubert dropped Marie home. Sitting in the soft leather seat of his old silver Jaguar felt safe, like being in a warm, impenetrable cocoon. By then the rain had stopped and, as Olive had decided to walk back from the village to get some fresh air, or so she said, it was just the two of them in the car.

Hubert wasn't one for chit-chat. He wasn't one to talk feelings or sentiment. So it was a pleasantly quiet ride back to Darkwood, and they witnessed a partial rainbow as a stray shaft of sunlight broke through the otherwise slate heavy sky. Marie might've taken it as a sign from Barbara had she believed in such hippy-dippy, airy-fairy nonsense.

They rolled up outside the cottage and Hubert pulled on the brake. 'She was a good sort, your mother,' he said, pursing his lips together, staring straight ahead, nodding ever so slightly. And that was that.

'Can you let Olive know I'm going to bed?' Marie said. 'She'll probably think to pop over to check on me. Tell her I'm okay and I'll give her a call tomorrow.'

'Will do,' Hubert said. He seemed to be gearing up to say something else, some words of wisdom he'd gleaned from years of burying loved ones, maybe.

Marie waited a moment, and when it became clear that Hubert had nothing more to offer, no wisdom, no comment of any kind, she creaked open the passenger door, forced a smile, and hauled herself out.

'Thanks for the lift.'

'Anytime, biggun.'

Marie turned back. 'What was that?'

'I said, Anytime, love.' There was nothing on the man's face to suggest otherwise.

She misheard, was all. Crazy, tiring day. Nothing left to do but sleep it off, wake up tomorrow and start the long process of figuring out who she was now.

'Okay, well, goodnight,' Marie said, and clunked the heavy car door shut. She turned and walked toward the empty house, watching out of the corner of her eye as the old man manoeuvred the Jag back onto the narrow road and away.

***

Inside, there were too many changes to describe the place as Marie's childhood home. It had received something of a facelift following Barbara's lottery win. Nothing structural, mind you, just a late twentieth century (as was) makeover: antique pine units and blue tiles in the kitchen and floral prints literally fucking everywhere else. Or 'country cottage chic' as her mother liked to call it. It all looked so very dated now.

Marie was in school halfway across England by the time the renovations started and, frankly, was glad not to be there. At eleven years old, it felt to her as if the last of her father was being painted over. Surfaces that he'd touched, where she imagined parts of him still existed in some form, were sanded down and varnished in foreign tones, while feature walls replaced any scuff mark reminders of him.

Despite the overhaul, there remained a few subtle touches of the old place here and there: the log burner, the attic hatch, the angled curve of the stairwell. These things were still undeniably Darkwood. But most were not.

A university photo of a much younger Marie holding a fake rolled up certificate took pride of place between the patterned plates on the kitchen dresser. Alongside it was one of Barbara standing in front of an iceberg, evidently taken while cruising the Norwegian fjords, and a framed letter from some ageing quiz show host she'd befriended online. Relics of her mother's adventures were everywhere, evidence of how the older woman had flourished in the absence of the younger. It all felt too much, and at the same time not enough.

Marie picked up the picture taken onboard the ship. In it Barbara beamed from ear to ear while proudly standing next to a tall man in uniform who Marie took to be the ship's captain. How happy her mother looked.

Happy without me.

She tried to stifle the notion, but it was stuck, just as it had been ever since the day her mother packed her off to St Jude's. She placed the picture down.

The lottery win hadn't been quite the slam-dunk it first appeared. Five families hit the jackpot that weekend. It wasn't a rollover, so each won a tad over 1.1 million pounds. A chunk of that went on the house renovations, another chunk on Marie's board and fees at St Jude's, and the rest Barbara seemingly blew left and right on holidays and long weekends at self-help guru retreats, health spas, and meet 'n' greets with people off the television.

The final figures weren't in from the solicitor yet, but by Marie's estimation there wouldn't be a whole lot left, not after the cost of the funeral and getting the garden cleaned up and a few bits that needed to be done to the house. But she was grateful to have a roof over her head as that at least bought her the time and security to figure out her next steps.

The kitchen grew dark, so she went to the window and gazed down the overgrown garden toward the raggedy hedgerow that separated the Darkwood plot from the fields below.

'Such a mess,' she said out loud, referring to the state of the garden, only realising afterward that she was correct on both literal and figurative fronts.

That was a job for another day, as were they all. Today surely had to be the hardest and it was almost over. Tomorrow she'd begin the unenviable task of rifling through her mother's paperwork–the legal stuff, the financial stuff, the personal stuff–which was about the last thing she wanted to do, now or ever. But, like house maintenance, some things just couldn't be ignored.

In the heart of the brambles, a shadow, or rather a deeper shadow than the others, a shadow within a shadow, gave the impression of a gap in the wild green wall of growth. An opening. A tunnel. She stared harder, trying to make sense of the shapes in the grey. But before she could get a lock on it, the light faded further and darkness took the hedgerow and its secrets into the realm of night.

For the first time in as long as she could remember, Marie pulled down the kitchen blind. It was a simple act that served no purpose. There was nothing or nobody to hide from, not even a scarecrow in the lower field. A handful of cattle, perhaps, but even they were more interested in grazing than the comings and goings of the people in the house next door. And besides, at this time of night they were likely safe and warm in their sheds.

Still, it felt right. With the blind drawn she was reassured by the sense of being closed in. Or of something else being closed out. She didn't want to see the windows and their cold, dark emptiness. It felt akin to looking into a black hole, a portal to nowhere.

She plugged her phone in to charge, pressed the side button to switch it back on having turned it off for the funeral, and laid it on the worktop. As she waited, she noticed her mother's calendar on the wall, times and places written on it in different colours, some on days past, some on days yet to come. Plans never to be fulfilled.

In her mind she replayed what Hubert had said: 'She was a good sort, your mother.' And just as she had with the young vicar's eulogy, Marie tried to reconcile the words spoken with the woman she'd known, the woman who'd sent her away and lived happily ever after.

The phone woke up with a lurching buzz. It cycled through its startup procedure and she mindlessly watched for no other reason than she was too tired to take herself upstairs. The familiar home screen appeared, then populated with the usual array of apps. Finally, the bars indicated a mobile signal and 5G connection. She made a mental note to log on to her mother's Wi-Fi in the morning which, she reminded herself, was in fact her Wi-Fi now.

After a moment, the phone buzzed several times more and a message showed that over the course of the day four calls from an unidentified number had been missed. This brought the total number of calls from an unknown caller over the last week well into double figures. No message had been left in any instance.

Marie switched off the vibrate function, then placed the mobile face-down on the worktop where it could stay until morning. Tomorrow she had calls to make, but at that moment it was just one more thing on a really long list of things she didn't care about. She flicked off the light and went upstairs.

***

The watchers watched. A skeleton crew of three.

Broadleaf would be back soon and demand an update and they would have all the answers, all the latest information, and she would be pleased with them.

They would show how good they were at their jobs even without being managed up close.

'Where is she?'

'Shush.'

'You shush!'

'Both of you shush. She's upstairs.'

They jostled and repositioned in the hedgerow until they settled into a comfortable arrangement where they were each satisfied with their view.

'Shouldn't we tell her?'

'Tell her what?'

'About the goblin. She needs to know, don't you think?'

'Not for us to decide. Watchers, not do-ers, remember? That kinda thinking gets us pulled into sluice duty.'

The smallest of the three sat back, folded her arms across her chest. 'You want us to watch while the girl gets killed in her sleep? Then what? Report back on how it happened? Anyone'd reckon you as working for the South.'

'Don't be overdramatic.'

'Fine. Tell me he's not coming for her.'

The biggest of the three said nothing, but she knew the little one was right. She looked over her shoulder, back toward the gate, its gentle swirl of twinkling light: still there, still open. No sign of Broadleaf or the others, though. How much longer could they be? If the goblin did show, there wasn't a whole lot the three of them could do by themselves except watch and wait and shove their fists in their mouths to stop from screaming out.

'Here,' the middle one said, passing a pouch forward to the others containing the last of the crunchy chestnut biscuits.

'Thanks,' the biggest and littlest replied, taking turns to reach into the pouch.

Then they sat back and watched some more.

9. NO REST FOR THE WICKED

Midday came and went by the time Marie was awoken by a curt *rap-rap-rap* on the front door. She clambered out of bed and pulled on a pair of jeans, threw a loose cardigan over the t-shirt she'd slept in, then made her way downstairs.

Father Colin was the last person she expected to see through the glass panels of the front door the day after her mother's funeral. But there he was, backlit by a halo of sunshine, his tall silhouette looking particularly vicar-like in the black attire of the clergy, as if he went around dressed like that at all times, just in case.

'Hello, Father,' she said, upon opening the door. She wrapped the cardigan around her torso and crossed her arms to disguise the fact she wasn't wearing a bra. 'This is a surprise. I thought you had a Saturday morning sermon to deliver.'

'Yes,' he said, and the young vicar smiled. 'As the name suggests, that was this morning. And now I'm here to see you.'

Marie glanced at the clock on the hallway wall and was suddenly embarrassed at having slept so late.

'Just a courtesy visit, Ms. Fisher. To check you're alright after yesterday. I know the days after a funeral can feel like an anticlimax. Especially when the person you said goodbye to was a close family member, and all those people you couldn't get rid of in the days leading up to it tend to disappear when the main event is over.'

The vicar made a gesture with both hands–poof!–like little bilateral explosions. 'They either think they should give you space or don't know what to say. Human nature, I suppose. Happens all the time. Anyway, I was in the neighbourhood.'

There was nothing patronising in his manner, but the kindness of his words hit a nerve. It occurred to Marie that, in the nicest possible way, he was lying as there was no neighbourhood here, just a handful of cottages clustered within a half mile of each other on a narrow and winding stretch of road. He was here by choice, she knew, not chance. She felt a sudden sting high up in her nose and sniffed it away.

'Thank-you,' she said, giving her forehead a pass with the back of her wrist just for something to do. 'I'm fine. I have a fridge full of food thanks to your parishioners being a bunch of feeders, and stacks of paperwork to get through, so-'

'Does it need to be done today?' the vicar said with a curious tilt of his head.

'Best not to leave it too long or I won't be able to face it.'

'Yes, but does it need to be done...*today?*'

Marie studied the young man's face. She was picking up a vibe of some kind, though nothing she could pin down. Before she could figure him out, he spoke again.

'Okay, okay. I can see you're on to me,' he said, raising his hands in mock defence. 'Honestly, Ms.

Fisher? My motives are selfish. You'd be doing me an enormous favour by inviting me in for a cup of tea. I can't for the life of me shake off the ladies at the vicarage. I'm loath to use the word torturous, but I'm sure if they had their way they'd strap me down in a comfy chair, take turns giving me shoulder rubs and manicures while discussing the gospels. And, forgive my language, Christ knows if I see another teacake I may vomit. It's a bit, how can I say? intense. Know what I mean?'

This new vicar stood on the porch in such a confident stance that Marie didn't think for a single second he was incapable of fending off the likes of Edith or Edna or whoever. There was a masculine energy about him, an undeniable, palpable force. A kind of strength that even the dog collar and all the self-deprecation in the world couldn't hide.

And something in those eyes. Where they blue or green or-

From inside, a buzzing cut through the moment. Father Colin's gaze searched beyond the hallway to the stairwell, and up. Then, when the buzzing stopped, he looked back at Marie, raised his eyebrows and smiled. 'Tea?' he said with a glint, less like a member of the clergy, more like one of Barbara's game show hosts.

'Um, yes, okay then,' Marie said, moving away from the door and gesturing awkwardly for the vicar to come in. She cursed herself for not thinking of an excuse fast enough.

In the kitchen, and after flicking the kettle on, Marie checked her phone which was face-down on the counter where she'd left it. She was confused to see nobody had called, but remembered that even if the phone did ring it wouldn't buzz, the vibrate function having been switched off the night before.

'Anything important?' Father Colin asked.

'No. Nothing at all, actually.'

The vicar, tall as he was, dominated the low-ceilinged kitchen as he stood politely by the table.

'Please,' Marie said. 'Take a seat.'

He pulled out a chair and sat himself down.

'Sometimes the quiet can be a blessing,' Father Colin said. 'Sometimes not. Which is this?'

'A blessing, I suppose.' She discarded the phone and tinkered about pulling mugs from the cupboard and teabags from a jar on the countertop. 'Sugar?'

'Sweet enough,' the vicar said, with another of those looks.

Too young, she thought, batting away the very idea of it. Too...vicar-y.

After making and passing the young man his hot drink, Marie pulled out the chair opposite Father Colin and sat down. Even though they were in her kitchen, sitting at her table, she waited for the vicar to speak. After all, it felt like this was his gig to emcee.

She could tell Father Colin was doing the thing that therapists do, where they say nothing so eventually you feel the need to fill the quiet with words.

Two can play at that game, she thought, reflecting the young man's smile right back at him, fully intending to stare him out, only to draw her eyes away a moment later and pretend to be idly glancing around the room. Seemed she was losing her touch.

Despite this, or perhaps because of it, the vicar caved first. Which gave Marie some small and admittedly petty satisfaction.

'Are you planning to stay in the area?' he said.

'I don't know. I haven't decided yet.'

'And your husband? Will he be joining you at some point?'

Father Colin must've noticed how this last comment affected Marie: the stiffening of her back, the subtle straightening of her posture in the chair. 'I'm sorry, your mother spoke about you at church on occasion. She told me about your wedding; didn't you get married abroad on a beach? Anyway, she was sad to have missed your special day, but she spoke so highly of you both. And I couldn't help noticing-' He nodded to where her wedding ring ought to have been and where the flesh still held the indented shape of the gold band that she'd left on the bedside drawers back in London, along with the keys to the flat.

She covered her left hand with her right.

'I'm sorry,' he said. 'I've spoken out of turn. Forgive me.'

'No, it's fine. We…Shaun's busy with work at the minute. So, no, he won't be joining me. One less sheep for your congregation, I'm afraid, Father.'

'Oh dear,' the vicar said, leaning back in the chair. 'Is that what you think of us? Out on the prowl for fresh scalps? I promise that's not why I'm here.'

'Why are you here?' Marie said. It came out more harshly than she'd have planned, but she chose not to correct herself or apologise, instead leaving it to hang there. Let the man of God fill the silence, she thought.

Father Colin looked down at where he now held his mug of tea with both hands and Marie thought she saw sadness creep across his face. Or maybe he was thinking of how to say what he was about to say without upsetting her further. Which was probably a wise decision given the headspace she was in, the mood Shaun delighted in describing as 'caustic', as if she were a kitchen cleaning product or a chemical spill.

'I thought you might understand what it was like to feel out of place, Marie,' he said, looking up at her across the table, unblinking.

The way he spoke her name sent a small jolt of adrenaline through her stomach. This man had gone from formal to intimate in less than a breath. Before Marie could answer there was a knock at the front door. She held the vicar's gaze just a couple of beats more then pushed her chair back. She was about to go out to answer the door, but there was no need as Olive was already in the process of letting herself in.

'Coo-eee,' the older lady called from the hallway. 'Anyone home? Marie? Are you in? Only me.'

Olive appeared in the kitchen doorway carrying a fresh pint of milk and a couple of glossy magazines under her arm, with a shopping bag dangling from her elbow. 'There you are!' she said. 'Oh, hello, Father. Didn't know you'd be here. Has the kettle just boiled? Lovely.'

As Olive made herself at home, clearly knowing her way around, Father Colin got up. 'Actually, I should be getting back,' he said. 'Goodness knows what the volunteers will have done to my vestry. Mrs. Poulter was eyeing up the bookshelves last I saw. I'd better go and check she hasn't rearranged it all according to the scriptures, or wherever she gets her ideas.'

'You haven't finished your tea,' Marie said, only half-heartedly.

'No, no. I'll leave you ladies to it. Nice chatting with you, Ms. Fisher.' Marie noted he'd returned to the formal option. He gave Olive a nod. 'Mrs. Wells.'

'Father,' Olive said in a no-nonsense tone, too busy lifting items out of her shopping bag to pay him much attention.

The vicar insisted he was perfectly able to find the front door by himself, so Marie didn't follow him into the hallway, but she did listen out for the creak and click that indicated he'd gone. And when she was sure he was well on his way down the road, she went and turned the key in the front door. As peaceful a place as this was, she wasn't used to people dropping in unannounced.

'How long since Father Colin took over as vicar?' Marie said, back in the kitchen.

'Ooh, a few months. Dear old Rev. Wallace–you remember him?–well, he upped and retired. Last minute decision, I understand. Took himself off travelling on a whim and decided he wasn't coming back. Anyway, they brought this new guy in pretty quick after that. Didn't want to leave the place empty for long, I suppose. Seems to be settling in okay, though. The ladies certainly like him.'

'Yes,' was all Marie replied.

'Here.' Olive placed a package on the worktop between them. 'No pressure, now. But I know you came up here in a bit of a rush, so I thought you might be missing these. For when you feel up to it.'

Marie gently tore open a neat wrapping of tissue around the parcel to find inside a large pad of artist's paper, a box of acrylic paints, and a packet containing a selection of different sized and shaped brushes. She couldn't remember the last time anyone had done anything for her that was quite so thoughtful.

'Only when you're ready, mind,' Olive said. 'When the time's right, you just paint it down, girl. Okay? Get it all out.' She pointed to her head. 'And paint it all down. Hubert and I, we'll be here whenever you need us.'

Marie swept away a tear. 'Thank you,' she said. 'Means a lot.'

'Right then. That's enough of that. Find me some plates, young lady. I brought cake.'

'Who are you kidding?' Marie said. 'You know this place better than I do.'

Olive pretended to be shocked at such an accusation, meanwhile reaching a sly hand into one of the overhead cupboards, then removing it again holding two saucers. 'Would you look at that,' she said, with a wink. 'You go light the fire. There's a nip in the air after yesterday's rain. I'll bring these through.'

Marie did as she was told. It felt good to follow instructions after a week of tough decisions and supposedly being in charge. Of having to behave like an adult. When what she'd wanted was to defer responsibility to someone else, someone who knew what they were doing.

After they'd eaten their oversized wedges of carrot cake, the fire crackling in the wood burner in the corner, Olive drew Marie's attention to the framed painting on the wall by the window. It hung in pride of place where, to anyone entering the room, it was the first thing they'd see.

'She loved that painting,' the older woman said. 'Never stopped talking about her talented artist daughter.'

Marie gave the painting no more than a cursory glance. She knew it well. The hours she'd spent getting the shading just so on the face peeking out from behind the foliage, the blended reds and oranges that brought the flames to life, the swirls of grey that gave the smoke curling through the trees such a feeling of movement.

No, she needn't look at it long. She'd given her life and part of her soul over to getting that painting finished in her last weeks at university and it came as no surprise to her that Barbara had gotten a thrill from showing it off, like some kind of trophy. Like a selfie with a cruise ship captain. Like a framed letter from Bradley bloody Gimble. It cheapened her work, somehow, tarnished it.

'Never trust a goblin, am I right?' On saying the words, Olive lifted her near-empty mug to down the last of her tea. When she lowered it again, she seemed to notice Marie's confused expression. 'That little fella,' she said, pointing. 'Behind the bushes. That's a goblin, isn't it? Looks like one. Doesn't matter. Whatever it is, it's wonderful. Very atmospheric. Almost as if you could jump right in.'

Never trust a goblin: what a peculiar phrase to come out of nowhere. And yet, it was one that echoed with familiarity.

'Right,' Olive said, then, not giving Marie time to think on the matter further. 'I'll be off. Heaven forbid Hubert starts wondering why his dinner hasn't magically appeared on his lap.' She pushed herself out of the armchair and gathered the plates and mugs in that way she had, seemingly incapable of not tidying up. 'You be alright?'

'Uh...yes, yes. I'll be fine.' Marie forced herself to take her eyes from the small hidden figure in the painting. She followed the older woman out into the hallway. 'Thanks, Olive. For everything. I really appreciate it.'

'You're most welcome, dear. Now, you just let me know if you want any help going through your mother's things.' She gave Marie's arm a squeeze and walked to the door. 'We're down the road if you need us or if you just want to talk.'

Marie nodded and Olive left, closing the front door behind herself with a click.

Back in the living room, Marie returned to the painting. On the windowsill was a magnifying glass her mother used to do the crossword. She picked it up, leaned in close to examine the small figure hidden amongst the painted foliage, half in shadow and camouflaged, eyes looking straight out from the image and into the real world.

Strange how when she'd been painting the thing she hadn't categorised the figure as anything or anyone in particular. It was an abstract representation of a being, a part of the green, a metaphor for our existence, a riff on the garden of Eden. But, yes, now that she thought about it, it did sort of look like a goblin. Although she couldn't quite put a name to it or understand how a character like that could end up in her work without her explicit say so.

She remembered what Father Colin said about not needing to deal with her Mother's paperwork today and decided to take the rest of the weekend for herself. Tomorrow, she thought, she would sit in the garden and paint the things around her. Her art had always been the way she grounded herself. 'Paint it down; get it out,' as Olive had said.

That night, Marie's sleep was poor quality and fitful. She dreamed of Barbara sailing off on the Titanic, waving from the stern as Marie called to her from a dock. She dreamed of her father–faceless, but undeniably him–disappearing into the Yorkshire Dales. She dreamed she was being chased by a swarm of wasps, furious and fast and eager to sting. And she dreamed, randomly, of Father Colin smiling much too sweetly and inviting himself in for tea.

Next to her on the bedside table, Marie's glowing mobile lay silent, unmoving. It wasn't the phone call that interrupted her sleep. Above where she lay, through layers of wallpaper, plasterboard, beams and floorboards, a pulsing vibration hummed. It teased her into near wakefulness then ceased, allowing her to drift into the next dream before the dull throb started again, calling, whispering, demanding to be heard. Over and over the sound penetrated the ceiling into the dark bedroom below.

It would stop before dawn and she wouldn't fully remember the sound itself, but something about the intermittent disturbance would stay with her, a bothersome almost-memory just out of reach, as ephemeral as her dreams.

10. THE MACHINE GODS

The fall of Diamond. Verbal account given by the last known historian, Johan Floralai, eye-witness to the events described below:

'You should know, the machines continue to thrum, still every bit as independent as they were designed to be. You thought yourselves smart, you men and women of the West. But that city of yours revealed its fatal flaw when it came to matters of your own necessity, did it not?

'Some of you got lucky, sure enough, those who sought sanctuary elsewhere when the end came. Most wound up dead. Not much meat on city folks, but it's enough when they harvest you by the thousand.

'Then, and to this very day, below ground and beyond the perimeter so as not to weaken the city herself, your unmanned drills continue apace. Grinding rigs tunnel blindly. Conveyors roll coal and ore from the business end of excavation to the factories where rows of white-hot furnaces stand gaping wide, hungry for more. Ton after ton. From ground to flame to sky. Quite the simple process. Congratulations.

'In the absence of its creators, only oil-spackled thumbprints on tools, strewn where you abandoned them, tell of the existence of the human engineers of Must.

'Those fiendish oafs who crept out of the shadows fancy themselves the engineers now. Learning on the fly, picking up the necessary to stop the towers crumbling, to prevent the smoke belchers from ceasing their awful work.

'They relish destruction, you know, the rank stench of the dead and unburied, the squeal of livestock. Always hungry. Every stray soul, lost and afraid, a meal.

'Let the place blacken and fester! they say. As long as the wheels spin and the fires rage. So what of aesthetics? We have no purpose for such fanciful grot. May a layer of ash and sludge be a burial shroud upon our foes.'

(Brief interruption as oxygen is administered to JF. He is advised by the medic to remain calm and take deep breaths).

'You ask me what they want of the machines and of the city, to which I say, you're missing the point. To the new gods of Must, by-product is everything. They place no value on that which they cannot eat or destroy to their advantage. Darkness is their default. The heat of the furnaces alone is enough to stave off any chill, were they to even be troubled by it. Which, mostly, they are not, their thick skin and padding feet not given to sensitivity.

'Since you ran, the Southern invaders have cranked up output to keep things on an even

downward slide. With the forests of the West gone, bar a few stragglers, the smoke above Diamond stirring with poison, soon they'll be hard-pressed to tell day from night. Imagine that if you can.

'Then, they'll reach further, even beyond the other gates, and they'll feast on what they find there. It's what drives them, you see, the taste on their hideous tongues, and the hope of not just having their world, or the core world, but all worlds, all lands, all folks big and small and walking and fluttering and humming and anything besides. Grub is grub in the eyes of the South. Take is take. They fear nothing when the greed is upon them. And that should be reason enough to terrify every one of you.

'You think yourselves safe, now. You are not. You think you've built yourselves a hidden fortress. You have not. They'll find you here as soon as anywhere, alter the Eastern landscape as easily as they have the core. My place in this battle may be over, but yours most certainly is not.

'All that's left for them to do is to keep things turning, keep things burning, avoid foolish misdemeanours that might result in the tightening of a neck rope by their own, and monitor the levels in the air as their master

instructs. Nothing to it, really. Time is on their side, as are the climbing numbers.

'Someday soon, the dark one will leave his kingdom and roar through the gate to rule over all you've left behind. The first step to his new world order.

'A half trip of the sun. More or less.

'But a tension builds on the streets of Must. Even to the tough skinned goblin crew of the South, a season feels like too long. Supplies are low. In a year, they haven't feasted. Not like the times of plenty, when each glistening tower opened up to a fresh wave of meat.

'Last rations, that's what I heard. One season, maybe two.

'For now, the city is theirs. Not fully hosting the South ones, yet. Only the grifters, the engineers, the forerunners, readying the place before the others arrive. It would appear they've been allowed to handle matters without close oversight for now, granted only the occasional check-in from on high, or a fly-by from that sharp clawed and tatty winged loon.

'They won't admit it, but she gives them the shivers, that one. How she crouches high atop her nest of scraps, rambling to none but herself. Too filthy to griddle, too quick to catch. Off limits for magic reaping, such was the order from the other side. That's what I hear, anyhow.

So they tolerate her odd ways, stay out of her sights as best they can.

'No misdemeanours. No hangings. Turn and burn. Turn and burn.

'A season or two at full tilt, and the core land of Diamond will feel almost like their own. At least, that's what they have to believe.'

Conversation terminated as per advice from medics. Documented by Submariner H. Quinn, prior to the late historian's unfortunate passing.

Entered into the East record: 312.18.056

11. THE GATE, SHE MOVES

'It's happening,' the smallest of the three said, digging an elbow into the middle watcher sleeping by her side and nudging a boot into the biggest at her feet. 'Wake up, wake up!'

'Darn it,' the biggest said, rubbing her eyes. 'Already?'

All three were awake, now. All three looked to the gate. It was indeed starting to flicker.

'What if it goes where we cannot?' the middle one said. 'Like a burning place or the smokiest barren land or where the city dogs are?'

'It hasn't yet.'

'One time it will.'

'Correct. One time it surely will.'

The smallest stood up and fluttered toward the portal to the West. She felt the air shake with the coming change, like waves on a pond.

'Don't!' the middle one said.

'It won't hurt me,' the smallest said. 'This gate's magic be Queen's magic and she loves us, still.'

'Come away,' the biggest said, in a firmer tone than the other.

The smallest was torn. She badly wanted to sneak a last look through the gate before it became another gate, somewhere else. She wanted to see with her own eyes the girl in case it was her last chance to do so. But the biggest watcher wasn't to be disobeyed. So with her head drooped, the smallest hovered back to the watch spot and sat down between the older and bigger two as they waited for the inevitable to happen.

'What if it doesn't reappear at all?' she said, in a voice smaller than even she. 'I don't want to see it go for the last time. I couldn't bear it.'

'Watchers must watch,' the biggest said.

'Even that which they do not wish to,' the middle one added. 'Who else will remember for the others if not us?'

The three sat huddled as one, quiet as rocks, resigned to the task at hand. The atmosphere rippled in increasingly fervent bursts, the gate itself glimmered, the wrought iron frame shook more and more fiercely until the three feared it might explode and end them in a spray of shrapnel. But they knew that wasn't how this worked.

Louder and louder it got. A tap to a rattle to a roar.

When the sound reached its peak, the smallest put her hands over her ears and the others followed suit shortly after. As they did, the gate and its frame and the surrounding air imploded and disappeared with such force it took everything in the immediate vicinity with it, freeing up fresh space for whatever existed on the outer edges to rush in and fill the gap. Like the gate was never there to begin with.

The three felt the pull as their tiny bodies were jerked forward in the sudden rejig of woodland particles. The older two weren't so new to this as to imagine they were close enough to be in any real danger.

The smallest wondered, if she had still been within the gate's sphere of vanishing at the time of shift, would she also have been taken to the new place? Would she, too, reappear in the gate's new location, transported any number of heifer's lengths across the forest? The thought of it excited her and frightened her, but mostly confused her. How was it possible for a thing to be there one moment then somewhere else the next?

This was not a question the others cared to ask. They knew from harsh experience that anyone too close at the time of a gate move would be shredded by enchantments beyond their wildest imaginings, a security put in place not only to make the gate more difficult to find, or impossible to plan attacks around, but to confound and destroy any who might wish harm to those on the other side.

Queen's magic or no, loving monarch or no, some things were not meant for dabbling. Better the smallest watcher didn't learn that the hard way. There were few enough left of them as it was.

'What now?' the middle one said, brushing dead leaves and twigs from her skirts where they'd scattered during the shift's influx. 'Do we make for the hollows? Should one of us wait here in the event Broadleaf returns? Protocol states-'

'I'll stay,' the biggest said.

'No, I'll stay,' the middle one said. 'She needs you to get her home.'

'I'm not a baby,' the smallest said, offended by the suggestion that she needed protecting.

'No, you're not.' The biggest touched the shoulder of the smallest. 'But you are the most special of us. You are the future, little 'un. Do you understand?'

The smallest watcher conceded to this. She knew it was the truth. And really, honestly, she wasn't bothered who took her home just so long as she got there. She was missing the soft cushions of her bed, the warm embrace of her family, and a belly full of Milda's fine tasting stew. Maybe there was honour in watching, but there wasn't much comfort, all told.

'That's decided, then,' the middle one said. 'You two head back and I'll stay here another half-light. If there's no sign of Broadleaf and the others then I'll be behind you quick as a blink.' She reached out with one of the sacks and shared the remaining biscuits and juice between the three of them. 'For the journey.'

'Half a light,' the biggest said. 'No more. Don't make me risk a team to rescue you.'

'I won't.'

They parted company, the biggest and the smallest making tracks through the air toward the Faretheewell hollows, the middle one staying put. They might've stuck together had they known a Hummer squad was en route. Not that it would've made any difference.

12. SUBLIMINAL

The garden at Darkwood had always been Marie's safe place. During the hours of daylight, that is. Nighttime being something altogether different. Barbara had been only too happy to give her daughter the freedom she so obviously craved, leaving her to run wild as long as she kept within the borders of the plot.

It made sense, then, that it was out on that same grass beneath the aluminium sky where Marie chose to be in order to quieten the noise of the last few weeks. She leaned back, tasting the air. If she was lucky the rain might hold off until lunchtime. Though an earthy aroma and cool breeze said otherwise.

She set up the old easel of hers that her mother had never gotten around to leaving out with the bins, taped a fresh sheet of paper to the board, squeezed out blue and green and a little burnt umber from their metal tubes onto a makeshift ice-cream lid palette, and looked around for an area of the garden that might capture well on the page.

If she blurred her vision she could trick herself into believing she saw the outline of her father mowing the lawn or raking up leaves, pulling up dandelions, roots and all. He was still here in many ways. Though Marie knew the snapshots she held in her mind were no longer true memories. They were memories of memories, facsimiles, images sent through the machine of her brain so many times it was impossible to tell if she was remembering events that occurred or was manifesting images from a photo album, projecting them as if they'd happened in front of her own eyes.

She dabbed the brush in the paint, no plan in mind, just pent up feelings itching to get out. God knew the gallery wasn't chasing her for fresh work. Not after the last time, what with Shaun's outburst at the opening and everything that came after. So she followed where the paint took her, swirling greens into browns and blues into reds, allowing the brush to dictate style and content, and it felt good not to be invested, to not try so hard to control the end result.

The first time Marie saw Father Colin that day, the vicar was by himself sauntering along the road in a direction that took him away from the village. From her vantage point, looking up the slight slope of the garden, she could see about a ten yard stretch of the dry stone wall that acted as the boundary between Darkwood and the road out front. Anything to the left of that was blocked out by the cottage itself.

The young man didn't appear to notice her, then, and she certainly didn't make a point of drawing attention to herself, preferring instead to let him drift by like a black swan, silent and serene. It was only when he walked out of view that she realised she'd been holding her breath.

The second time she saw him, he was heading back the other way. Only this time he was flanked by two of the volunteer ladies, Edith or Agnes or whatever the hell they were called. They walked–no, glided–as one, as if coasting on greased rails or floating six inches off the ground.

Despite herself, Marie was mesmerised by them, the way they moved past the property not speaking to each other. She watched until a nearby cow let out a startled grunt and caused the drifting group to turn simultaneously to look.

Father Colin, on seeing Marie sat by her easel, paused the unusual procession and acknowledged her with a smile and a gesture that was somewhere between a wave and a salute. 'Ms. Fisher,' he called out. 'Good day to you.'

The volunteer ladies said nothing, did nothing except stand steadfastly at either side of the young clergyman. From this distance they seemed oddly vacant, though they were most definitely looking right at her. At that moment, it occurred to Marie that looking and seeing weren't necessarily the same thing.

'Hello again, Father,' she said.

Her skin tingled as tiny spots of rain began to land on her face, her forearms, and on the painting in front of her. Not enough to cause damage or streaks. Still, for more reasons than she could articulate it felt like the right time to go inside.

'Any danger of a cup of tea, Ms Fisher?' the vicar said

Marie began packing up her paints. 'Can't I'm afraid,' she said.

She peeled the paper off the board, rolled it up and balanced it on top of the box of acrylics and pack of brushes. As inexplicable as it was, she didn't want him in her house. 'A friend's popping over in a bit. Need to get cleaned up, you know how it is. Another time, perhaps.' She made a point of making it not sound like a question.

The vicar and his two lady friends swivelled their heads in unison to follow Marie as she navigated her way quickly across the garden, laden with art supplies and the folded down easel carried awkwardly under her arm.

'Oh yes?' Father Colin said, so, so calmly. 'Which friend? You know only a few people as I understand it.'

Marie stopped at the edge of the cottage at the point where, if she'd continued on, her view of the road and the unsettling visitors would be lost. Was that a dig? Was Father Colin mocking her? He certainly seemed to be doing his darndest to suppress a smirk. *Game show host* was all she could think.

Just then, the sound of an old telephone rang out through the back door: a lifeline, a distraction that bought her a second or two to think.

'Hubert,' she said after a beat, with all the breezy confidence she could muster. 'He's lending me a few tools from his shed so I can get started on taming this jungle.' She jabbed a thumb over her shoulder toward the garden and its mess of summer growth. As lies went it wasn't too unreasonable.

'Ah, Hubert,' the vicar said. 'Hubert, Hubert, Hubert.'

From inside the cottage the phone continued its rattling cry.

Drrrring.

What began as occasional spits and spots had rapidly turned to a persistent drizzle. Still, Marie and the vicar (with his two volunteer helpers) all stood looking at each other from opposing sides of the wall, as fixed and unmoving as the wall itself. Chess pieces awaiting a turn.

Drrrring.

'I'd better get that,' Marie said.

'Yes.' Neither Father Colin nor the volunteers showed any signs of walking on. 'You'd better get that.'

Then, as if the spell was suddenly broken, Marie drew her eyes away and walked briskly to the back door. 'Goodbye, Father,' she said, not looking back.

Inside the kitchen, she elbowed the door closed behind her. She dumped the easel down. But before she could place the other art supplies on the counter her shaking hands failed and sent them clattering across the tile floor.

'Fucking fuck,' she muttered between panicked breaths. She locked the door, trying not to feel stupid about doing it.

Drrrring.

The phone continued to ring on the table. It would've gone to voicemail long before Marie had gotten to it if she hadn't disabled the function since returning to Darkwood. The same message showed on the screen as before: 'Caller unknown'. She answered it anyway.

'Hello?' she said.

A pause.

'Hi.' Shaun's voice was hesitant. Not like him at all.

Marie looked around the kitchen, unsure what to say. She scratched at a mark on the table, a knot in the wood, then closed her eyes and concentrated on calming her heart rate to something close to normal.

'Marie? Are you there?'

'Yes, I'm here. Where are you calling from, Shaun? I don't see a number.'

'I'm at work. Halfway through a meeting with the Ratcliffe guys. I popped out to call you. Said I needed a piss. Just wanted to see if you were okay after, you know, everything.'

Marie nodded, not that Shaun could see it. It was more a self-soothing motion, as if to say, Yes, Shaun. I know. Everything.

'How are you? How's the house?'

'It's a house.' Marie didn't like the tone in her own voice but declined to go back and correct herself. Let him worry. Let him think she was still mad at him even though the truth was she didn't have the energy to be angry at anyone, and had barely given their broken relationship a thought since the funeral.

'And you? How are you? In yourself, I mean.'

'I'm fine. Why are you calling, Shaun?'

'I wanted to check-'

'Sure. Great. You checked and like I said, I'm fine. But I could do without the barrage of calls.'

'Barrage of what?'

'Calls, Shaun. Just so you know, if you ring me again from an unknown number I won't be answering. In fact, if you call me from a known number I won't be answering.'

'That's...yeah...okay, Marie. Okay.' He sounded flustered. Confused, even. 'I get it. But I didn't think it was a crime to see how you were getting on. It's been two weeks.'

Marie looked up at the ceiling in disbelief, slowly shaking her head. She said nothing.

'You make it sound like I've been harassing you or something. Christ, Marie, this is me. *Me*. Not some random guy. You wanted space. I gave you space. You want me to leave you alone from now on? I'll leave you alone. Just don't make me out to be the fucking weirdo just 'cause I still care about you.'

'Space?' She let out a howl. 'Every day you've called, Shaun. Every bloody day.'

Before Shaun could defend himself against the accusation, the phone buzzed against Marie's ear, making her pull it away from the side of her head. She looked down at the screen to see the same 'caller unknown' message.

But there was something else. With each buzz the house seemed to vibrate as if another phone, upstairs perhaps, a device perfectly in sync with this one, was ringing at exactly the same time.

'I have to go,' she said, hanging up to the sound of Shaun saying something, but being cut off mid sentence. Then she answered the new incoming call.

'Hello?'

There came a sound down the line, a raw and messy sound, like static. It must've been a broken connection, an error of some kind.

'Hello?' Marie said again.

More static.

Then, clear and sweet-sounding yet somehow distant words were spoken in her ear. 'By your hand,' they said. 'Do not falter.' After which the line went dead.

She looked at the blank screen, thought about the words: *By your hand. Do not falter.* But they held no meaning. A crossed line. A glitch, nothing more. Suddenly, the phone felt like an alien thing, a doorway for those she didn't want to let in. She held the side button and watched it power off, then dropped it in her pocket.

A little over an hour later, Marie was summoning up the will to go through one of her mother's boxes from under the bed when she was halted by a knock at the front door. She was halfway down the stairs when she saw Hubert through the glass panel. When he caught sight of her, he smiled.

She was about to turn the key in the lock and find out the reason for this unexpected visit, but something–maybe instinct or an abundance of caution–made her hand pause.

'Hey, Hubert. Just give me a minute. This door jams sometimes.' She rattled the handle pretending to try the lock, and then glanced up at the older man, looking him in the eyes.

'Hiya, love,' he said, so, so calmly. 'Got those tools for you in the car.'

13. THE FETCH

There was a time when Marie believed in mysterious things. She was small, then, and being a child all things were possible. Not yet had she gathered evidence to the contrary. But also, she wanted to believe. Actively chose to. Believing being far more interesting than not.

But the blunt realities of life took their toll, knocking (as they are apt to do) such fantasies out of her, slowly and steadily, a little each day, until the notion of Nessie or Bigfoot struck her as absurd and she realised she'd left such preposterous fictions behind.

And yet.

The man on the other side of the door looked and sounded exactly like Hubert. So much so that Marie would've opened the door gladly and welcomed him in were it not for the sick feeling in her stomach and the knowing that she'd lied to the vicar, that she hadn't been expecting the old man at all.

Strange, too, that he would offer the exact same reason for being there as the one she'd made up out of nowhere only an hour earlier: tools from his shed. Proof positive in her eyes that the person at the door was not what he appeared to be.

She pretended again to rattle the key in the lock. 'It's not going to budge,' she said. 'Let me check in the kitchen. I think there's a spare set in the cupboard.'

'You want me to go around back?' the man who looked like Hubert said.

'No, that's okay. I'll just be a moment.' She pulled the key from the door and left the man staring in through the glass panel as she walked swiftly away. Once out of sight, Marie leaned back against the kitchen cabinets and exhaled. She wanted to call Olive, but her mobile was upstairs on the bed, and could she remember the number? Could she fuck.

She looked around and, on seeing the landline phone on the worktop next to a large pot of utensils, cautiously lifted it out from its charging cradle.

Please, God, she thought. Please let Barbara have the number saved in speed dial.

Every button beeped when she pressed it, which made her wince and shush the bloody thing. She scrolled through the phone's memory. *Please, please, please.*

'Any joy?' the man called through the letterbox.

'Not yet,' she shouted back, hands trembling. 'Gimme a sec.'

Then there it was, stored under O for Olive Wells, and Marie felt an unfamiliar wave of gratitude toward her dead mother for doing something right for a change.

She clicked the little green handset button and listened to it dial through.

'Pick up, pick up, pick up', she muttered, tapping her foot furiously on the tile floor.

'Hello?'

'Olive,' Marie said quietly, not wanting the man at the door to hear. 'It's Marie.'

'Alright, love? Funny, I was just thinking about you.' The older woman didn't sound upset or troubled. She sounded just as she always did.

Marie suddenly felt ridiculous and wondered if the events of the last few weeks had finally caught up with her and she was, in fact, having a breakdown. There was no doubting the women in her family had form.

'Is everything...okay at your place?'

'As far as I know. Hubert's out faddling with his lawnmower. Spark plugs arrived and, you know what he's like when-'

'Hubert's there?'

'Yes, love.'

'Are you sure? I mean, you're sure he's there?'

Yes, love. Out in the garage. Last I checked he-'

'Could you put him on?' Marie said. 'If you don't mind,' she added, realising she ought to at least try to hide the alarm in her voice.

A few moments passed. Marie wasn't sure if Olive was thinking of what to say in reply or if she was going to find Hubert. But then she heard footsteps down the phone and she knew the older woman was walking through her house. Then, there was the opening of a door and other muffled sounds.

'Olive? Are you there? Olive?'

'He's gone,' the older woman said. 'Must've popped to the shops.'

Marie listened. She heard Olive go outside and call out for Hubert. Then, a beep.

'Oh, that's my loaf,' Olive said. 'I'll have to call you back.'

'No, wait.'

'What's this about, love? You alright?'

'He's here, Olive.'

'Well, that's okay then.' The older woman sounded relieved, and a moment later, confused. 'So why would you be calling him here?'

'I don't know,' Marie said, pinching the bridge of her nose. 'It's wrong. All wrong. It's him, but it isn't. I can't explain.'

Marie turned so her back was against the wall that separated the kitchen from the hallway. She lowered the phone to her chest and glanced over her shoulder toward the man at the front door. The man that looked like Hubert.

But the man no longer looked like Hubert. On the other side of the front door's glass panel stood the smiling face of Father Colin and he was once again flanked by the church volunteers, who were most definitely not smiling. All three of them watched her turn back to the kitchen and out of view.

'Marie?'

The thrust of the voice from the phone against Marie's chest startled her. She lifted the handset to her ear. 'He's the vicar now,' she whispered.

Something in that statement seemed to affect the older woman. Marie got the sense that she was gathering herself.

'Is he in the house?' Olive said, her words measured, deliberate.

'No. He's at the front door. Outside.'

'Go to him.'

'What?'

'It's alright,' Olive said. 'Take the phone with you and put me on loudspeaker. I want to talk to him. You'll be fine. Just don't let him in.'

Marie counted to three in her head. Then counted to three again. On her third count to three she pushed herself away from the kitchen wall, turned around and went back out into the hallway and over to the front door.

'There she is,' Father Colin said. 'Are you going to let us in now? Kettle on. Chop chop.'

'I have someone who wants to talk to you.' Marie pressed a button on the phone, putting Olive on loudspeaker. 'Okay, he can hear you.'

'Leave the girl be,' Olive said.

The vicar's smile didn't fade, but something in his eyes changed, like a veil dropping, a subtle fading of the veneer.

'Where is my Hubert, and what have you done with him?'

Still, Father Colin smiled, though a slight twitch began to pull at the corner of his mouth.

'I'll ask one more time, where is my husband?'

'Make the girl let me in and I'll tell you,' the vicar said.

'Don't do it, Marie. He's lying. He's nowt but a filthy lying fetch. You keep that door shut tight, do you understand? There's not a damn thing he can do and he knows it.'

'What's going on?' Marie said. 'Where's Hubert?'

Father Colin leaned in close to the transparent door panel and breathed on the glass. In the mist that formed there he drew a simple face: two dots above a curved mouth. 'Open up, girly,' he said.

His words awoke something in Marie, something that had remained dormant for a long time. She stumbled back from the door and tried to remember what this feeling was, but it was just out of reach.

'Leave her be,' Olive said again. 'Begone, fetch, else you want me and mine to deal with you.'

'You and yours?' The vicar laughed. 'There are no *yours* left, foolish bint.'

That was the break Marie needed. She pulled her gaze away and bolted up the stairs, leaving the smiling vicar and his lavender-scented sidekicks outside on the porch. Not wanting to be seen through any of the windows at the front of the house, she huddled on the landing against the bathroom door.

'Are you there?'

Marie switched the speakerphone off and spoke into the handset. 'Yes,' she said, catching her breath. 'I'm upstairs.'

'Can he hear me?' Olive said.

'No.'

'Good. Right. Now then.'

'Olive-'

'Yes, dear,' the older woman said. 'I know. You have questions. I had hoped there'd be more time to explain and for you to get used to the idea of what I have to tell you, but, well, here we are.'

Marie heard the sound of the silver Jag starting up out the front, so she tiptoed to the window and peeked around the curtain just as the vicar and the volunteers drove off.

'He's gone. He's taken Hubert's car.'

'Which way?'

'Towards the village. And towards you. Oh God, is he coming to you?'

'Don't you worry about that, love,' Olive said. 'I've faced worse than the likes of him in my time.'

'The likes of who? Who is he?'

Before the older woman could reply, a light buzzing sound distracted Marie from the conversation, and she looked up. She followed the sound across the ceiling to the corner where it seemed to be the strongest.

'There's something in the attic,' she said, more to herself than anyone else.

'You should go and have a look,' Olive said. As if this were perfectly normal and to be expected.

'In the attic?'

'Yes, dear. The attic. I think you'll find your father explains it all rather well.'

14. LIBRARY OF THE FORGOTTEN

The attic felt out of bounds even now. The hatch, too high to reach by standing alone, had a lock built into it that required a key, one that Barbara kept in a jewellery tin in her underwear drawer. As far as Marie knew, her mother never bothered with it either, that whole other part of the house they'd all but forgotten about, and had left it like so many things to fester. Surely nothing of importance could be up there?

Marie found the tin and the gold-coloured key and carried a cushioned stool from her mother's dressing table, placed it under the attic hatch in the hallway and climbed onto it. The extra foot and a half enabled her to reach the lock with ease. She clicked the key clockwise before carefully lowering the wooden hatch then hopped off the stool and wrestled with the loft ladders, unfolding them first one way then the other until they concertinaed down to the floor.

How fitting that for thirty years her mother chose to keep the door closed on whatever existed up those steps. But then that was her talent, Marie realised. Ignorance ruled Barbaraland with an iron fist and its message was clear: avoid what makes you uncomfortable. Better to shove life's inconveniences in a cupboard or attic (or boarding school) and sail away.

Each wooden tread creaked as she pulled herself up and into the semi-darkness of the room above. What she saw shouldn't have come as a surprise. Houses have attics; it was hardly a shocking concept. But still, the sight of the vast open cavity tucked under the eaves, the knowing that this whole other place had existed above her this entire time, gave her reason to pause in wonder.

Around the room, piles of books sat stacked on top of each other, on the windowsill, on the floor, old and leather-bound and calling to Marie to pick them up, to leaf through, to explore.

By opening the hatch she'd disturbed air that had remained motionless and untouched for decades and in the swirling motes she got a sense of her father. A familiar scent, albeit a stale one, took near thirty years off her in an instant and would've sent her tumbling backwards if she hadn't gripped firm on the ladder rail. She needed to focus. She needed to get her shit together.

Just a room. Just another room. No ghosts here, only books.

She pulled herself up through the hatch and knelt on the rough wooden floorboards. The attic was practically the length of the cottage itself, the roof above her head propped up by sturdy oak trusses. A small window looked out over the road allowing in just enough light. Marie noted that she saw that same window every time she walked up to the house and yet never had it occurred to her to try out the view from the inside.

Another of those feelings came over her: an ache in her chest, a longing for something she couldn't recall. She pictured her father going about his day, creaking across the dusty floorboards, journal in hand, cutting a path through the sunbeams, nosing though his own literary detritus. This place, having avoided the indignity of Barbara's post-win floral overhaul, was inescapably her father's room and here it seemed he remained.

She saw, then, that all the books were journals, their leather bound covers held closed with either string or leather twine. Dozens and dozens of them. And she knew that the scent of books was what most reminded her of her father. Always writing, always carrying a journal with him wherever he went. George Fisher and his words were as inseparable as two things ever could be.

She pulled herself up to stand, ran a finger through the powdery layer that coated the nearest stack, and the thought occurred to her that dust was little more than dead skin cells. She brushed her fingertips on her jeans then rubbed her hands together for good measure.

She headed for the light, looked through the window over the front garden and onto the road that ran past the house. Partly because she wanted to check the vicar wasn't squatting out there, watching. But also to get a handle on her position in the world. To ground herself in reality.

Where to start, she wondered? There were almost too many. When on earth did he find the time to fill so many pages? There might've been an order to them but Marie couldn't latch onto any logical pattern so she picked one up at random, unfurled the length of leather twine wrapped around it and opened it up to a page part-way through.

***

On the day 9th April 1991

I wandered the woods early this morning while Barbara took Marie to the dentist. The other place had called to me as it often does, promising companionship and adventure and, as there was barely a thing to eat at home, I decided to see if the good people of Faretheewell were open to a visitor.

Lucky for me it was bake day and I filled myself to the gills with buttery pastries and the sweetest fruit jams. My good friend, Dale, traded drinks if I helped him clear the guttering on his cottage, which I did, gladly, and I wiped the moss from the corners of his coloured glass windows while I was up there. Old habits, and all that.

We talked about shallow things as neither of us were in any mood to open the floodgates on our losses. His boy asked about Marie and when they could again play in the stream together. They had such fun the last time and I have to admit it made me happy to see my daughter with a friend for once, given she lacks a sibling to share these things with.

And while Dale could undoubtedly sense my mind was on other things, he did his best to entertain me while I was with him, for which I was grateful. I would go back tomorrow but I fear I may overwhelm him.

So instead I write. To remember, and also to forget.

***

Marie had to stop. The sudden heaviness she felt at reading her father's words, seeing his swirling handwriting on the page, was almost too much. Through the writing she heard his voice. He was here with her, talking to her from the book in her hands.

She tilted her head back and let a tear streak down each cheek.

After a moment she read on.

***

On This Day 12th April 1991

How it destroys me to watch my beautiful bride in pain and be unable to mend her, and to know she no longer finds comfort in my company. More and more she drives me away, demands I leave her to wallow in her grief, and much as I hate to admit it even in the written word, I'm relieved to go.

It does a man no good to feel he is of no use. Each of us needs a purpose to our being. Barbara may feel I'm wasting my chances or prefer that I go out into the wider world in search of a career, in the pursuit of greater wealth, security for us and our child. But to label me a 'two-bit window cleaner' when she is well aware I work only to fund my writing? Something I do for all our sakes?

I know she speaks from a place of profound sadness when she says these things. However, knowing this makes the words no less hurtful.

Only so long can one be expected to carry such a burden before we all suffer under the weight of it. Suffer and break. Is there a limit to how much I'm expected to take before I too am granted, in the minds of others as well as my own, permission to dwell some on my own concerns? Must it always be about supporting her?

Yes, I suppose it must.

***

Marie Closed the book and placed it back from where she'd taken it. She looked around the dimly lit attic and went over to another pile of journals on a desk in the corner and picked up one of those. The dates showed these were earlier volumes.

***

On this day 4th September 1987

So many corners of Darkwood call me back to childhood. To date, much of the work I've done on the place is superficial, afraid as I am of altering the spirit of it. Will this become ours or will it forever feel as if we are guests in my parents' home?

Tomorrow I shall tackle the garden as that is where I suspect my dear Dad would be least proud of my efforts. I'll imagine him telling me to 'get your arse into gear, lad,' as I take a pair of shears to the summer growth. That I can do, though I don't imagine I will salvage the vegetable patch. While I inherited much this past year, alas, my mother's green thumbs died with her.

My darling Barbara grows larger by the day! How proud I am of her.

***

Marie flicked ahead to the last few pages. There was nothing in the volume she held in her hands from the day she was born, it stopped short by a week or two. But it gave her an odd feeling knowing she had been curled up inside her mother as her father wrote the words she read.

***

On this day 20th March 1988

I've chosen not to involve my wife in the affairs of the other place. Our child is due any day so it would serve no purpose other than to upset and alarm her further. And in light of her change in mood these last weeks no good can come of the additional stress.

I pretend to be leaving the house. Tell her I have a job or need to pick up supplies from the shop in town or whatever. I of course make sure she has all she needs before I go. I slip down the lane to the side of the property where if I stoop behind the hedgerow I cannot be seen even if Barbara were to be standing at the kitchen window, which invariably she wouldn't be. Rarely now does she leave her bed until mid-afternoon.

As wondrous a world as it is through the hedge, as different as it is from our own, the problems they have there are no less worrying than any we face here. The turbulent nature of politics, it seems to me, is universal. As an outsider I try not to get involved.

To satisfy my own curiosity I've decided to attempt to map the layout of that other land in some simple way using what information I've gleaned thus far. I cannot believe this is the first time I've thought to do so. It will likely not be an accurately scaled representation as I couldn't possibly walk the entirety of it. I'm told it would take a full day to cross from West to east (perhaps a quarter of that on a scooter) and Barbara would certainly miss me were I to be gone that long.

Given its name, I am minded to draw the perimeter as diamond-shaped and the four compass points the folks there refer to suggest that also. More than once I've been described as a West-Gater. An interesting term that flows easily from their mouths. But what is slowly becoming clear to me...(cont.)

***

Marie traced a finger around the edge of the map which was drawn on the back page in pencil. What it lacked in detail it made up for in style. Her father sure did have a knack for conveying the fantastical. The elements he'd captured of the place he described were magical and made Marie wish she could read more of the story.

She was about to close the book and choose another, perhaps even pick up from where this one left off, when she spied what looked like the page of a newspaper tucked into a paper pocket inside the journal's back cover. She slipped the paper out and unfolded it and saw it was a partial page of the Yorkshire Evening Post, dated from March 1988. The article had obviously been clipped out and kept for some reason. It showed a grainy picture of a young blonde boy ('Daniel Evers, aged 7 at the time of his disappearance'). The headline read: Father of Missing Child Arrested.

She studied the boy's face, the half-smile, the sad eyes. Seven years old was no age to look so beaten down by life. She folded the clipping back along well-worn lines and returned it to the cover pocket, closed the journal and placed it down.

Her attention was then drawn to a small wooden box on the desk between stacks of books. She picked it up, opened it on its fragile hinged lid. Inside the box was a coin, or a medal, or something in-between. The object was round and flat and looked to be cast out of silver. It had a loop at the top which could, if you wanted it to, fit a length of ribbon or chain or take a pin to attach it to a lapel. The design on the face of it showed what looked like overlapping leaves or the wings of an insect, and although it was clearly very old it shone as if it had been left there only yesterday.

Marie took the coin from the box and turned it over in her hands, reading the inscription on the reverse: 'Given to William, In thanks, HM JVii'.

William was her grandfather on her father's side. He'd been in the army during the war so Marie assumed the medal dated back to that time, though who or what HR JVii was she didn't know. She made a mental note to ask Olive about it when she called her in a while. Olive had a mind for remembering those sorts of details.

Hanging from the back of a chair next to the desk Marie spotted a satchel made of worn brown leather, with a long strap and bronze buckle fastenings. She placed the coin-cum-medal back in its box, nestled it into the velvet lining and closed the lid. She unhooked the satchel from the chair and lifted the flap and noticed a couple more journals inside. Deciding she was done breathing in long-dead skin cells, she slipped the wooden box in there with the books, slung the satchel strap over her head and across her body and headed back toward the hatch.

She suddenly craved daylight and fresh air so told herself she would come back later, that she could climb the attic stairs any time she liked from here on, having broken the seal on the out of bounds rule. But for now she wanted to sit in the kitchen with a cup of tea and read through more of her father's words and absorb them at her own pace.

She was almost at the bottom of the creaking ladder when the satchel began to buzz.

15. FRACTURED

Deep inside the castle, in a cupboard in a cell in a room, a clawed hand extended to a jar on a shelf. Not any jar, mind. None of your commoner muck. Time again for the draining, a shift gone by since the last, plenty long enough to recoup some.

A blasted head pain bothered the squat and grumpy fella doing the taking. He was planning on when he could sup the ale again, knock this fuzzy-eyed ache away with a shot of the good stuff. More concerned with clock-off, a swift-footed doddle to the booze house, than what an end-stage shitterbug might be dreaming about.

He took the jar and held it up to the light, gave it a rattle: still going, if only just.

He opened the machine, raised the lever to access the slot where the jar would fit snug, like a tongue in an eye socket, moved the wires to the side, fumbled with the switch. He'd done the trick a hundred times and would likely do it a hundred more.

Last step was to open the jar.

-

Atop the nest she'd built on the highest city peak Mae sharpened her blade, stroking it back and forth on a rock she'd scored in the wastelands. Round and round she swirled the edge, taking it down by microns, bringing it to the most perfect point, fit to carve a shrew liver.

Broadleaf watched. If she'd been taken for food or harvest it would be over by now. Evidently the effort the freakish thing was going to was for her benefit, the knife and the show of its deadliness designed to instil fear and make her talk. It wouldn't work.

If in doubt, do nowt, as Pappy would say. Let the game play out and deal with what might come, as and when it does.

'That old fool,' Mae said, turning her gaze from the blade to Broadleaf. 'Can't help you now.'

The young fairy blinked, said nothing in reply.

'We hear you, unhidden one.' The dark-eyed fairy leaned down until forehead to forehead with the other, not the width of a grain between them. 'Doubt not, you'll give us what we need, now or later,' she said, drawing the blade under Broadleaf's chin. 'Up to you.'

-

At the machine, the fuzzy-headed engineer checked his settings and gave the vacuum chute a kick, to be sure it didn't catch like the last time. He clamped a leathery fist about the golden lid, turned it.

It opened with a pop.

-

Mae lurched backward, her vision fixed on a point in space that didn't exist there, a place not within her eye-line. Her arms dropped flaccidly to her sides.

Inches away, Broadleaf gasped and pulled back from the fearsome sight. Despite her bound wrists, she rubbed at her neck, the pin-prick wound from the blade.

She looked up at the crazed and rotting fairy and wondered what in the name of all Diamond was going on.

-

Halfway down the attic ladder, Marie felt a pulsing buzz against her hip. It came from the satchel she'd taken from the attic that held some of her father's artefacts. She maybe should've waited until she was back on level flooring before opening it, but then she maybe should've done a lot of things.

Holding firm to the ladder with one hand, she opened the flap of the bag with the other. She looked in and watched as the small wooden box containing the coin-medal jiggled about in there, rattling against the journals, jumping this way and that. Marie took it out, held the box flat in the palm of her hand.

Pressing it to her belly, she managed in a one handed move to open the lid where, inside, the silver object quivered, pulsed, a living thing, a beating heart.

She wanted to touch it, to stop it jumping clean out of the box. She unfurled a finger and-

CRACK!

The lightning bolt surged from the coin into Marie's fingertip and in an instant sent her six feet across the landing, where she fell in a heap on the floor.

-

So little time to speak and cry on borrowed waves and yet and yet she's here and now and grasping with whatever there is to show and scream and try.

And try, she must.

Again she sees the girl.

'Tis she.

Clearly now. So clear that something is altered. Something is through. Broken through.

Now or never.

'By your hand.' She thinks it harder than ever before. Shows with all she has and all that is given and borrowed. Forces it between the gap.

The girl must know. Or else.

To do the act. To meet her there in time and space.

She feels the sliver of air and takes the gift from whomever or wherever. Thinks not where the gesture originates. Just takes and borrows. To use and ride the wave and push it out and tell the girl and hope and hope.

'Do not falter.'

Is all she can say.

-

Mae stood staring upward, her body trembling. An abysmal stench, likely the wings, made Broadleaf wonder if the greying fairy was alive in the slightest.

Alive or dead she wasn't paying any mind to the world around her. If she were she'd notice the young Faretheewell captive slip her binds and slowly, carefully climb from the nest.

One of Broadleaf's own wings had taken a hit during her undignified flight from the hollows. Unsure if it would hold her weight, she scrambled like a tree mite down the outer face of the building and into a broken vent cover some way below, while not taking her eyes off her captor.

-

Marie saw it then: the gate and the green world beyond it. And she remembered.

-

The girl, she knows.

She sees.

She-

-

The engineer rammed the lip of the glass against the machine's seal, perhaps harder than usual, taking his head pain out on the machine and the bastard thing in the jar. He twisted it in place and flicked the switch, and boom his job was done.

It writhed in there as the suck took out the whole purpose of the thing. It writhed and he watched, still getting a kick out of the job after so many times. But the eyes on it. Darn, if they didn't creep him all the way out.

'Stop looking at me,' he growled.

But it didn't, and he had to go do some made up task to move away from the sight of it. He reminded himself it wasn't in any position to harm him, half-dead and ugly, spitting its last. Powerful once, perhaps, but look at the state of it now. No, better not look. He rubbed his weary eyeballs and popped a handful of bandiroot pills to take the edge off the fuzz.

-

Mae dropped like a bundle of rags amongst the scraps and tatters that wove together to form the nest. It took a moment for her sight to return. She felt around blindly, orienting herself, waiting for the flashing lights to subside and the wails to stop ringing in her ears.

'What did we do?' she said, resting her head on her knees.

'Need not worry about that, sister of mine. Rest now.'

And it was a while before the dark fairy even noticed the green skull was gone.

16. ALL OF US RUN AWAY SOMETIMES

Marie gripped the bannister and staggered downstairs. However long she'd been unconscious on the landing the sunset had taken hold, the afternoon light gone the way of the warmth, over the horizon and away. She massaged her lower back while thinking herself lucky not to have broken her neck in the fall.

'Did you read them?' Olive's voice was a soothing balm in the weirdness.

'I skimmed a few. Brought some down to read later.' Marie took the kitchen landline over to the back door and looked down the darkening garden to the mass of hedgerow at the far end. 'There were so many. I had no idea.'

'And what did you learn?'

It sounded as if Olive was deliberately holding back. Something about the overly calm tone of voice, the waiting for the younger woman to catch up. There was wisdom there, a deep understanding.

What did I learn? Marie thought. She conjured the memories, the flashes of places and things, of joy and tragedy. She sensed wonder and terror, not just from the journals but seeded in her mind by the touch of a coin, too much all at once to make sense.

Outside, shadows climbed the garden. Arms of brambles reached through the hedgerow, pointing and beckoning, skeletons swaying in the breeze. Marie placed a hand against the window. 'A gate,' she said. 'I remember a gate. Down there.' She tapped gently on the glass even if the older woman on the other end of the phone couldn't see her do it.

'Okay.'

It didn't occur to Marie to ask why none of this came as a surprise to the older woman. Her mind was occupied with repairing connections, lost over years and seemingly, violently, reforming in real time. 'Hubert,' she said, recalling the man at the door. 'Where's Hubert?'

Olive sighed. 'I'm afraid he's probably dead, dear.'

The statement shook Marie out of her distracted state and she found herself standing in the kitchen once more. 'What do you... What?'

'Reckon so, love. A fetch sets its mind on you, chances are you're done for. Filthy buggers.' The old woman sniffed, as if drawing a line under any possibility of tear or tantrum. 'Anyway, best thing now is to get you away. Looks to me like he's taken to you. Likely he knows what Darkwood is and where it goes, which can only mean one thing: he's on the side of the South.'

'South? Like London?'

'Oh, sweet girl.' Olive's smile, sad at it was, somehow carried through the phone line. 'No, not London. Another South. Tell me, what are the dates of the journals you took?'

Marie reached in the satchel which had remained strapped across her body since before she'd been thrown from the attic ladder. She pulled out the books, checking the start and end of each. '1993 to '94,' she said, before slipping them back inside the bag and fastening the buckle. The dates triggered a thought, a memory, which Olive interrupted.

'Ah, yes,' the older woman said. 'That ought to do it.'

The low rumble of a car engine and the crunching of tyres on gravel drifted through from the front of the house. Marie turned to see Hubert's Jaguar pull up outside.

'He's back,' she said. 'What does he want?'

'Anything he can get his grubby hands on. Just you remember, he lies. And he can only get in the house if you let him.'

Marie lowered the phone handset to her chest. Olive said something else but all Marie could hear were the footsteps growing ever-closer on the path from the road.

Despite having her back to the hallway and the front door, she could feel the eyes of the vicar boring holes into her. Refusing to give him the satisfaction of seeing her look, she swung the kitchen door shut then involuntarily clasped a hand across her mouth.

There was no time to think, to fumble a decision, so she went with her first instinct and hurried to the back door and ever so carefully turned the key. She opened the door as quickly and quietly as her trembling hands allowed, crept through the gap, closed it behind herself and tiptoed across the grass toward the hedgerow.

She remembered that she still had hold of the phone with Olive on the other end and lifted it to her ear. 'I think I need to find the gate.' As Marie said the words aloud she knew this was where her thoughts had been heading all along: *find the gate and go through.*

The line beeped twice then fell silent.

'Olive? Olive?' She realised she'd gone too far from the base unit and the bloody thing had cut out. 'Bollocks.'

She dumped the phone on the grass and began feeling around in the wild brambles and overgrown hawthorn for any area that gave way a little easier than the rest. She figured she had a minute, tops, before the man calling himself Father Colin guessed what was up and came to check around back.

Sometime since falling from the ladder, a memory had come back to Marie of crawling on hands and knees and of clambering through this very hedge. Not just a simple memory, though. She could feel the excitement in her stomach, the rush a small child gets when their parents stop watching them for longer than they possibly should, freeing said child to go further than they otherwise might.

'I see you,' the vicar called from the road. It seemed her minute was up. 'Don't be running away, now, girly. Ain't no better place to go. Shitsville, that-a-way.'

Marie ignored him and kept on searching, kept on crawling and scratching about in the dirt, the satchel dragging along in the grass beside her. She hoped against hope that what Olive had said about him not being able to get in without her say so extended to the grounds as well as the house itself. And while that seemed unlikely, he had yet to breach the perimeter.

'Let me in, let me in,' the man taunted.

Marie felt something small but heavy hit her leg. Then another something caught her on the neck. Was he throwing gravel at her? She glanced back over her shoulder just as a stone whistled past her face, then another smacked into her arm.

'Ten points,' he whooped. 'Ding ding!'

The church volunteers were also with him, more of them than before. Marie counted four, maybe five, now. The bastard was recruiting! They, too, picked up handfuls of stones and drew their throwing arms back and fired.

Marie pushed herself into the hedgerow, deciding that even to end up on the other side was better than squatting down here as target practice. The deeper she went, the fewer direct hits she felt, until the stones could no longer reach her. She shuffled on and on expecting to pop out into a field full of unimpressed cows. But then she caught sight of the ornate wrought iron gate in the midst of the tangled hedgerow and she knew she'd seen it before.

The vicar's voice was faint, though still calling to her to come back, come back, and something about that resonated inside and upset Marie more than anything.

As she neared the hidden gate, a sheen formed between its bars, twinkling lights danced and the tang of spent gunpowder and woodsmoke drifted toward her through the branches and vines.

She thought of Olive and of the unholy man screaming at her from the roadside. She feared what it meant to leave the cottage unguarded, but the pull of the gate was stronger. It spoke to her of a green and welcoming place, a place to wander unobserved, to explore the unexplored. Most of all it conjured images of her father crawling through with a journal under his arm and leaving his worries far behind.

Come back, come back.

She tried to believe she wasn't running away. And even if she was, was that so terrible? To leave a bad place, a bad situation, for a better one? Wouldn't anyone?

Near enough to touch the gate, now. A current flowed, crackling and fizzing, and she felt her hair float away from her scalp. Dale, she thought. Her father's friend. But then she remembered how his little wooden cottage with the pretty stained glass windows burned down.

In a heartbeat, she remembered tree trunks that talked kindly in a forest so green it took your breath away. An army with wings, a picnic, a wishing well, and a goblin caught in a trap.

She remembered running and running and running some more.

Faretheewell, she thought, the name coming to her in a wave of knowing. Like it had always been. Like she had never forgotten. After all, how could she forget such wondrous things? She could not. She did not. It was there in her head the entire time.

Diamond. Like the map in the journal her father drew.

She pushed open the bars of the gate and crawled through the universe of stars.

17. NOR'WESTER

What met Marie as she emerged wasn't green or lush or welcoming, it was desolation. There were no trees (no live ones, anyway) or trickling streams, no cottages with stained glass windows, no picnics or freshly baked bread, no bustling paths or markets. Any people who at one time might have been here, along with everything else, were gone.

She staggered to her feet and moved forward away from the gate in a vain attempt to get her bearings or to sniff out the merest hint of life. She walked what could've been twenty yards (hard to tell with no obvious landmarks and visibility akin to chicken broth). She spun on the spot. Here was nothingness, little more than a collection of smoldering waste piles, splintered tree stumps, and smoke clouds that churned and turned the sky black.

She wondered if the visions that had been thrust so forcefully into her mind's eye only a short while earlier, of Diamond and the forests of Faretheewell, were in fact put there by the vicar as a trick.

He lies, she thought, remembering Olive's warning.

But then she remembered something else the vicar said: 'Shitsville, that-a-way.' He sure as hell hadn't lied about that.

The air scratched her eyes and caught in her nostrils every time she inhaled. She fumbled in her jacket for anything she could use to breathe through–a handkerchief, a glove–and pulled out a ball of white and blue paper which she immediately recognised as several intertwined facemasks, once commonplace. Less so, now.

Marie thanked her younger self for being too lazy to ever clear out her pockets as she disentangled one of the masks. She placed it over her face and fed the loops over her ears. It was far from ideal but it would have to do and was a vast improvement on breathing the foul air raw.

She looked across the landscape, in turn covering her eyes or casting them downward to avoid being blinded by the smoke and microscopic debris that blew all around. For a moment, the ground felt unsteady. A mild tremor took Marie off guard. She held her hands up, kept her feet rooted in place until it passed.

Even with a mask it was clear she couldn't stay here, so she turned back and prepared to face Father Colin if that's what had to be done.

But wait.

She turned again the other way, looking for the glittering lights that had shone from the gate's opening, a beacon in the otherworldly fug. But it was gone. The gate and her way out was gone.

***

Marie stumbled from the dead forest and after a while found herself in open terrain, a barren dust bowl that looked to stretch for miles. To her right she spied a city as dark and lifeless as the forest she'd left behind. No lights lit up the skyscrapers, no sounds of civilisation came to her across the wasteland. The city, were it not for the billowing smoke stacks, appeared every bit as abandoned as the rest of this godforsaken shithole.

A gusting wind did its worst to usher her toward the dark towers and presumably empty streets. It tried in bursts to buffet her in the direction she knew, as sure as she knew anything, was south.

No, she thought. Not there.

The paper mask wasn't the kind to filter out fine particles. They got under it and around it and rasped at her throat and her chest, making her want to clear it away while she tried her hardest not to.

With every hunched step, Marie prayed she was walking toward something and not just further and further away. Not that she had another option. With the city on one side, a forest of ash behind, and a storm blowing in from her left, she had no choice but to keep going straight ahead.

Around tall stones and stacks of boulders, the wind sang. Soon, something else, a voice, muscled its way in and it came to Marie that her mother used to call her 'Hunnybun'. She couldn't recall the last time she'd heard it said. Certainly not since she left for St. Jude's. But in the fraction of a second it took to remember, it went from a lost thing to a powerful truth: *Have fun, Hunnybun.* The words became stuck, looping her brain for kicks.

Her eyes were streaming, now. The polluted air, she decided. Fallout from the city's gargantuan belching chimneys. Another strong gust rocked her sideways, almost sending her tumbling. She needed to pause, to breathe.

Some way in the distance, an arrangement of stone slabs held firm against the swirling eddies and Marie veered towards it hoping it might offer protection from the poisoned air. She squinted through dust covered lashes, lifted her arm and wrapped her inner elbow around her mouth and nose as an additional barricade to keep the pollutants from reaching the flimsy mask and, beyond it, her lungs.

Each time she looked up the stone slabs weren't getting any closer. She knew it was a fool's errand. Chasing a goddamn mirage. She'd die here and stay here and nobody would ever know. Still, on and on she went. Step after choking step.

The stone slabs weren't getting closer.

Until they were.

***

Marie scrambled under a stone slab that lay across others like a lintel, sliding down into a lower level. Once inside, the gusting winds abated, giving way to ear-ringing calm, and the whistling sounds of the dead desert were replaced by her own ragged breath. She found she was able to lower her mask, to gasp the air. She at last gave herself permission to cough.

Only when she felt her breathing return to something close to normal, her eyes beginning to adjust, did she think to look around to check nobody else was at home. But there was nothing to fear, just a space the size of a small garage, a dirt floor, sandstone walls. The only break in the shell of the structure was the narrow entrance that she'd somehow managed to fit through. There were no other windows or gaps of any kind.

She sat down to rest a while.

***

By the time Marie jolted awake, the light from the entrance had faded so much that it was only just visible in the darkness. She stood and, feeling for the rough stone above her head, trod carefully over to the opening. The wind still blew south. She could tell by the way the dusty topsoil swept by. The opening faced that way too, toward the city, which was, she knew, the only reason she wasn't suffocating on clouds of ash.

Another sound added to the dulled but ever-present whirling and whistling from outside. Marie turned her head to listen. It was hard to make out at first but got more distinct with every passing moment. It was a sound she'd heard before.

What had her father called them? She thought back to a journal entry she'd skimmed through while in the attic, one she'd assumed was fiction, that hadn't meant much at the time.

Hummers. That was it. The word was foreign but the angst it caused in her was not.

She leaned closer to the opening and cautiously searched the leaden sky for movement, but it was too dark. Unless these so-called hummers wore hi vis and headlamps she knew she'd never see them up there. And it seemed unlikely they'd be so accommodating. Although, she thought, no less likely than what had already come to pass.

The sound came in fluctuating waves, louder or quieter depending on the gusts that rattled by the stone shelter. A minute went by, then two, then five, until Marie realised the noise–*the hum*–had grown quieter. She gave it another minute to be sure. They hadn't gone over the top of where she was crouched so they must've flown to the side. Probably they were going towards the burned forest. What was there for them in that desolate place, Marie couldn't imagine.

She picked up the mask from the floor where she'd dropped it earlier. It was covered in dirt and black smears from the foul outside air. She felt around in her jacket pocket and found a couple more crumpled up masks, the first one she unfurled was in a sorry state and completely unusable, the second was better. She checked the ear loops were intact which, thankfully, they were. Last hope, she thought. If she didn't get wherever she was going before this mask packed in then she was pretty much fucked.

'The only way out is through,' she said, invoking a phrase her father would use to encourage her on the last leg of a long walk over the hills. She pulled on the fresh mask, smoothing it across her nose and mouth.

'Wish me luck, Dad.'

She leaned forward into the gap.

***

Climbing from the shelter was a lot trickier than climbing in. Marie threw the bag out, then shuffled and wriggled herself up and through the narrow opening in the stone slabs and back into the wide open of the barren land. Some way ahead, a dust devil swirled in the semi-darkness accompanied by a mid-level sound like the whirr of a cheap hair dryer. Marie saw but thought nothing of the oddity, assuming it to be a natural phenomenon, a whirlwind whipped up from ground warmed by a long day in the sun.

On she went, no end in sight, no plan but one step after another. Each breath became more difficult until the dust and smoke particles ignored the mask altogether and found their way to her throat and made her gag, which made her cough and cough until coughing was all she did. She doubled over, covering her mouth and eyes with the front of her jacket and fell to her knees, gasping for air where there was none.

The whir of the dust devil was louder, now.

Marie's eyes wept brown dirt down her cheeks and onto her t-shirt. Near-blinded, a flicker of a thought came to her that perhaps she should have risked the city after all. The South, Olive had said. He works for the South.

If he came from the South then there was surely air to breathe, water to drink, food to eat? It was a moot point. She'd make it no further in any direction. She curled into a knot in a last bid to keep out the smoke.

The ground shook as the whirling dust storm blew nearer until it blasted up grit and dirt that rained down on Marie. She clutched her hands to her head. Something like a blanket was thrown over her, wrapped about her head and arms, bound around her waist, and she was lifted, pulled clean up off the ground. And then she was inside the dust devil, flying across the desert. She could just make out the floor moving beneath her through the weave of the cloth. She wriggled, but what held her in place held her firmly. After a while she didn't fight it anymore, her head dazzled by, and lost to, the sense of motion.

She felt herself thrown every which way as the dust devil carried her what must've been miles. Until finally she came to a halt and in the screaming wind she thought she heard someone calling her name, shouting, 'No, no, no!'

She realised, then, that she was on her feet and moving fast, still with the blanket over her, still half blind. She'd broken away from the dust devil and she was running free.

There were lights ahead, a doorway, a universe of stars.

She lunged at it with all she had. One last push. To get home or whatever else existed beyond. Can't be worse than here, she thought. Anywhere but here.

Pounding feet on dusty soil gave way to-

Nothing.

She was falling, flailing through the air, as if dropped off a cliff and rushing down and down until-

The cold swallowed her whole and she sank below, her body shocked by the sudden change. *Don't breathe. Can't breathe. Mustn't breathe.*

After a fight, she managed to shuck the cover from her arms and head and realised pretty damn quickly that here was no longer the dust bowl; here was underwater. She turned and flipped, frantically searching the blue blur for which way was up, but saw only a slightly lighter area and used what little she had left to kick good and hard toward it.

Too cold. Too deep. She'd plunged too far beneath to make it back before she absolutely, positively, had to take the longest, hardest pull of a breath and–holy mother of God. Her lungs sucked in the salty water. As the burn of it rolled through her chest she thought perhaps she was an elderly woman in her bed and having a stroke, or ten years old and in the throes of a fever dream. That all this was imagined. That she'd wake momentarily.

And it occurred to Marie that if she had to die anywhere, anytime, this would not be the worst of ways

to go. Not the worst of ways. At least she wouldn't die in a desert of filth-ridden air.

No.

Better to drown here in an ocean of her dreams.

With no kind of air at all.

PART THREE

1. FEW

Leddy Rickett checked the count: six more gone in as many suns. She didn't want to tell the old 'un, unsure how he would take the word of the further dwindling of their already decimated numbers. He'd lost so much it hardly seemed fair. But when he came to her at the meeting tree and asked directly where they stood, she had no choice. While Pappy Skylark may have been old, he wasn't stupid. He'd likely worked it out for himself anyway.

'Who?' he said. 'Say it straight, now. Honey dips are for strawberries, not bad news.'

'Three gate watchers. A couple of little 'uns out playing. Snuck away without asking and gone in a blink. And Broadleaf, of course. Safe to assume she isn't coming back. Been too long for that.'

Pappy shook his head and slapped a hand on his knee. 'Bastards,' he said, quietly.

Leddy held her fury in check. She wanted to find those responsible, burn them, take back what they had stolen from West Diamond: the life, the green, the hope. She would rip it out of their flesh and fix this. She didn't know how, she only knew she couldn't see another innocent snatched, knowing as she did what was done with them after. The thought of it brought her to the brink of a scream.

'Everyone stays indoors,' Pappy said. 'Group runs only, and then in the light and never, ever beyond the hollows.'

'Agreed.'

'And, Cerulean?'

A pause.

'Protect them. Please?'

Leddy nodded: *With my last breath.*

'Good,' he said. 'Now, let's get back and fix the windows and doors so those blasted humming heifer turds can't get a whiff of us.'

Pappy handed Leddy the sheet with the roll call. 'I'll walk with you,' he said. 'It'll do these old wings good to have a break.'

The ex-hummer took the square of parchment, folded it and slipped it into her pouch. Then the two friends set back in the direction of the hollow stump that had once been a troll called Oskar.

***

The wind had turned. The clouds from the city now swept back across the land, dimming the evening light so it felt more like sundown than middling time. Pappy and Rickett picked up their pace, both feeling the nerves coming off of the other and both knowing the vibrations in the air were not good.

They heard the hollow, smelled the burning, long before they saw it. Cries of little 'uns being snatched from their mothers' arms rang through the trees, shrieks of horror and pain.

Leddy broke into a sprint.

'Go!' Pappy called after her, somewhat needlessly. She was already far ahead.

Under her cloak Leddy Rickett's wings twitched with every step. When she was certain the old 'un couldn't see her, or perhaps she no longer cared if he did or not, she tugged at the ribbon, letting the cape fall, and by the time it hit the ground she was airborne, humming through the forest at a pelt.

When she got to the stump, the hummer crew were gone, having taken to the sky with those that were left of the village and of Faretheewell. Leddy darted from one room to another searching for anyone they'd left behind, hoping to find a child cowering in amongst the furniture or a baby hidden in a drawer. But there were only the bodies of those who'd resisted and lost against the army of the North.

Pappy was right, she thought: Bastards.

She lowered herself to the floor when a groan made her turn. There by the door was Fig, the young green skull. He was bleeding badly. It looked as if he'd put up quite a fight.

'You're one of them,' he said, fear in his eyes but no will left to back it up with anything resembling action.

Despite the young fairy's flinches, Leddy leaned in close to examine his wounds. 'I was,' she said, lifting his tunic, stemming a bleed from his abdomen with the heel of her hand. 'Not anymore.'

'They took 'em all,' he said. Each rise and fall of his chest was accompanied by a gurgling sound, each word spoken through a spattering of red.

Leddy kept pressure on his belly hoping it was enough, and kept looking into the young 'un's eyes. 'I know,' she said. 'I'm going to get them back. Just you concentrate on staying here with me. Okay?'

And he tried. Leddy could see he tried. But trying wasn't always enough and after a moment the gurgling stopped. She drew her hand away.

The humming soldier rushed at her out of nowhere and grabbed Leddy around the throat and by the hair, pulling her into the inner heights of the hollow trunk. Leddy's wings kicked into gear halfway up. The two fairies paused momentarily, eyes locked.

'You're supposed to be dead,' the soldier said.

The surprise evidently affected her grip as Leddy slapped the grasping hands away. She knew that face, those eyes, that mouth. Knew it better than most. 'Free?' she said, rubbing her neck. 'Gunwing Free?'

Surprise turned to disgust in a click and the soldier pulled her arm back to strike. 'Squad Leader Free to you, bitch.'

Free swung hard, with purpose, but Leddy swerved and the punch landed in the spongy lining of the trunk. Leddy backed up some, held her arms forward. 'Can we not?' she said. 'I don't want to fight you.'

The younger squad leader laughed. 'Oh, that's fucking priceless,' she said. 'Give it up, traitor. Come with me to the city and I might ask Borealis to let you keep your wings. For now.'

The hummers steadily circled each other.

'I'm not sorry I left, Free,' Leddy said. 'I had good reason. But I am sorry I hurt you.'

'Ha!' the soldier rolled her eyes.

'No. I should've told you. But what if I had, Free? What then? You'd have had to leave, too.'

'You take my choices away and reckon it makes you a fucking hero? Spare me.'

'And if they'd caught you and punished you for my crimes? How was I supposed to justify that?' Leddy said.

'Yeah? Well, I'm over it.' The young squad leader pulled out her blade and lunged for Leddy Rickett.

'Don't do this, Free. Don't-'

Before Leddy could finish, her former gunwing–former lover–was upon her, the blade flashing through the air in an arc that would've taken the tip of the weapon down through her clavicle. Likely a fatal wound, were it to have found its mark.

Leddy grabbed Free by the forearm, placed the still-bloodied palm of her other hand on the younger soldier's chest and waited, holding her gaze, until the intensity, the shared emotion, made Free drop the knife.

'Cerulean!'

Leddy turned. On the floor of the hollow was Pappy. 'You don't have to,' he said.

Free used the distraction to wrench her arm from Leddy's grasp and darted out through a hole in the stump, clutching her chest as she went.

Fuck. Leddy descended the full height of the hollow in a blink. She was hesitant to approach Pappy in the doorway. She saw he was looking—not angry or afraid, just looking. She pondered briefly the option of darting out of a window herself and humming away, not facing the conversation she knew needed to be had. But she decided against it. She'd done too much running already.

'I don't know what to say.'

The older fairy placed an arm around Leddy Rickett's shoulders, glanced at her wings, gave them an appreciative nod. 'Oh, don't you be worrying, now,' he said, calm as you like. 'I've known who you were from the start.'

2. EAST

It took Marie a little while to come around from a profoundly deep and dreamless sleep. The first thing she knew was that her wrists hurt. Then, that she couldn't move as she wished. A feeling surged within her that she was trapped in a box, buried alive, and the burst of terror that followed woke her quickly and with a scream.

'It's alright, miss,' someone said. 'Safe now.'

Marie saw, then, that she was restrained. Canvas straps buckled her arms to a hospital bed. She wanted to pull the rubber mask off her face, to stop the hissing of cool air against her mouth and nose, but the straps only allowed her enough range of movement to reach her torso. She looked down to her feet where another pair of straps snaked out from under the sheet. She jerked her knees up and felt the tug around her ankles.

'I'm sorry, miss,' the someone said. 'We had to be sure. You understand? Not much longer now.'

She gave back into the weariness and dropped her head back onto the pillow. Uncommon sounds filled the space around her. Inside the room, the *tink-tink-tink* of monitoring equipment, and beyond it, a dull swoosh like giant doors opening and closing. Bubbling, too (a fish tank?) All these things in combination took on a hypnotic lilt which, when combined with the fact she'd been doped up to the eyeballs, sent her rolling back to a place of calm. She didn't tug at the restraints after that.

It was later–how long Marie couldn't guess having drifted in and out of sleep numerous times–when the door opened and a group of people entered the room. They talked quietly among themselves, standing at the bedside. She would've listened in a while and kept her eyes shut were it not for the coughing fit that gave her away.

'Alright,' one said, holding the mask close to her face and helping her lean forward, gently rubbing her back. 'That's it. Deep breaths, now. Nice and slow.'

'Can we get these damn things off, please?' another said.

And Marie felt hands fumbling at the straps, after which her wrists and her ankles were free.

She reached up and wiped away the tears brought on by coughing, after which she was able to look around the room properly for the first time. Three men and a woman looked back at her. Most of them were dressed in pale green lab coats. The other, one of the men, wore what appeared to be black and grey army fatigues.

The woman in the lab coat, who Marie took to be a medic of some kind, dragged over a stool on wheels and sat next to the head of the bed. 'I'm just going to shine this light in your eyes, Ms. Fisher.' The woman pointed a dazzling pen torch, flashing it left and right.

It was far too bright for Marie's barely woken state. She turned her head away, raised a hand to block the beam.

'Give her a minute,' one of the men said.

'I need to check for neuro deficit.' The medic flashed the light again.

Marie pushed the woman's hand away, firmly and with clear intention. She looked up at each of the people crowding over her in turn.

'She's all there,' the man in fatigues said, who was standing further away than the others, watching from the door. 'Christ, Gen, give her some room to come round.'

The woman scribbled on a clipboard then got up off the stool, pushing it away. 'Fine,' she said. She gestured to the others in lab coats to follow. 'Half an hour. But she doesn't leave this room.'

The man in fatigues stepped aside to allow them through the door. 'Roger that,' he said.

It was just Marie and the army man in the room, then, and Marie pulled the sheet up to her shoulders, having become acutely aware that she was dressed only in a hospital gown.

The man took the stool and sat some distance away. 'How are you feeling?' he said.

'Where am I?'

'East,' he said.

'What does that mean?'

'Here,' he said. 'This'll explain it better than I can.' The man stretched forward, leaning over the bed.

Alarmed by the sudden invasion, Marie shrunk into herself and tried to bat the man's arm away.

'You're okay,' he said, raising a hand, then pointing a finger as if to say, *watch*.

Marie looked. She realised the wall to her left was not a wall at all, but a large rectangular window hidden behind a set of folding blinds.

The man tugged on drawstrings that dangled to the side and the blinds lifted, revealing a wide open landscape of rippling blue.

'Are we-' she failed to find the word for it.

'Underwater,' the man helped her out. 'Yes, we are. You're quite safe, though.'

He didn't say any more than that, instead allowing Marie the courtesy of time to take in her surroundings. Outside the window, which she could see was made of glass a foot thick, an ocean went about its day. Unfazed were the shoals of fish that swam past, untroubled by her presence were the urchins and anemones that crawled over corals or waved their spiny bodies in time with the currents. Crops of tall plants softly billowed. The entire display was lit by beams of light dappling down from above.

She had the vaguest of recollections of falling.

'How did I get here?' She turned back to the man, finding it difficult to draw her gaze from the window and the sights through the glass. 'There was a dust storm. I couldn't breathe.'

'Yeah. Not sure what you were thinking going out in that. Damn lucky you got caught out in a nor'wester, else you'd have choked up long before you did, and I'd never have gotten to you quick enough.'

'A what?'

'Nor'wester,' the man said again. 'Wind from the north-west. Usually get those when the North gate opens. Sometimes they just happen by themselves. In any case, wind comes down from that way, takes the pollutants back south where they came from. Doesn't clear it entirely, of course, but better than it would be otherwise. Buys you a bit of time. Not much, but some.'

There was a look about the man, the bone structure, the chin, that Marie recognised. 'Do I know you?' she said.

But the man just smiled. 'Give me a minute,' he said. 'There's someone else wants to meet you. You up to having a visitor?' He barely waited for her to respond before speaking into a box in the wall. 'She's ready. Tell him he can come down now.'

'On his way,' came the crackling reply.

While they waited, the man helped Marie swap out the rubber mask for a tube that fed the oxygen up into her nose, which she found much less of an irritation. After that it was only a matter of a couple of minutes before they heard multiple sets of footsteps on the corridor outside.

When the door opened again, the medics from earlier walked back in along with an older man and woman who were dressed in regular attire, neither military nor medical. The older man strode over to the bedside with an outstretched hand.

'Ms. Fisher,' he said. 'Or can I call you Marie?'

She took his hand. 'Marie's fine,' she said, still somewhat overwhelmed.

'Thank-you, Marie. Yes, you won't remember, but we do know each other. I was a friend of your father's back in the day. Your mother too, briefly. My condolences, by the way. So much loss. Poor woman.'

'I'm sorry, how exactly do we know each other?' Marie had never been to this or any other underwater place before. She felt sure she would've remembered that.

'Like I said, you were too young. I don't expect you to have any memory of your time with us. But this is my wife, Reenie,' he gestured to the older woman beside him, who smiled back at Marie. 'And you've met my boy, Dale Junior. Or as we call him, Rock.' The man squeezed the shoulder of the man in fatigues. 'You two kids would play together for hours, you know. Before we left for the East. Right pair of troublemakers you were.'

'So that would make you-'

'Dale Senior, yes. Or just Dale to most folks around here.'

She felt her eyes fill. 'I thought I made you up.'

'I expect you did,' Dale Senior said. 'The gate has that effect. But don't you worry, there's time for all that later. For now you just get your strength back and we'll get you fed and watered, and we'll see where we are then. Okay?'

Marie nodded.

'Good,' he said. 'Later, it is.' And with that, the group left, leaving Marie and the younger Dale alone once more.

As the room returned to almost-quiet, apart from the *tink-tink-tink* and the bubbling sounds, Marie looked to the man in fatigues, Dale Junior, or Rock as the older man had said he was called. She knew without doubt that she knew him. Knew his face, recognised it, remembered it. It was the face of a friend she'd gone in search of but hadn't found. A face that had disappeared from her memory.

'I'm sorry I wasn't there to meet you that day,' he said, as if reading her thoughts.

And for the first time in the better part of three decades, Marie knew she hadn't lost her goddamn mind.

3. REASONS

It was nighttime in the ocean when the woman medic came back to check on her patient. Marie hadn't been asleep. She'd been watching moonbeams dance down from the surface, trying to figure out the layout of the other metal structures of this huge submarine habitat the people living here had constructed. So when the door opened with a gentle creak, she turned to look.

'You dropped this out on the plains where Rock found you. He thought it must be important so we saved it. He made sure to keep it dry on the way down. I'm Genevieve, by the way.' She handed Marie the satchel, still with the journals inside.

They were indeed dry, Marie saw as she looked around and under the leather bound books, shoving them to the side. 'There was another thing, a box?' she said.

'Can't say I saw one,' the medic said.

She seemed genuine, which bothered Marie. Either she was lying and good at it or the object had fallen out of the bag and was somewhere out in the desert slowly but surely being buried by dust and ash. Either way, she felt a deep sense of loss at no longer having the coin in her possession. It had been her father's and he'd clearly thought it valuable enough to keep.

'Okay, thanks for this,' she said, drawing out one of the journals, opening it at a random page.

'Your dad liked to write?' Genevieve said.

'Huh?' Marie was already engrossed in an entry. 'Oh, yes. It was kind of his thing. Wait, you've read these?'

The woman lowered his gaze to the floor. 'I'm sorry, yes. We entered them into the record. Believe it or not, those books,' she pointed at the journal, 'we consider to be important historical documents. With the historians gone, it's up to us to save them for those that come after.'

'Historians?' The word meant something to Marie, beyond what it actually meant in dictionary definition terms.

'Did you ever meet a troll? Before they got turned, I mean. They were the beating heart of Diamond, so Dale says. Never knew one he didn't like, apparently. Good folk. Long memories and the best of storytellers. The keepers of knowledge. Which is why they got targeted by the South.'

Marie had returned to flipping pages of the book when she stumbled by chance across an entry she recognised, one she'd read before. In it her father wrote of meeting a troll named Johan. After a moment she laid the book down.

'What did Dale mean when he mentioned my mother?' she said.

'You should probably talk to him about that,' Genevieve said. 'I only know this information because of what he's told me and what's in the record. Better you hear it firsthand. I think maybe we should leave it for now.'

'Leave what? My mother never knew about Diamond. She never went through the gate.'

Genevieve started to look uncomfortable as if she'd overstepped a mark or had gotten herself into a conversation that would end up some place she didn't want to go. 'Everything that happened with the baby.'

'What baby?' Marie said.

'I thought you knew. I wouldn't have brought it up if-'

'What baby?'

They sat for a moment with the *tink-tink-tink* and the bubbling sound until the medic eventually blew out a lungful of air in resignation.

'She was pregnant when she followed your father through. Not pregnant with you; with another child. We don't know if it was the gate that did it, but she hadn't gone far when her body decided it was time and she birthed the poor little thing in the forests of Faretheewell. Your father found them together only as he was returning to the gate, by which time the baby-' Genevieve held her hands up. 'It was just too early. I really am sorry. I thought your mother would've told you about this.'

'Barbara wasn't much for sharing,' Marie said. 'So where was I when all this was going on?'

'I believe it was before your time. You came after.'

Marie placed a hand on the open pages of the journal in her lap. 'She let me think she'd destroyed this when I was a child. I was so angry with her for that.'

'Maybe she wanted you to forget, too.'

'Too?'

'Like she did,' Genevieve said, as if her answer was supposed to make perfect sense. Then, when she saw that Marie wasn't getting it, she went on. 'She didn't want to remember so she chose to let the gate do what it does.'

'For fucks sake,' Marie said. 'Does anybody in this place talk plain English?'

The medic sighed. 'The West gate affects people,' she said. 'Doesn't harm you, as such. But it has the power to, how's the right way to put it? allow you to forget over time, if you choose to.'

'Right?' Marie said, slowly.

'So, if you visit Diamond, as-'

'Barbara,' Marie prompted.

'-As Barbara did, and you don't like what you see, when you go back to-'

'Yorkshire.'

'Yes, when you go back to Yorkshire you can simply let it fade away from memory. Or you can actively choose to remember, in which case, well, you get the idea.'

Marie pictured her mother, then, laying on the sofa watching TV. She thought of the words her father had written about the woman he loved–*his beautiful bride–*

and about how much he'd wanted to make her happy, to help her get better. And a sudden sense of clarity came to her mind, a fresh perspective, one that brought with it a surprising new emotion in regard to Barbara: pity.

'She was depressed,' Marie said quietly, exploring what this new understanding meant.

Genevieve shrugged. 'Sounds like an experience some might want to forget.'

'And she pushed me away.' A tear made a break for Marie's cheek and she swept it away.

'Maybe she thought it was her job to protect you. You were a child, after all. Maybe she knew to look after you she needed to get well. Or if she couldn't get well then the next best option was to push you away, ensuring you were okay despite her?'

'Gah!' Marie slammed the journal shut and threw it back in the satchel. She furiously rubbed her face. 'Where's Dale now? Older Dale. Dale Senior. I need to speak to him.'

The medic glanced up at the window behind Marie. 'Looks to me like that's a scout returning from a mission. My guess would be they'll be in debrief just as soon as he's dry and dressed. Which means they'll be over in C-Pod a while.'

Marie followed the medic's line of sight to see a person in diving gear pulling himself hand-over-hand down a guide rope from the surface toward one of the other underwater structures. 'And Dale Junior? Rock? Where's he?'

The medic didn't move or answer.

'Show me.'

'I'm not sure that's a good idea.'

'Show me or I'll go and find him myself.'

'Alright.' Genevieve reached over to a shelf for a pile of folded clothes and threw them on the bed. 'But you might want to put these on first.'

4. CITY DOGS

Leddy tore herself away from Pappy Skylark in order to leave for the South. This was her battle to fight, not his. The fact that the old 'un had skills was not in question. Still, she wouldn't put him at risk like that, not when she held herself responsible for the goings on at the hollows, crazy as that may sound.

She knew she wasn't the South. It wasn't she who had ordered the invasion and destruction of the green lands. She'd done her fucking job as a soldier of the North–a hummer–and the dark alliance had been formed without her say so. Too late she'd learned that she was flying on the wrong side, morally speaking, but it wasn't too late to endeavour to make amends. Never too late to try.

She stuffed a fistful of packed moss into a length of silk ribbon and wrapped it around her face, knowing that once beyond the last of the protective forest the choking poison would become unbearable. She tied it tight in a bow at the back of her head.

Pappy watched her as she hummed away.

It had been a while since she last tested her wings, long-haul, but they remained strong and held her aloft with little complaint. She'd forgotten the rush of true high altitude flight, to see the ground change beneath you as you broke through the air. She'd missed it. Too long spent in the guise of another, however good it might've felt to shed her tainted Northern skin.

She followed what little of the sun made it through the black clouds, across the dead landscape, until she reached the edges of the city. There she darted into the remnants of a small copse of trees and hid amongst the dry and broken branches, and took a moment to gather her thoughts before entering Must proper.

Leddy had just about calculated the best way to enter the walled city, and the direction to go in to stand the least chance of encountering those dark ones occupying the city streets, when she heard a whimper from behind a cluster of the dead wood. Thinking it might be a stolen Faretheewell little 'un she hummed toward the sound, then slowed when she saw a heap of dark fur curled up on the ground, nestled at the base of a rotten trunk.

'Oh, hello,' she said to the young pup that laid there. No matter its size, the dog still dwarfed the fairy. It was afraid, and likely injured. Leddy flew closer, and after allowing the animal the chance to adjust to her presence she reached out and slowly, cautiously stroked its snout.

She knew that, as the population of Must dwindled, the dogs and cats and other such creatures kept by the people as household companions found themselves abandoned, let loose to roam or to die at the mercy of the greedy Southern invaders. And when the forests of the West disappeared, and the central plains dried out without the forests to protect them, there was nowhere left for the animals to go.

She felt the poor pup's loneliness through her fingertips. Like plunging her hand into a puddle. We all suffer, she thought. Even the dogs.

'Where's your mama, little 'un?' she said. 'Can't leave you here by yourself. Are you hungry?' She looked around at the barren ground. There was nothing. So she pulled a couple of berries from a pouch in her waistband and dropped them in front of the animal.

The dog swallowed them with barely a chew, tiny as the berries were in comparison to its size, and Leddy felt its gratitude then. The creature looked up, hope in its eyes.

'Okay,' she said, dropping another berry. 'Just the one more.'

These were the feelings she didn't mind sharing, the feelings of friendship, of joy, of trust. Moments like this, her gift was a gift, not the curse that brought her to her knees with shame from the hurt that she'd wrought on so many. She'd refused it, then, avidly and actively choosing to not feel, not to see.

And then there was the man. The scout. What was there to say about him? She knew how he felt. How could she not? That he imagined he was taken with her and hoped of things that simply couldn't be. Not if he knew her as she knew herself. If that were the case he wouldn't be taken with her at all.

But she enjoyed him, so. The way he studied her with his eyes. Even inside the steel and glass orb he wore over his giant head, his intentions were clear. She didn't touch him if she could help it. The power of it would threaten to knock her sideways.

Another noise, then, behind her. Leddy turned to see a pack of dogs, full-grown and angry. No, not angry, defensive.

She hummed upward, palms facing the pack. 'It's alright,' she said. 'He's here. Look, he's right here.'

The animals eyed her warily, crossing the floor beneath her over to where the pup was now on its paws, its tail whipping the air.

Happy little fella, Leddy smiled to herself, then remembered the task at hand. She left the dogs to their reunion and flew up and over the walled perimeter and into the streets of Must.

5. NOTHING TO LOSE

Genevieve had given up trying to talk Marie out of it by the time they reached the lowest deck of C-Pod. The medic pushed open the door and went through first and Marie followed closely behind. The room had the same view she had seen from the hospital bed, through large windows looking out into the open ocean. There was only one other person in there, a man sitting at a bank of computer screens and tapping numbers into a keypad on the desk. He looked around and smiled at the woman in the green lab coat before noticing Marie, after which a look of concern descended over his face.

'It's fine. She's with me,' Gen said. 'We're looking for Rock.'

The reply didn't come from the man sitting at the desk, it came from behind the two women, from the scout in fatigues who had just walked in through the door after them. 'She was supposed to stay in the medical bay,' Rock said.

'What was I supposed to do, restrain her again? As far as I'm aware she's not our prisoner. Understandably, she has questions. Anyone would.'

The scout walked past the women and over to the man at the desk. He looked at the images on one of the screens and at numbers on another.

Marie wondered if she should speak as the silence dragged on. The man known as Rock, who she remembered as a boy with another name, ignored her like she didn't exist or as if she was an irritation best avoided.

The scout checked his watch then looked at Marie, then at Genevieve. 'You've got four minutes,' he said. 'We've got mission prep and the others'll be on their way over. I don't want her here when they arrive.' He ushered the two women to an empty desk, of which there were many, and gestured for them to sit. He perched himself against a different desk, neither sitting nor standing, looking every bit ready to pounce into action should the situation require it.

He folded his arms across his chest. 'Fire away,' he said.

There was too much Marie wanted to know, she couldn't think. The man looked at her with what she perceived as increasing impatience. 'Where are we?' she said at last.

'You fell through the East gate,' the man said. 'After I picked you up from the central plains of Diamond. And while we're asking questions, I have one: what in the fuck were you thinking?'

'Leave her, Rock,' the medic woman said. 'She wasn't to know.'

'Fine. What else?' He looked at his watch again.

'How do I get home?' Marie said.

'You don't,' the man said. 'Next?'

'I can't stay here. I have a house and people who will be looking for me. Just show me the way back and I'll figure it out myself. I'm not asking for an escort, just a signpost and a fresh mask to get through the smoke out there.'

The scout repositioned himself slightly against the desk. 'Okay,' he said. 'Let's suppose we give you the kit to go topside, and you manage the climb to the gate. Which, might I add, is a pully-lift of some hundred feet, or thereabouts. How strong are your arms feeling, Ms. Fisher? Suppose you make it all the way up, then out into the core world. You've got a day's walk across the plains, at least, in the southerly winds. Ain't no way my father's gonna let you take one of the scooters. We'll be taking them ourselves for the mission.

'Anyway, suppose you do somehow miraculously walk to the West on foot, and that the gate isn't having one of its more erratic days, and it didn't jump and vaporise you as you went through-'

'Yes,' Marie said, straightening her back. 'Let's suppose all that.'

Genevieve sat between Marie and Rock, looking back and forth between the two as they stared at each other, Rock annoyed, Marie indignant. Even the man further away at the computer screen looked to be working extra hard to avoid getting involved.

Rock broke the moment, turned to a monitor on the desk behind him.

'Don't,' the medic woman said.

'Doesn't look like I have a choice, Gen,' Rock said, tapping something into the keypad, rolling a mouse clicker around on the desk.

Marie saw an image appear on the screen, fuzzy blobs of green and brown, shadows and light, moving back and forth, impossible to decipher but familiar all the same. Along the lower edge of the image, numbers ticked by. A date stamp, perhaps?

'Rock, turn it off,' Genevieve said. The medic left her seat and went to press a switch on the console, but the scout blocked her arm.

'What would you have me do, Gen? Send her back? She needs to see.'

The blobs of green parted, exposing a face, and Marie knew that what she was looking at was foliage and the face she saw was that of the vicar, Father Colin. He pointed an index finger at her through the screen, seeing her but not, and the finger appeared malformed and bulbous as it tapped on the fish-eye lens.

Rock turned a dial and Marie didn't just see the taps but heard them.

'Is that-' She considered her words. 'Wait. There's a camera on the gate?'

'Hello?' The vicar spoke into the lens. 'Anyone there? West calling. Can you hear me?' He smiled the same smile Marie had seen through her front door. Then again with the tapping finger.

Genevieve went to interrupt but the scout held up his hand: No.

'I'll assume you are watching this, my salty friends,' Father Colin said after a pause. 'I shall also assume the girl is with you.'

Marie clenched her fists. How she wanted to land a punch on that smug face, hear the crack of that nose.

'Kindly tell the thief I have someone here who would appreciate muchly her returning and bringing with her what she stole.' The vicar drew back from the lens and puffed out his cheeks and mimed with his hands the breaststroke as he pretended to swim away.

The medic shook her head while Rock sat perfectly still.

'Wanker,' Marie said under her breath.

A few seconds later the vicar reappeared, suddenly close, not smiling, just staring. 'Say hi,' he said.

He pulled away and another face was thrust forward, filling the screen.

Marie gasped.

'Don't do it, Marie,' Shaun said into the lens. 'Don't believe a word-'

The vicar, who held Marie's husband firmly about the neck, then yanked him back out of sight of the screen, leaned in close once more. He looked through the lens as if seeing Marie there, knowing there was something intimate about the moment that would make her insides squirm.

He didn't speak again, only winked, then vanished through the foliage as quickly as he'd first appeared.

Rock clacked something into the keypad and turned a dial which made the image rush forward at high speed.

'I have to go back,' Marie said. 'You know that, right? I have to help him.'

Without responding, Rock slowed the racing images on the screen until he reached a certain timestamp, pausing it so the same green and brown blurs on the screen froze in place.

'Fuck's sake.' Marie slammed a palm on the desk. 'Are you listening to me?'

'That was recorded several days ago,' Genevieve said, softly.

Rock set the film running again. 'And this was yesterday,' he said.

Marie looked back to the screen where she saw the branches separate and Shaun approach the lens.

'Marie, if you can hear me, and God I hope you can, come home. It's safe. I got rid of him, the man, the vicar. There was a fight and I-' Shaun ran a trembling hand through his shaggy hair. 'I hit him, Marie. I grabbed a shovel and hit him, and he ran off. I called the police from the house and they came round but he's gone. Please come home, let me know you're okay. I love you, Marie. Come home.'

The scout froze the picture on Shaun's face looking out of the screen with pleading eyes.

'My husband is dead, isn't he?' Marie said.

Neither Rock nor the medic answered, which was an answer in itself.

'You think that he-' she pointed at the screen '-is the fetch?'

The two Easterners shot each other a glance as Marie studied the face on the screen.

'Marie, where did you hear that word?' Genevieve said.

'What word?'

'Fetch,' Rock said. 'Where did you hear that from?'

'My friend. My neighbour, Olive. That's what she called the one pretending to be a vicar. She called him a fetch, and he sort of answered to it.'

And there they went again, glancing at each other, Rock and the doc, as if sharing some private joke.

'Olive who?' Gen said, more kindly that Rock would've asked, Marie imagined.

'Wells. Olive Wells. Why?'

The scout switched off the monitor with a snap of a switch. 'You are joking me,' he said, then laughed. 'Shine a fucking light.' He pushed himself up off the desk and marched to the door where he was met by Dale Senior and a half dozen others Marie didn't know.

'Where you off?' Dale Senior said, before noticing Marie. 'Oh, hey, Ms. Fisher. I'm afraid you don't have the authorisation to be in here. Genevieve, please escort the young lady back to her room.'

'You might want to hear what she has to say,' the medic said.

'Thank-you, doctor. But this is no place for landsiders, you know that.'

'Doc's right, chief,' Rock said. 'Might be new info to factor in.'

'Such as?' Dale Senior lifted a somewhat bedraggled looking cigar from his shirt and rolled it between his fingers, then ran it under his nose before returning it to the pocket from which it came.

'We might have ourselves a historian.'

'No shit?' Dale Senior said. 'Where? How?'

Rock shrugged. 'How, I've no idea. Where,' he nodded at Marie. 'Befriended this one, apparently.'

'Name?' Dale Senior said.

Marie didn't have the faintest idea what this conversation between the two men was about, but they seemed energised all of a sudden.

'Get this,' the scout said. 'Olive Wells. Called the goblin a "fetch" of all things.'

Dale Senior clapped his hands together. 'I'll be a slippery fluke.'

'So what does this mean?' Marie managed to say during a pause in the talking.

The older man approached and put his arm around Marie's shoulders, and for an instant it almost felt like her father giving her a hug. She pushed him away. 'Please can someone just explain to me what in the hell is a fetch?'

'Doppelganger, Ms. Fisher,' the medic walked up behind her and whispered. 'A copy.'

'I know what doppelganger means. And Olive? What's she got to do with this? She's pretty old. Wouldn't hurt a fly. And she said the fetch killed her husband. Wait, did you say goblin?'

'Husband?' Rock said.

'Yes, her husband, Hubert. What was that you said about a goblin?'

The scout went over to the nearest screen and typed into the keyboard until a page of text appeared on the monitor. 'Got him,' he said. 'Not husband; Guardian. Hubert Greensleeve, formerly of Faretheewell upper stream. Some royal blood there, I think. Chief?'

'Which would track,' Dale Senior said, scratching lazy fingers down his stubbled cheek. 'Longest I've known any keep cover was a few months. They must've been hidden, what? Thirty years?'

'At least,' Rock said.

'Ain't no regular magic, that.'

'No, sir, it is not.'

'Won't change matters, son,' the older man said. 'Gotta pull the plug, either way. Levels are up. A move is on the cards.' He called over to the man at the computer at the far end of the room, 'Whatcha got, Greg?'

'Tipping into the high hundreds,' the man said. There was worry in his voice, Marie noted, restrained but there.

'And scout Vogler just reported back that another of the hollows has taken a hit. We go now or we don't go. South'll be ramping up to mobilise for sure.'

'Which hollow?' Rock said.

'I think you were there last week? Where the green skull marks all cluster.'

But Rock was gone, out the door and away.

'He sure does care for those little fairy fellas,' Dale Senior said. 'Which is why we have to do what we have to do. Turn those blasted diggers off and end the burn. Soon as that's done, we'll set to getting you home, young lady, okay? Until then, sit tight. Our people will take care of you.'

***

'I want to go with them,' Marie said as she walked alongside the woman down the tubular corridor in the direction, she assumed, of the medical bay. She didn't say that she had nothing else to fight for, nowhere else to go, nothing to lose. And she didn't mention the voice that echoed in her thoughts of a trapped and desperate someone crying out for help–for her help, specifically– or that she knew without question that the same desperate someone would be found somewhere in the heart of the dark city.

If she told Genevieve any of that, the medic would be inclined to not only keep her in a room away from the others but to lock it tight.

So, yes, she kept those things to herself. For now, at least. Until she understood for herself what was going on.

'Do you have a death wish, Ms. Fisher?' Genevieve said. 'Because there's an excellent chance they won't come back. Must is crawling with Southerners who won't be letting our guys switch their machines off without a fight.'

'I owe them some payback.' Marie pictured Shaun on the monitor and imagined him dead.

'Indeed. Well, as honourable as that sounds, I should warn you they have a penchant for flesh, the uncooked variety, and they'll be hungry.'

'I'll risk it.'

'Not just risk, Ms. Fisher. They'll know we're coming and will in all likelihood be ready. Ah, here we are.' Genevieve held her hand out to signal they had arrived at the room.

Marie went inside.

'Do you want any supper?' the medic said. 'I can have some sent down if you like?'

'Marie smiled. 'That's okay,' she said. 'I think I'll try and sleep. Might read some more of my father's journals. I haven't taken it all in yet.'

'Alright. If you want anything, press this button.' Genevieve touched the box on the wall by the door, an intercom, and after Marie said she understood, she was left alone with her books and the rippling view of the moonlit ocean and shoals of fish swimming outside.

Helluva thing, she thought, building a civilisation deep beneath the ocean waves. But then these were city folks, and she'd gleaned some small insight into what they were capable of back in the desert when she viewed the skyscrapers and smoke stacks from afar. How much of a reach would it be to imagine utilising those same skills here?

She wondered how long they'd had to plan it, to implement it. The medic, Genevieve, had suggested as they walked between levels that the move was out of necessity and done hurriedly, that the engineers and skilled trades had diverted all efforts to the project. She said she remembered being told to pack her favourite toy as a child and had to choose between a bear and a doll. She eventually went with the bear and spent the next six months in a state of anxiety about what had become of the doll.

No way for a child to live, Marie thought as she listened, understanding the feeling in the pit of her stomach of losing one of two things you care about, and that you cannot imagine life without.

***

On this day April 30th 1994

The people have spoken. Word from the city is that time is short and if they stay they will most certainly get caught up in matters of the South. Their spies are everywhere, I hear. So it might be that I am unable to return soon, if ever, to my beloved Diamond.

I made a promise to a friend, however, that I must keep. So I shall.

If only I could've saved the boy.

***

After reading a month's worth of entries in one of the journals, Marie dimmed the lights and lay still under the covers. The final, most recent entry, the last her father ever wrote, stayed with her: *If only I could've saved the boy.*

She followed the lines of underwater structures, the tunnels leading from one pod to another, from one level up to the next. The rope to the surface was visible as a glistening silver thread rising from a cylindrical pod some five or six levels up. Marie's eyesight wasn't the best, but through circular portholes in that pod she could make out rows of wet-suits hanging on hooks, and a mesh-frame storage unit containing gas tanks.

She cast her mind back to earlier when the other scout had returned. She hadn't been paying it much attention given what was happening at the time, but now she thought about it, he had swum under the pod and up into it, as if there were a hatch or a moon pool there. She squinted to focus on the area in question, but it was in shadow and impossible to make out.

'Tomorrow,' she'd heard one of the others say as she left the computer room.

'First light,' she believed Dale Senior had replied.

The medic hadn't clarified when Marie asked about the mission, instead changing the subject to matters of a less sensitive nature, about the weather up top.

Marie made the decision to wake herself early and fiddled with a small travel clock that sat on the bedside drawer. She'd go and speak with Dale Senior in the morning and make him see. Tell him the city was calling her. That she had a mission of her own even if she wasn't sure what that was yet. She had to go with them. Simply had to.

The shimmering light of a thousand moonbeams travelled by her window, dancing through the clear water onto the ocean floor. And Marie slipped into a faraway sleep and dreamed of her father and his words:

If only I could've saved the boy.

6. THE WINDOW CLEANER

George Fisher was a man of his word. As far as he was concerned, a promise made was a promise kept, a debt always repaid (more or less). And while Barbara liked to accuse him of selfishness or flights of fancy, George knew himself better than that.

So when his friend from the other place whose company he so enjoyed wanted badly to see his world, to spend time there and watch him work, George felt obliged to make it happen.

'Tells me abouts the biggun lands,' this friend would say. 'What be the tallest of tall places you takes your bucket and sponge?'

So fascinated was he with the ancient architecture of George's world, and how it was to climb up wobbly ladders and clean the highest of windows, to see the sunrise from a rooftop, he'd make George tell the stories over and over, get him to describe it in detail, listening each time with eyes wide and mouth agape in wonder.

And so it was that one quiet morning George left his wife and child sleeping, called for his friend through the gate and hid him in the van with the ladders and hose. They drove to St Cuthbert's, the greatest of the churches in the region, and where George had a regular thrice-yearly gig making the stained glass shine as it should.

On any given day in Yorkshire, the other-world folk would stand out like a marching band. But get there early, he thought, and nobody would notice an extra gargoyle sitting atop the roof, if the little fella didn't move around too much. And he was right, nobody did.

That day, the sunrise welcomed the strange visitor by showing him just what it was capable of. George thought his friend might weep at the beauty of it. So quietly the creature sat, taking it in, balanced on the roof edge, shuffling along each time the window cleaner moved his ladders to the next colourful arch.

Lunchtime came and the two ate sandwiches of ham and pickle, shared a bottle of pop, the gargoyle and the man both perched high above the green of the surrounding countryside. They talked as they often did about something and nothing, passing the day as friends do: together, unhurried.

'Why does you ever thinks to leave here?' the little fella said. And the man didn't have an answer for that.

Later, when the sun had begun to set, shadows lengthening, it was time to head back. George Fisher dried off the last sparkling pane with a chammy and gave his friend the nod.

'I gots to ask you something,' the gargoyle said. 'Before we goes, like.'

'Ask away.' George smiled.

'Where does you keeps them secrets of yours?'

'What secrets are those, my friend?'

George had secrets, of course, as do we all. But he wasn't about to give his up so easily, even to a friend. Especially without clarification as to which ones the gargoyle was referring. Rookie mistake, that.

The creature leaned in close, head tilted on its thick, leathery neck. 'Bookish secrets,' he said. 'Where you writes us all down. Where be they, friend?' That last word–*friend*–did not sound friendly in the least.

In the quiet that followed, distant music played overlaid with drunken cheers. A wedding, perhaps, or a birthday party.

The eyes of the creature seemed colder than before, his expression blank as stone, and there was a palpable shift in mood. It occurred to George that he didn't know this friend of his half as well as he thought. In that moment he was less inclined to share so much as a slice of cheese with him, let alone his most closely guarded treasures.

The breeze picked up, a chill in the air. George knew he had to get the squat Diamonder home as leaving him here in any circumstance wouldn't do. 'Time we got back, fella,' he said, keeping his voice jovial so as not to arouse an unnecessary sense of feud. 'Here, take my arm and climb over.' He hoped he'd imagined the darkness in his friend's eyes, but knew deep down he hadn't.

The gargoyle wasn't for taking George's arm. Instead he sat back on the slates and dangled his stubby legs over the guttering and, looking up at candy floss clouds, let out a series of gentle tuts.

'Now, why you gotta bees like that?' he said. 'Tells me, George. Tells me where you keeps 'em. Else I'll finds 'em myself, and then what do I need you for, hmm?'

The window cleaner's mouth flapped open. No sounds came out. Nothing of use, anyway.

'Well?' the gargoyle said after a moment.

George kept quiet, suddenly regretting his decision to bring the creature here. What damage could he do? What harm could come of it?

'I'm not altogether surprised, to be honest,' the gargoyle went on. 'Just disappointed to find you as pointless and whining as the rest.'

At some point in the conversation the creature had begun speaking in proper words and his grammatical tics were gone. He was hardly the bumbling character George had taken him for.

'The journals, George.' The gargoyle snapped his clawed fingers in front of the man's face. 'Where are they? And the token? Reckon ya know what I'm talking about. That too if you don't mind.'

The creature wasn't wearing a watch but tapped his wrist anyhow. 'Last chance, George,' he said.

'I'm not giving you a sodding thing.' George finally found his vocal cords, and his balls.

'Shame,' the gargoyle said. 'Thanks for the sandwiches.'

And with a swift kick of his padded foot, he knocked the ladder from its perch against the roof line and watched with a cool gaze as the man flailed against the inevitable, his flightless arms flapping, until the scales tipped and gravity got its way and the ladder, and the man balanced on top of it, dropped thirty-five feet in no time.

Alas, George Fisher met the tarmac head-first.

7. THE WORST OF WAYS

Two Borealis walked the full length of the centre shelf, each step kicking up a fine plume of dust. Blank faces gawped out, swelled by pickling brine and awash with whatever expression they had the misfortune to die wearing. She tapped on every other jar, occasionally breathing on the glass then polishing it clean with her sleeve.

She wanted to see them clearly. And, dead or otherwise, she wanted the little fuckers to see out. For their beady black eyes to witness a world that would never again be theirs. For them to know exactly what they'd lost.

She checked the light: nearly time for her final audience with the king. She'd take him a delicacy. How he enjoyed his meat treats, folded and rolled and speared onto cocktail sticks for easy pickings.

'Bring me my squirrel!' he'd say, and they'd know what he meant even if he himself didn't.

The middle shelf was a place for adolescents; not so small as the little 'uns lower down, not so tough as the top-shelf fully grown. She decided on a juicy looking specimen and took note of its position, thinking to let the cook know to prepare it in readiness for the meeting. She'd lace it with the poison en route.

'Free's back, Ma'am.' A young gunwing barged breathlessly in through the swinging pantry door, before realising they might've just got themselves grounded. 'She brings news. Apologies, Ma'am,' they backtracked. 'Thought you'd want to know.'

'Yes, that's alright,' Borealis said. 'I'll be there in a moment. And, gunwing? Gather a team. Do it quietly. Get me haulers, the strongest and most discreet. Have them meet me on the uppermost floor. I have a certain cargo that needs flight and protection.'

'Yes, Ma'am.'

Borealis leant her face against a jar just as soon as the nervous recruit was gone. She stared eye to eye at the bloated and preserved woodland fairy inside, wondering how such a weakling might be blessed with magic inherent, while her stronger Northern kin had none. How vulnerable these little 'uns were to the forces. Not like she upstairs who sat endlessly decaying yet never dying, in a state of elemental bliss.

Queen's magic. The thought of it sent a ripple of anticipation through her soul, if there was such a thing. The people could take the steel castle for however long it lasted, but they couldn't take her prize. And the South could have their land, sure enough. She didn't care. Two Borealis quite frankly couldn't have given a damn about the wants of the small-minded.

She would speak with Free, who would tell her what she already suspected, that the people were coming. She would communicate this to the South, who would order the next phase to begin. And she would see to it that it was done. She would tell the engineers to set it in motion, and they would do as they were told because they were runts, mere foot soldiers, forerunners of the real South.

She knew this would be the order of things because she'd always known, from the beginning, that this was how it would play out. Because the people were people. Incapable of anything else. Likewise the South, whose greed knew no bounds. Constrained by type, all of them. There was no other way this could've ended, any which way you came at it. It made the hummer smile to know they were finally here at least, at this point, after building up to it all this time.

She examined the half-open mouth of the adolescent Faretheewellian, its tongue swollen and blue. She didn't recognise it from any of the others, but even if she did it would've made no dent.

There was only one jar that mattered to Borealis, the contents of which shed a light more powerful than a hundred sacks of the desiccated, powdered bones of these meagre wastrels. Perpetual wish energy. Queen's magic. Each time she saw the living carcass was a thrill unmatched. And that jar was not for pickling brine or weak little fluttering shitterbugs. It was an apt cage for royal livestock, the source of eternal greatness, and it was for Borealis to keep.

8. UP AND OUT

Rock pulled himself up the rope and glided through the water toward the rippling light, with two people ahead of him and two behind. He felt his father's gaze upon him from the large window of the viewing platform. Dale Senior would never say it out loud for fear of manifesting his deepest concerns, of willing them into life, but Rock knew he worried for his son each time he left the complex.

'There's bad folks out there, lad,' he'd say when Rock was a boy, hinting at experiences the much younger Dale could never possibly comprehend.

Now he knew. Now he comprehended only too well, having watched them on the monitors and through the glass of his own visor in the core world, as they picked up his colleagues–his friends–by the hair on their heads and dragged them screaming away.

The team of five each heard the same communication through their helmets. 'Heads up, everybody. Piss-poor surface weather. Take it easy on the pull to the top. Be sure to clip on.'

'Aye that,' the scouts replied.

When they breached the surface, the white caps and rolling waves made manoeuvring from guide rope to lift the most difficult Rock had experienced in a long while. But one by one they latched their ties to the wire that hung alongside the dual pulley ropes, and waited their turn to clip their boots into the one-way wheels that would lock tight and hold their weight and roll upward with ease with every new pull. One by one they hauled themselves out of the water and up. No sooner were they clear than they each turned the dials on their wrists to pause the flow of gas. They lifted their visors and breathed the ocean air instead of wasting precious oxygen which they would later need.

As they ascended, the scout at the front, a fearless man named Brynn, called the steps: Left, right; reach, pull. Brynn had at one time been Dale Senior's trainee, in the days of city-living. He was now their most experienced scout.

They found a rhythm. While their thighs took the brunt of it, their hands gripped and slid steel grappling holds along the ropes ahead of them. After a while Brynn no longer had to say the words, the rhythm just was, and they moved in a continuous motion.

The group paused several times on the climb to the clouds as was standard. Even the most active and strongest among them could only haul some thirty feet in as many minutes in full dive kit, the tanks being the most limiting factor. Rock often wondered how rapidly he could ascend if he were to try it in only his underpants. Likely in one go, he decided, and quicker than it took him to put on a wet-suit and gear.

Maybe one day they'd work out an easier way, but for now this was it. This was how it was. So they pulled and hauled and pushed with their thighs and paused and breathed and continued again. Left, right; reach, pull. Only going as fast as the slowest of them.

The gate hung horizontally in the mist of the low-hanging cloud. On clearer days it was visible from the ocean surface, an impossible hatch in the sky. On the darkest days it would disappear altogether and you'd have to climb halfway into a storm to find it. This day was some way between and the rectangular shimmer came into view as they neared the cloud base. The sight of it was a reassurance to the scouts - nearly there, it said. Just a little ways more to go.

As he felt the cloud mist on his face, Rock took a last look down at the ocean below, then ahead of him, where Brynn was the first to disappear through the shimmer, then Katya. A dozen pulls more and Rock was at the gate, feeling its crackling aura even as he lowered his visor. The hint of ozone would stay inside the helmet at least until the oxygen had done a full cycle, probably longer. It was the kind of smell that stuck.

He unclipped from the guide wire, gripped the gate frame and pulled himself through.

***

The grinding wind and fine debris ricocheted off Rock's visor. Inside the protective metal dome, it was as if he were putting his ear to a conch shell the way the winds of the plains shushed and whispered around. He watched as the last two scouts emerged through the gate.

Brynn signalled to the nearby shelter, a large stone slab resting atop other stone slabs where they parked solar scooters out of the abrasive air, and the five trod heavily toward it.

Rock examined the panels on the roof for damage. The unavoidable scratches didn't appear significantly worse from what he could tell. The low light levels were a concern, however. How much charge it was possible to obtain under these blackened skies was anyone's guess.

Katya was the first to enter the shelter. She lowered herself in through the gap and a moment later the others heard her shriek through their headsets and they rushed to help her, fearing that a goblin or hummer squad had discovered their hiding place and was waiting for them to arrive.

What Rock found when he slid down into the shelter was far from what he expected. There, in full dive gear was the woman from the West. And he'd be damned if she didn't just raise a gloved hand and wave.

9. STEEL CASTLES

'I can't hear you,' Marie said, tapping her helmet.

The scout grabbed her shoulder and pulled her near, clicked something on the side of her head, which was followed by a crackle and a slight hiss. At first Marie thought the man had pulled out the air hose and she wondered why he'd want her dead. But then he spoke and she realised he'd merely turned on the comm system so she could hear the others.

'What the hell, lady?' he said. 'You have to go back right now.' He thrust an aggressive pointed finger at the opening and presumably toward the gate.

'I'm coming with you,' Marie said.

'The fuck you are.'

Brynn stepped between them and Marie recognised the man as one of those she'd met the night before.

'Marie, is it?' he said. 'You come with us and we cannot guarantee your safety. Do you understand?'

She nodded inside the heavy dome.

'And you get in our way, we will do what is necessary. Clear?'

Again, the nod.

'Our mission is bigger than you, bigger than any one of us. I cannot emphasise that enough. Rock,' the older scout turned to his colleague who had already walked away in frustration. 'She comes with us or we abandon. And there isn't time for that second option.'

'She took Wolstein's dive gear.' The scout seemed particularly enraged by this detail, swooping his arms for effect. And Marie thought that of all the spare suits on the rail she could've chosen, perhaps she'd picked the absolute wrong one. The one that would trigger something in this man and piss him off the most.

'That she did. Not that he needs it anymore. But she also got up here all by herself. Gotta admit, Rock, girl's got skills. As I recall I dragged you out of those waters plenty of times when you were learning to haul your arse up the pull.'

'Woman,' Nova said. She was the last scout to slide down into the shelter. She'd heard the conversation through the comm from outside and was now standing at the base of the entrance brushing the debris from her suit.

The others looked at her. Even Rock, who had yet to lower his arms.

Nova felt the shift in attention and glanced up. 'She's not a girl; she's a woman. Just saying.'

'I'll take care of myself,' Marie said. She wondered if her tone sounded to them as it did to her, like she was ten years old.

'Glad to hear it,' Brynn said. He turned to the group. 'Right. That's that. Five of us, two to a scooter. We get into the city via Norwich, turn down Third until we reach Grosvenor. Stash the gear first chance we get. You got a mask, Marie?"

He was smiling then, and Marie felt a warmth in him she liked. An approachable nature. Forgiving.

'No,' she said.

Brynn gestured to Nova who dug into a pocket at the rear of her suit and retrieved a folding mask of rubber with filters built in on each side. Marie cautiously took it from her.

'It's fine,' Nova said. 'I have a spare.'

'Thanks.'

Marie felt around the back of her own suit and finding a pocket there fumbled the mask down into it.

Brynn reached for Marie's wrist, studied the dial for a moment. He didn't appear perturbed by what he saw, which Marie took to mean that her tank levels were satisfactory.

The older man gave brief introductions. 'You already know Rock. This is Chappers, Katya, and Nova.' Each raised a hand at the mention of their name. 'Good. Now we're all pals, can we get a hurry on? Air don't grow on trees around these parts.'

The man called Chappers wrenched away a large tarp which Marie hadn't even noticed given how it blended into the sandstone, revealing three sturdy motorised bikes rested up against one another. The woman called Katya unplugged wires from each. Charging ports, Marie thought, wishing she'd had the foresight to bring her phone. Would she get a signal here? Doubtful. Still, her fingers twitched out of habit, at the familiarity of sensation that was to hold the device in her hand, to stroke the screen, to scroll mindlessly.

The scouts wheeled the bikes, or scooters as Brynn called them, to the ramp that led up and out the entrance. Rock climbed through into the caustic breeze and pulled as one by one the others fed the scooters into the gap. Then when the last scooter was gone, Nova, Katya and Chappers climbed out, leaving only the older man and Marie in the shadows of the hiding place.

'You'll be with me,' Brynn said. 'Stick close when we get to the city and do as we say. There's things in there you'll wish you hadn't seen. You get lost, we won't be able to help you. Got it?'

'Yes.'

'Good.'

***

Marie was in the dust devil again as they rode full-pelt across the dry dirt of the central plains, only this time she was upright, spooning behind the older scout on the seat of a solar scooter, heading South into the wind. Scratching particles battered the glass of her helmet as they cut through the blustering air. Like being in a car wash if the water and soap were replaced by grit and sand.

They'll know we're coming.

She pictured a dark city with shadows to spare and dark creatures squatting in every corner. Creatures that hunt you and eat you.

They'll be hungry.

She had a feeling in her gut of how it was to be chased, that humming sound growing closer, closer, closer still.

The Goblin. She felt positive now that's what they'd said. She knew a goblin once, had painted him into her work without realising. *Never trust a goblin*, Olive's mantra, and what the people of Marble Falls believed, without even knowing why.

How was it possible to believe something so absolutely, to know it's true without evidence, without proof? Faith, she wondered? Or a kind of cellular memory? She wasn't sure either existed, not entirely. And yet she knew she was being summoned to this dark place. That she would sneak from the group the first chance she got to go in search of the voice. And the boy.

Brynn tapped Marie's leg, then her hand around his waist: *Hold on tight!* and he accelerated the scooter, swerving a pile of stones, a dead branch, a rolling tumbleweed. Through the dust clouds and smoke, Must's ominous skyline came into view.

***

When they arrived at the city limits, the convoy paused. As quiet as the scooters were, any sound now might spell the end of the mission and the end of them. There was no-one, but still they climbed off and rolled the bikes the last stone's throw, eventually parking them against the high perimeter wall.

Rock took out a map, the old fashioned paper kind but laminated, he unfolded it and pressed it up against the wall for the others to examine.

Marie listened in through her headset as they spoke of road names and tactical shit like what to do in the event of an ambush. She paid close attention to anything they said that might lead her to her own targets, help her complete her own missions. Though she didn't give much thought to how she was going to get out after she'd done whatever it was she intended to do. Hardly seemed any point. That's how nebulous plans worked, she told herself. Could go any which way, including arse over tit, in which case no number of exit plans would help.

Rock put the map away and the scouts filed into the dark street ahead. Here was a wide avenue, made mainly of what were at one time industrial units and storage facilities, two and three storey buildings. Some had toothless mouths of smashed windows, others remained relatively intact, some had boarded the glass over either before or after the damage was done. The smoke and grime had tarnished the signs but many were still just about readable: Store-U-Like; Gunner's Hardware; Tile It.

Strange how even here in this far away world the people still had their things. This could've been any street in any city Marie had ever been to. Gotta buy those hammers, those sofas, that carpet from somewhere. People and their stuff, she thought. People and their goddamn stuff.

The group stayed close to the buildings, not venturing out into the middle of the roads. Nova took point and Rock followed behind, then Chappers and Brynn. Marie found herself with Katya most of the way, with the scout making sure to keep this unexpected guest from the West ahead of her at all times.

They reached Third Boulevard, by Marie's estimation, within half an hour. Up until then they had yet to encounter anyone or anything besides themselves. But as they turned the corner and saw the first of the high-rises sink itself up into the black clouds above, Katya grabbed Marie by the waistband on her suit and slammed her against the nearest building. The scout put a finger up to the glass dome covering her face: *Shhh.*

The others had stopped, too. Rock noticed Marie's confusion. He pointed to something on the ground a little further ahead, slumped against a doorway, then he also signalled for her not to make a sound.

The group edged forward on a diagonal, stepping for the first time onto the road itself. Slowly, slowly.

Marie picked up on a noise then. From beyond her helmet with its constant hiss of air and the rise and fall of her own breathing which gave her the impression of being inside her own head, she heard it: a rasping snort. And as the group drew level with the shape they were trying to avoid, the noise coming from it growing louder, Marie realised it was a living, moving thing. A breathing, snoring thing.

'Goblin,' Brynn whispered through the comm, presumably for Marie's benefit. The others would no doubt know exactly what it was without needing to be told.

And so she saw it, this creature she believed in but couldn't prove. The thing she knew existed but couldn't remember how she knew. And it gave power to the notion of forgotten things and the idea that she should follow her instinct, follow the voice, the cry for help. Join the fucking dots.

'Southern scum,' Katya added. For context.

Marie studied the goblin, a squat little creature with padded feet and clawed fingers. It wore a uniform of sorts, like that of a steam engine driver of old: dungarees, a rough linen shirt, a tatty cap slipping off the top of its fat head as it slept. Next to the creature a brown ale bottle lay on its side in a puddle of its own contents.

'Bastard's pissed up,' Chappers said.

'Shocker,' another voice, maybe Nova, replied.

'Alright, that's enough.' Brynn signalled for the group to cautiously move on, so they did, leaving the snoring heap of goblin behind.

A little ways further down the wide boulevard Rock creaked open the door to a shop with large frosted windows–still intact owing to the roll-down security mesh–and went inside. The others too.

Marie glanced up before following the group and read the word 'Jeweller' on the sign that swung from a pole at a ninety degree angle from the frontage. This was confirmed when she looked around the shop's interior and saw rows of watches and rings under glass, precious stones and chains pinned in place on padded velvet display cushions. Goblins weren't in the business of theft, then, she thought. Apart from the obvious land grab.

The scouts began removing their helmets and suits. Nova reached over and clicked and twisted the dome from Marie's head, which was just as well. She'd somehow managed to wrangle the thing on back in the ocean compound, but didn't have the slightest clue how to get it off. Guess she figured she'd be dead long before that mattered.

Dressed in base layers, Rock opened the map again. 'West for two,' he said. 'Grosvenor's some fifty yards or so on the left.'

'No hummers, yet,' Katya said. 'They hiding or what?'

'Not exactly their style, is it?' Chappers kicked off the last of his dive suit.

Marie got her first good look at him and she was surprised at how young he was. Couldn't have been a day over eighteen. Still, he carried himself like a soldier, was as tall as Rock, maybe taller.

'Like we said, there's a fair chance they know we're coming, so expect pushback,' Brynn said. 'I wouldn't put much past 'em. They might be out on a raid or back in the North or holed up in one of these here skyscrapers. Eyes and ears open, team.'

'And the goblins? Where the fuck are they?' Nova said, straightening her black vest.

'Best guess? Concentrating their numbers around the machinery. They'll want to protect that above all else.'

'Machinery?' Marie said. So far little of what she'd heard made much sense. But she pictured a jar being thrust inside a metal fascia, jammed up against a rubber seal, a lever being pulled. She wanted to understand at least that. To get the image out of her imagination and into reality.

'Those clouds of shit above our heads?' Rock said, barely glancing Marie's way. 'The reason you'll need a mask when we step foot outside? The machines did that. We turn off the machines, the fires go out, the smoke dies down. Mission accomplished.'

This didn't answer her real question. She moved on anyway. 'But the goblins will want to stop us?'

'Yes. And it's us-' he drew in the air with his finger, circling the group of scouts '-not you. You're just extra baggage.'

Marie tried to ignore the last comment. 'Why will they try to stop us- er, you? Why would they want Diamond ruined?'

'Spoken like someone who's never been to the South.' Rock was clearly done with the conversation and with what he seemingly perceived as the inane ignorance of a reckless spoiled girl from the West. 'Are we leaving?' he said to Brynn as he pulled his facemask from the pocket in the back of his dive suit.

'Aye, we are,' the older scout said. 'Nova, Kat? Take the side street and come at the Grosvenor from the service entrance. Should take you in through a staff area. Chappers and I-'

'Uh, what? You are joking?' Rock said.

'-Chappers and I,' Brynn continued, 'will go in via the basement doors, here.' He pointed to somewhere on the map that Rock wasn't looking at as he had his back turned, his hands on his hips, indignant over the order of things.

Marie realised that this angry stance had a lot to do with her.

'And you and Ms. Fisher,' Brynn went on. 'Will go in through the main foyer. We'll meet up there. Everyone know what they're doing?'

The others, everyone but Rock and Marie, nodded.

'Okay. Now remember this is a stealth operation. You've got your sticks but only use them if you have to. Only if cornered. If you can run then do so. If you can hide, even better. If you can avoid being seen in the first place then gold frigging star to you. A horde of gobshites on your heels you don't need. A hummer squad, and you're done. Any questions? No? Okay, masks on, and let's go switch those ruddy smoke stacks off.'

10. GROSVENOR

The building was an architectural marvel. Modern, yes, surely not more than fifty years old, but harking back to another time aesthetically speaking. It put Marie in mind of the Empire State building, art deco and plush, elegant curves detailed in gold. There was money here, she thought. Lots of money. Not now the people were gone, perhaps, but at one time. Nothing looked this expensive unless someone had sunk a barrow load of cash into it.

She and the scout had barely spoken on the move from the jewellers. They'd kept low and slunk from one shadow to the next, one doorway to the next. There'd been no more goblin encounters and none of the hummers the team spoke of and that Marie remembered only as a fearful blur from childhood, the sense of being chased, of running, running, running until she felt ready to throw up.

The heavy glass door, embossed in gold with Grosvenor House, was held ajar with a length of pipe and opened easily when the scout pulled at the handle. Too quiet, Marie thought. Too many shadows. Better to face the thing than wonder when it was going to get you.

Rock leaned close. 'Stay behind me,' was all he said.

Inside, the foyer continued the building's homage to the glory days of early twentieth century design. Marie forgot for a moment why they were there and turned on the spot, crunching on the smashed crystal of a fallen chandelier, taking in the green and gold and black, the swirling lines and elegant mirrored feature walls, marred only by the long-dead trailing plants left to crispen in their vases.

Rock grabbed her arm, ordered her to stand still.

She heard it too, then, the sound of footsteps, of many feet approaching. She followed the direction from which it came–the stairway with its magnificent marble treads and brass handrails swirling up from the foyer.

Rock looked around for where to go, to hide.

The footsteps, so many footsteps, grew louder, closer.

He pulled Marie over to a door and tugged at the handle but it didn't open. He tried another, a little further down the same wall. Again, it was locked.

'What do we do?' Marie said, herself searching for doors, for exits.

'Back outside,' he said, dragging her to the large glass entrance.

But the door had closed behind them, had clicked shut, and even as Rock tugged and pushed the handle either way it wouldn't budge.

The air shook with the sound of quick feet spiralling down, of hurried conversation, mumbling and shouting, jostling and barging. Then there they were, the goblins, swinging on the handrail to turn the corner into the foyer and toward the main doors where Rock and Marie stood. They kept coming, more and more of them, each of them half Marie's height, a third of the scout's, showed no sign of slowing, their leathery padded feet slapping across the marble floor.

Rock shoved Marie to the side. She wasn't ready for it so tumbled to the floor and held her arms over her head awaiting the inevitable attack.

The goblin at the front of the oncoming stampede ran at her. He swung something on the end of a length of string, a hunk of wood or some other such thing, around and around. She could hear it whistle, building pace, cutting a circular path through the space. The heavy object on the end would make one hell of a crack in her skull, she knew. She waited, braced for it.

The goblin launched the object on the string. But it didn't follow a path toward Marie, hunched on the ground. Instead it zipped through the air, landing heavily against the wall above, rebounding onto the floor where the creature reached to pick it up. The moment of eye contact between the two was fleeting but enough for Marie to know he was not there for her.

The throng of creatures hit the door as one and they swung outward, releasing the goblins out into the empty street. The scout and Marie watched from opposite sides of this spectacle until every last goblin–too many to count–were gone.

What the fuck? Marie wanted to say. She didn't need to. Her face said it for her and the scout's reflected the same sentiment back. After a beat, they stood and dusted the crystal shards from their bodies. Rock looked through the door to the street and at a trail of dust left by the fleeing workers.

Marie looked at the wall where the projectile had struck above her. There she saw a green button. 'Press to exit,' the sticker below it read.

Rock lowered his mask, let it dangle around his neck, and Marie followed suit. The air in the building wasn't compromised like the air outside. Not so fresh as one might associate with a walk in the dales, perhaps, but equally not like sitting downwind of a power plant. In short, it was tolerable.

'What was that about?' she said, referring to the goblin stampede. 'Aren't we on their hit list?'

'Not today, apparently.'

A moment later, more footsteps, different sounding ones, and Nova and Katya appeared in the foyer.

'Shit on a stick,' Nova said, bending over, hands on thighs, catching her breath. She lowered her mask, as did Kat. 'Thought you were breakfast for a sec. Guess they already ate, huh?'

'Never known them not be hungry,' Kat said.

Rock had wandered over to the base of the staircase. He opened the map and flipped it to read something on the reverse. Marie followed, somehow less afraid of him, now, as if the adrenaline rush of near-death had reset them both or at least shown her that there were worse things in this place than a scout with an attitude.

'Which floor are the machines on?' she said.

The scout seemed to appreciate the simplicity of the question. Was it a slight drop of his shoulders that told Marie that? Some imperceptible change in his manner? 'Eighteenth,' he said.

'Lot of stairs.'

'Yes it is.'

'There's power here,' Marie said. 'The button for the door.'

'Mm-hmm.'

'So maybe the lifts are working?'

The scout pondered this for a moment. 'Not worth the risk. If it's a trap, the last place I'd want to be is hundreds of feet up hanging from a cable. No, stairs is best.'

The other two joined them at the bottom of the staircase. There was still no sign of Brynn and Chappers but the scouts didn't come across as worried yet, so neither did Marie.

On the wall above the first stair was a plaque that listed the companies and departments that once resided on the different floors of the building. Marie went over to it and up close saw that other words had been scrawled into the plastic screen, tiny scratches, tiny lettering, barely visible at all unless you looked carefully.

According to the sign there were fifty-one floors in all. The first twenty or so, linked together on the sign by a late-addition curly bracket, were labelled in the scratched writing as being accessible to 'engineers only'. She wondered if it had always been that way, but figured not. She pictured the drunken goblin down the street in his train driver uniform, and similar worn by the ones who'd almost run her down only minutes earlier. Engineers, she thought. And she imagined herself beginning to understand.

From floor twenty-two up to the fortieth, again gathered together by a curly bracket, the scratched on label read 'Processing.' The word meant nothing to Marie. But something about it didn't feel good.

A gap of a few floors, maybe six, then the top handful were labelled with a symbol rather than words. Marie leant in closer, rubbed at the gouged out shape. It was a moment before she noticed the tall scout Chappers at her side, also staring curiously at the carved symbol.

'Is that-'

'A crown,' Marie finished his thought. 'I think it's a crown.'

11. THE ENGINEERS

The backstreets thundered with hurried stomping feet. Clusters of goblins ran, as much as they were able, from the place they were toward the place they needed to be. They tried to be neither happy nor sad about the turn the day took. End goals were no different however you got to them. And besides, fighting chance this would bring about a feasting sooner than expected, which was never a bad thing.

Still, they muttered their mutterings: 'The people are coming. Smell 'em from here.' And: 'They drive us out and stop the dig and slow the burn and hinder us, hinder the ruin. Lord will not be happy.' And: 'We will swing for this.' Because if there was ever a thing a goblin liked more than food it was a grumble.

But the one near the front saw determination on the face of the leader. 'The ultimate plan? Are our options dwindled such? Is that what we are to do, now?'

The largest and least fuzzy-headed held his tongue for a beat. He toyed with the truth or the lie of it. 'Yes,' he said. 'We'll not be hanged for the likes of an Eastern sea dweller and a scummer thief from the West. Order came and who are we to question?'

'Not I.'

'Indeed. Nor I.'

The steelworks had long since fallen derelict without the people there building and making as they did. The goblins, enough of them to reach the top of the highest conveyor lift, were they to stand on each other's shoulders, scurried between the creaking structures and abandoned piles of scrap and ore and rusting cars. Only a fraction of the bodies stomping through the dirt knew where they were heading. The special few, kept in the loop out of necessity. The notion of never trusting a goblin was not reserved solely for the West.

The pit was deep and cold and dripped with groundwater at the base of it, not somewhere anyone from the South would go out of choice. But this wasn't about choice. The time had come to do what had to be done.

The lead goblin took the sack from over his shoulder where it had clacked back and forth on the run from the steel castle. It had entered his thoughts that it might fulfil its purpose on the way here, that the rocking of it could trigger the switch and set it off. He studied it, turned it over in his sweaty clawed fingers, followed the coloured wires and felt sure it was functional despite the dash. He flicked the toggle switch from the 0 to the 1 position and the numbers came up as they were supposed to.

'You.' He thrust the device into the leathery hands of the nearest subordinate, pushed him toward the open shaft. 'Fire it up.' He signalled to others to man the rope that lowered a flat wooden platform into the hole.

'And if I can't get out?' The goblin trembled at the idea of it.

'Then know you went for the good of the mighty cause.'

12. BY YOUR HAND

The staircase was eerily quiet but for their footfalls. The eldest and youngest of the scouts caught up with the rest at around the seventh floor with some tale about a burst pipe and a flooded basement. They all paused every five flights, for Marie's sake mostly. It took less time than she'd expected to reach the eighteenth, and they grouped on the landing only when they were sure nothing untoward was waiting for them on the other side of the door.

It wasn't locked or chained through the handles, no effort had been made to prevent non-engineers entering the supposed engineers-only rooms. This struck Marie as odd. If these machines were so precious, their function so critical to the goblins and to the South, surely they'd not run away and leave them at the first sight of a handful of people? People they could quite easily overpower. None of it made sense.

Still, there was some element to this place she knew as if she'd been here before. The look of it and smell of it stirred a feeling in her she couldn't draw the shape of.

By your hand, she thought. Do not falter.

The scouts discussed their moves: search the floor in pairs, track down the control room, pull the levers to halt the machines. Easy as.

Marie went over to the plaque similar to that on the wall of the ground floor. Again it labelled the levels. Processing. What the hell was processing? The crown was clearer on this one. Yes, it was most definitely a crown.

She noticed that Brynn and Chappers had gone. Shortly after, Katya and Nova disappeared along a different corridor. Rock gestured for Marie to follow him as he was ready to go. 'You're with me,' he said. 'Gotta be quick. Stick close.'

'I'm not coming with you,' she said.

'You can't stay here.'

'I'm not,' Marie said. 'I have something I have to do.' Though even as she spoke the words she wasn't sure what that something was. She tried to pin down the feeling that called her up the stairs. Like trying to recall a dream moments after waking: there but not. And within that feeling was a nonsensical logic she knew the scout wouldn't get no matter how she explained it. She didn't understand it herself. She only knew it, as much as she knew anything.

'The machines are the priority. Switching them off, that's the priority.'

'No, it isn't.'

'What's so important?'

'There's something I have to do.'

'Are you a spy?'

It was an odd question, but on reflection a fair one, and for the first time it occurred to her that these thoughts were put in her head for a reason, and how was she to tell if that reason was bad? It didn't feel that way, though, not to Marie. It felt important, vital, necessary. Not nefarious in the least. But still, perhaps-

'There's someone I have to help. I think I'm here to rescue them. Maybe more than a single someone. It's hard to say.'

'Who? From where? This is a massive building, Marie. And we didn't come here on a whim. We came with a plan. And right now you're fucking it up.'

She didn't have answers. She only knew she had to keep climbing the stairs, up the floors, and go somewhere, do something, help someone.

By your hand. Do not falter.

She knew this building. Knew it inside and out. Though if you asked her where the janitors cupboard was, which direction the bathrooms were, she couldn't say. And yet, she knew this place as if she'd been here her whole life.

'I have to go.' She climbed the stairs and left the scout calling after her.

'Where? Where are you going? We can't wait for you,' he said.

And Marie wasn't even sure she cared.

***

The sign for Processing hung at a crooked angle from a nail that must previously have held some artwork or other. Marie had lost count after ten or twelve floors, but figured this was somewhere in the mid-thirties. She listened at the door, then took a careful look though the clear panel into the wide antechamber on the other side.

There was nothing. No sounds or movement. So she pushed through the door. On the walls of the antechamber were smears and hand prints the shape of a goblin's, which Marie took to mean this was a thoroughfare of sorts, actively used by the squat creatures as they went to and fro about their daily business. She followed their direction of travel along the route of the most grime until she approached another doorway and a sudden stench filled her mouth with the taste of death. Her eyes streamed, her nasal passages revolted against the festering insult.

'My god,' she said, throwing a hand up over her face. The words 'who died' came to mind. No other smell like it. A month-old old sheep carcass left out in the summer heat.

She stopped in the doorway. No need to go in. Her eyes quickly adjusted to the sight in front of her: the hooks and blades, the chains and rows of cages, each the size of a shoe box, the brown spatters marking everything within reach of the central steel table. This, she knew, was an abattoir and there was nothing left to be saved from here.

The stench stayed with her up to the next level and the next. She climbed another couple of floors if only to put more distance between herself and the bloodied room. Marie couldn't say why she chose the door she did after that, just that it felt right, as it does taking a route through an office building or college campus or apartment block you've been visiting your whole life.

Knowing the way, just knowing it. Not having to remember it or think about it. An effortless act.

There inside was the same antechamber as on all the other floors. This time instead of following streaks of clawed hand prints she turned the opposite way, because that was the way to go. It had always been the way to go. Ahead, another door. Through it, a sound, a gentle hum. Machines, she thought.

She walked on, pushed the door open with both hands.

The hum grew louder, shifting in pitch from here to there like a car changing up and down through its gears. The room was dimly lit with no windows, the air stale with dust. Racks of shelves lined two of the walls, and on those shelves were jars, hundreds of them, crammed against each other wall edge to wall edge, floor to ceiling, and inside those jars something moved. In the far corner something else moved, something outside of a jar.

Marie's stomach lurched hard and fast. Her eyes darted to the winged creature as it hummed from one jar to the next, until it stopped suddenly. It, too, had realised that they weren't alone.

'Hey, hey, hey.' The words came from Marie's mouth as a reflex. She held up her hands in the same way, an involuntary action, defensive but equally showing she was no threat.

The humming thing lifted itself higher and beyond the reach of Marie even if she were to try to grasp at it, which she had no intention of doing. It wasn't so difficult to understand the need to draw back, to protect oneself, to go to a place of safety.

'I'm not here to hurt anyone,' she said. And then it came together in her head, one more key notch that fitted, another audible click in the barrel lock of her memory. 'You're a hummer, yes?' As she said it, Marie knew the implication. She might just as well have said *enemy*. You're my *enemy*, yes?

The tiny flying person, the hummer (the fairy?), stayed where it was. 'What are you here for?' it said.

'I'm not sure I'm in the right place,' Marie said. 'All I know is I'm here because I have to be. There's no reason for us to fight.' She stepped forward a cautious pace.

'Don't do it,' the hummer said, pointing a finger now.

'Do what?'

'I've no plans to hurt you either, but I will if I have to.'

'Okay,' Marie said, lowering her hands. She signalled to the rows of jars. 'And these? What are these?' But she saw even before the hummer answered that each jar held another tiny person. So many faces looked out at her, tiny palms against the concave inner surfaces of glass.

'I need you to leave,' the hummer said.

'I can't. There's something I have to do first. Only-'

The hummer's hovering stance was some way between hostile and curious, now.

'Only I don't know what it is. Just that I have to do it. I was told to come here'

'By who?'

'I don't know.'

'Don't know much, by the sound of it.'

Marie couldn't argue with that.

'How did you get through?' the hummer said. 'Southerners must surely have blocked your path on the way up. Or are you one of them? That what you are? A traitorous fetch?'

'No! No, I'm not.' It was as if she were learning a language, starting to get a feel for the sound and texture of it. 'I'm not a fetch,' she said, glad to at least know the meaning of such a thing.

'Then how did you get here?'

How did you get here? Marie rolled the question around and around. A question bigger than its component words. She knew what had led to this moment, of course, knew all the events that got her from there to here. Five minutes ago she'd learned her husband was dead, killed by a member of the clergy in a skin suit. Five minutes before that she'd covered her mother in dirt. Before that she drove from London, and before that she'd rubbed bar soap on her finger to loosen the gold band without leaving Shaun so much as a note.

It troubled her some why she wasn't more upset about any of it. Was she broken? Missing the chip in her brain that controlled the part of her that felt?

How did you get here?

Exactly what depth of information was required in order to answer such a question? Would the hummer like to hear about her humiliation at the gallery opening, perhaps? How she learned second-hand about the existence of an unknown sibling, whose heart failed in utero before they could take their first breath? Or the fact her father, her wild and free and dear father, whose shoulders she sat on, whose footsteps she followed for so many miles over hills and dales, whose words she believed in above her own, was so much more selfish than she'd given him credit for? How he'd fucked off to fantasy land just when Barbara needed him most?

Marie knew how she got here, she just didn't want to think about it in any detail or else risk crumbling to ashes under the weight of it.

'From the East,' was all she said.

And for some unknowable reason the fairy didn't enquire further after that. Instead it hovered back to the spot on the highest shelf where it had been when Marie first entered the darkened room, apparently returning to the task it was there to do.

The little ones in the glass jars moved to face the larger, more powerful fairy, they tapped on their cell walls, showing no more interest in Marie than in a discarded ale bottle on the ground.

The hummer positioned herself with her feet on the glass of the nearest jar, her arms across the brass lid. The small fairy inside (a child?) mimed with their hand a shoving motion. Push me off the ledge, it seemed to say.

'No,' the larger fairy said. 'You'll be injured. If I can just get this...open.'

Marie knew then what the hummer was doing, or trying to do. 'Let me help you,' she said. She stepped forward, paused, and assessed the hummer's response. 'Okay?'

A moment.

'Okay,' the hummer said.

By your hand. Was this it? Was this what she was brought here to do?

She took a jar carefully from the middle shelf which held upon closer inspection a very young and frightened fairy boy. 'It's alright, I've got you,' Marie said and turned the lid–speckled with pin holes–until she was able to lift it off.

The tiny winged child looked up at her with wide eyes. She placed the jar, without its lid, back on the shelf and backed off a ways.

The hummer hovered down and reached her hand in the jar, encouraging the little one to come out, which he did. He was nervous at first, then elated to be out of confinement.

'The others, quickly,' the hummer said.

And Marie got to work, cracking and popping the lids one by one as a growing swarm of young fairies rose up and filled the air, their voices chittering and squealing with excitement as they hugged each other in relief.

When all the jars were empty, the hummer turned to Marie and flew herself in close. 'I know you. The Fisher girl. From the West.'

A tilt of Marie's head told the hummer, yes, correct, but how was she to know that?

'Time was you'd have been at risk from me. Not so for a while. And assuredly not now.' She nodded up at the dozens of young fairies swirling freely above. 'Name's Rickett. I owe you a debt, Fisher girl.' The hummer called to the children, told them they had to go, and they all duly followed her to the door in an undulating swarm.

'I have a question,' Marie said.

As she rounded the doorway, Leddy Rickett looked back.

'What's upstairs from here?'

'Royal chambers,' the hummer said. 'Better you go back the way you came. Likely you'll not make it in. And if you do, you'll not make it out.'

'I think I have to. It doesn't feel...done yet.'

'Don't say I didn't warn you.' And with that the hummer and the young fairy swarm were gone and the darkened room fell silent, as empty as any one of the open jars.

13. POWER DOWN

Rock followed the sound of voices and eventually found the others in the room previously occupied by engineers. It reeked of sweat and booze, and the scout wondered how the creatures ever got anything done.

Kat and Chappers were studying the schematics pinned to the wall next to a bank of switches and levers.

'Where's the girl?' Brynn said, having noted Rock was alone, now.

'Woman,' Nova called from across the room. 'She's not five, Brynn. She's a grown-arse woman.'

Kat shrugged: *Nothing to do with me.*

'Fine. Where's Marie?' Brynn glanced at Nova for approval, which she gave in the form of a theatrical bow.

'Took off,' Rock said. 'Upstairs. Said she had stuff to do.'

'Christ, man. And you let her go? By herself?'

'I didn't *let her* do anything. She went. If I'd have gone without telling you it could've jeopardised the whole mission. So here I am, telling you.'

'Go after her. We can do what needs to be done here. Chappers? We've got this, yes?' Chappers gave a thumbs up. 'You've got fifteen minutes, Rock. Fifteen minutes.' The two scouts checked their watches. 'You're not out front by then, we leave you and the girl–sorry, *the woman*–behind.'

'Copy.'

'Watch out for more of those goblins. Just 'cause they haven't come for us yet doesn't mean they're not gonna. And you hear any humming, you get the heck out of there, girl or no girl.' Brynn purposely avoided eye contact with Nova. 'Agreed?'

'I hear you, boss. Fifteen minutes.'

'Not a minute more.'

***

Rock had an idea he was unlikely to meet further interference as he took the stairs two at a time. This place was empty, abandoned. The engineers, most of them anyway, had left their stations before the scouts had even arrived, before they'd even entered the Grosvenor. The hummers, too. The crew that passed them in the foyer he knew were the last of them. Call it a scout's instinct.

He didn't like the emptiness in his belly, the sense that this was all just a bit too easy. He knew that feeling. It was how he felt when the way across the central plains, that last leg before the East gate, was clear and you thought you were home free. When you thought nothing could stop you.

Only that was what they wanted you to think. To lower your guard, slow your pace. And that, invariably, was when they got you.

14. RESCUE

It had to be the penthouse. Please, God. Marie couldn't imagine her legs taking her up another flight even if a sniper were trained on her from the stairwell. She dragged herself up the last few risers by pulling on the handrails to get that little bit of extra momentum, gasping, lungs no doubt scored by the microscopic debris. Even with the greatest air scrubbers turning over the air, all the filters in the world, some of the outside pollutants had to be able to get in.

She crossed the antechamber, which was considerably more expansive than those on the lower floors, to a pair of giant frosted glass doors which were bolted shut. For a second she considered the need for a slide bolt on the outside. Bolts weren't put on the outside of places to keep people away. They were put there to keep in whatever was on the inside. So what was kept in this room in pride of place at the top of the tallest city skyscraper that they might not want to let out?

Fuck it.

Marie yanked the bolt to the side then lifted a second bolt that had been sunk into the floor. She opened the doors inward, and the first thing that hit her was how the room far from matched the appearance of the hallway and the rest of the hotel decor. It had been made to look like an old building made of stone, a castle, perhaps, with tapestries hanging from poles on the walls, furniture of gold and the plushest velvet, and wait. Was that a throne? It put her in mind of Arthurian legend, of swashbuckling movies from years ago. This wasn't a castle, not a real one, not what the monarchs of old might've seen with their own eyes back in the day. It was an approximation, a fantasy, a set.

She noticed that the inner aspect of the doors were not glass as they were when viewed from the hallway, but instead had been panelled with oak. Someone had gone to a lot of trouble, here.

'Can I help you?'

Marie spun to see a man, a human man, looking out over the city rooftops. She hadn't seen him at first, blended in as he was in his finery against the deep purple of the curtains that hung in swathes either side of the window.

The building shook, then, a tremor fierce and sudden enough to make Marie drop her stance, to bend her knees, hands out to the sides to balance herself. The man at the window, however, did not seem unduly concerned. He stood tall with one hand on the window frame, the other poked into a fob pocket at his waist.

'Not often I get to see this,' he said, referring to the view, smoke buffeting past the window on the breeze, the occasional grouping of hummers zipping by and giving the man no more than a passing glance. 'Rather beautiful in its own way, don't you think?'

***

Every step burned as Rock hit the mid-level floor running. How much time had that taken? Three minutes? Maybe four? No time to pause. No time to dick around. Get the girl and get back.

He shouted for the Westerner but no reply came. Where was she heading? All he knew was up. But there was a hell of a lot of up to pick from. He ditched this floor and went back to the staircase, took a second to catch his breath and then bolted up the next flight.

He heard the sound, faint at first, like a remote drone sub being tested in the lab. The sound ricocheted down the stairwell off the marble walls. A buzz.

Fuck, no. A hum.

But the swarm was upon him before the thought could run its course, before he could think to duck into a corridor, and it was to his great relief that he saw how, of the group, only one was from the North, the others being the type from the woods, the Faretheewell kind, and little ones at that.

The single hummer leading the squad damn near flew into the scout's face, stopping short with just enough distance between them that Rock didn't instinctively smack her away.

'Woah!' he said, only then realising just who it was he was talking to. 'Leddy. What are you doing here?'

The hummer was taken aback by the use of her name–her actual name, not the name she had given herself. Not the name that reminded her of the blue skies of her former home. Then she remembered how she'd told him of it back in the forest and she liked the sound of it on his tongue.

'I'm here for the children,' she said. 'You have to go. The South-'

The lights went out with a click. The staircase fell into darkness but for a few streaks of daylight from the glass dome at the very top of the building and the handful of open doors leading to hallways on several of the upper floors.

'It's okay,' Rock said, noticing the terror in the eyes of the young fairies huddling as one behind the larger, more powerful hummer. 'That's just my people. We're here to shut them down, the machines, the coal fires, all of it. But you have to go now. Take them out. I'll find you when I'm done.'

'Why are you going up? You should be going down. Come with us.'

'Can't. I have to get a bloody Westerner from up there. Some voice told her to go do something, to save someone. I don't know whatever the-' he remembered the little ones '-whatever the heck she's doing, but I can't leave her here.' He checked his watch again: six minutes gone.

Leddy seemed to consider this. 'Top floor,' she said. 'If she's anywhere she's there. But you fly down these stairs when you find her, you hear? And you get as far out of the city as you can.'

She knows more than she's telling, the scout thought.

'And remember,' Leddy said, guiding the young group flitting past the scout and downstairs. 'This is what they wanted all along.'

***

Another tremor, and Marie heard a smash followed by echoing tinkles from somewhere along the corridor outside. There goes another chandelier, she thought.

'I've come to help you,' she said to the man at the window. It occurred to her that he might expect her to curtsy, but she hadn't climbed all those stairs to cowtow to a single sodding soul. He looked like royalty, had been dressed up pretty to seem like a monarch, though Marie knew full well he was no such thing. He was no more a king than she was a fairy queen.

By your hand. Do not falter. She tried to shake the words from her head. Not over yet, she thought. Still not done.

'And how could one as small and weak as you help someone as mighty as I?' the king said. He turned from the window and looked straight at Marie, scorn in his eyes, contempt in his posture. 'What is it you believe you have to offer that I don't already have?'

'I believe I'm supposed to take you home.'

'I am home, girl.'

'My name isn't Girl, it's Marie Fisher. I came through the West gate. I know you were taken and my father wanted to help you, but he died before he could. I think him wanting to help you might have had something to do with that, with his dying. I haven't worked it all out yet. All I know is someone has been calling me here.'

Marie swept her sleeve over her eyes to relieve an itch.

'I think whatever they've told you about where you're from is a lie. I think your name is Danny. Danny Evers. From Yorkshire. And I think the reason I'm here is to rescue you.'

King Daniel slowly crossed the room. He looked Marie up and down and up again.

'You don't think I know what they do?' he said. 'How they use me to get what they want? I hear their chittering, girl. I know what I am to them. A puppet, a temporary wedge to keep any other from taking my place. They sing that bastard song and it works a while.' The man waves a finger in the air as if conducting, hums a few bars of a tune familiar to Marie but not quite identifiable. 'And they don't think I remember. But I do. Oh yes, I do. How could I not?'

He's closer, now, close enough to reach out and pull a hair from her head were he to choose to.

'Marie, was it? So your father died, Marie?'

'Yes, a long time ago.'

'Lucky you. You remember him, though?'

'Yes.'

'And did he beat you?'

'No!'

'Did he make you feel small? Worthless? Afraid?'

'Of course not.'

'No,' the king quietly echoed. 'Of course not. So you'll have to take my word that, even given the circumstances, for me here is better.'

'But the South will come.'

The king laughed as if some insight had tickled him. As if nobody could touch him now. 'And where do you think they'll go next?' he said. 'You think they'll stop at Diamond? Stupid girl. No, no, no. Here is but a holding station for the real advances. You watch. Next will be your precious West, and then where will you go? At least I had the time I was given to feel...important. To be looked after.' He sashayed in his velvet cape across to the chaise lounge and sat down. 'I'm tired. I think I'd like to take a nap.'

The room shook again, violently, and a painting of a waterfall dropped from its hook, splintering the frame as it hit the wooden floor.

A hand grasped Marie's arm and she spun to see the scout, Rock, with the open doors behind him. 'We have to leave,' Rock said, just as chunks of ceiling plaster started to fall around him like hail.

'Danny, please,' Marie said, the scout pulling her away.

'Close the door on your way out, there's a dear,' the man who was once a Yorkshire boy, but now imagined himself king of all Diamond, said.

Marie resisted the scout but eventually had to concede to his superior strength. And Rock did as Danny asked, pulling the doors shut behind them.

On the small table to the side of the chaise lounge Daniel Evers spied the plate of delicacies the courtier had brought up mere blinks before the girl so rudely interrupted his thinking time. With careful fingers he selected a cocktail stick, admired the skill that had gone into its preparation, before elegantly popping it in his mouth and teasing the meat from the little wooden spear.

He noticed the bitterness, of course, the nutty aftertaste, and had a fair idea what it signified. But it troubled him none as he picked out another tasty morsel.

'Mmm, always such delicious squirrel, here,' he said aloud. 'My compliments to the chef.'

***

'Hurry,' the scout yelled at Marie, who was still in two minds as to whether to go down or go back. 'This place is gonna fall.'

'Have they done it?' she said. 'These earthquakes? Does that mean they've turned off the machines?'

'No,' Rock said. 'But the darkness does. The lights going out means the power's out, which means they pulled the plug.'

'Or that the quakes have busted a fuse?'

'Yeah, I'd sooner go with what I said. Now can we move?'

Marie was taken with something across the hall, another smaller door which was slightly ajar. 'Just a moment,' she said. Despite the tremors, the sounds of destruction from all around, the scout's growing frustration, she went over to it and stepped inside.

A machine dominated one side of the room, floor to ceiling. Not a machine made by man. Something else. It made no sound, no power going to it, and the only light in the room came from a frosted glass slit high up in the wall, what was left of a window which had been partially painted black.

Also in that room was a cell made of iron bars, the door to which, too, was open. And in that cell was a cupboard. And in that cupboard was a dark and dusty shelf.

Marie felt a sense of being in the presence of another, someone who'd burned their voice box clean out, screamed loud enough for their cries to become part of the walls, the vibrations absorbed into the very fabric of them. She could almost hear it. It was a voice she knew.

She opened the cupboard doors wider, and wider still, to let as much of the weak daylight in as she could, until they overextended on their hinges, almost splitting the wood on which they hung. She searched every inch for the voice, as crazy as that sounded even to herself. But on the shelf was nothing, only dust, and the circular imprints left by a jar.

15. DO NOT FALTER

Atop the steel castle, Mae Skylark grasped at sections of her nest with both hands. The first tremor wrenched her from a deep slumber, the second alarmed her more greatly than the first. The tower shook and swayed a little. At the highest peak of it this was felt more than lower down, having the greatest sway of all. The nest, she realised, was not the sturdy bed she had thought it to be. The lurching and shuddering caused gaps to form and separation to occur. Any moment it would disintegrate altogether, her fortress in the clouds gone.

Ordinarily she might've flown to another. At least ten of the structures across the dark city housed her handiwork from back when she explored the black skies in vigorous flight, back when her wings were still young. Not so now, though. Not anymore.

'Jump, sister,' Eryl whispered. 'Jump and we might live.'

But Mae knew this to be a ploy by the dead one. 'You would have me die to be free of me,' she said. 'Don't believe I cannot hear the hope in your voice.'

'Would that be so bad? Are you not tired also, sister? We do not have to be this way.'

'Lord and Master would dip us in butter and rye seeds, have us on a cracker if he heard such guff. Shut up, sister. Shut up!'

But Eryl wouldn't and didn't shut up. The dead fairy was inside of Mae, heard her, saw her, knew her well enough to know it would only take a nudge.

In the end that nudge came from elsewhere. Another tremor rocked the castle and shook the nest until it wasn't a nest, only a collection of branches and flotsam that crumbled away and rained down on the streets below.

Mae tried in vain to work the wings she'd stolen. Then, when they failed, she tried with all her might to dig her sharp nails into the sloped roof. Finally, when her strength was gone, she slipped and scratched down the slope of glass and tumbled over the edge of the great chasm and gave in to the glorious rush as she plummeted through the air.

Happy now, sister? she thought.

But Eryl said nothing.

***

Inside the vent tunnel Broadleaf limped along, her broken wing numb after days of pain and scavenging and dodging the ones who might want to see her dead. They were gone now, she was sure of it. The ripples in the air had lessened since the last dark. The huge tower built by the people, pride of the city of Must, was nothing but a husk, an abandoned hollow. The commandeering gobshites and the humming army that defended them, provided them with the ways and means to work, were gone. Still, she crept. Hadn't made it this far just to fuck it all up now.

Another quake. The sound of glass shattering.

She pushed on quicker than before, dropped down a metal shaft with a clang, damn near broke her leg. She thought of her captor, the festering fairy on the rooftop, and wondered if that too had gone, had leapt from the tower before it fell.

How many downs had she taken? How many more until she reached the flat? Shaking dislodged flecks of rust and Broadleaf scrunched her fingers in her thick mat of hair and shook out the debris as best she could.

Another turn, another down, this one more of a slide.

And another.

And another.

Until at last she heard sounds of life, voices, footsteps. Not those of gobshites. She'd know those anywhere, the padding and lazy and stinking things. No, these were people. People! And others, besides.

Broadleaf followed the sounds, forward and faster, until she didn't realise she was running straight toward a vent. She hit it with such force that she forgot the numbness of her wing and her hunger. She was unconcerned by who it was she was running to, that they might as easily take her gift as help her, that the people started this and were the ones responsible for just about everything bad that had occurred.

None of that mattered.

Only getting to them. And getting out.

***

'I can't. Please wait. I can't,' Marie gasped, the scout dragging her by the wrist into the ground floor foyer of the Grosvenor building. They'd descended fifty flights in minutes. Twice she'd stumbled, and both times Rock caught her before she hit the hard marble stairs. Which was just as well. A landing like that didn't strike her as something she'd easily recover from.

'We're not stopping,' the scout said, also out of breath but wearing it well. He made for the doors, slammed into them. They didn't open. Then he remembered the green button and smacked his palm against it, pressing the thing full force.

Still the doors didn't open when they pushed. Or pulled.

Another tremor. Mirrored tiles fell from around the lifts with smash after smash.

'The power,' Marie said. 'You pulled the plug. The power's off.'

'Shit.' Rock looked around and ran toward the reception area where he manhandled one of the heavy steel-framed armchairs that were dotted around a coffee table, relics from the days when people worked here, and he dragged it squealing to the door.

Marie stood back a ways, watched as the man arced the chair through the air using the weight of it to hurl it at the glass, and it sailed on out, coming to land in the gutter. He stepped through, then held a hand out for Marie to take, which she did, carefully ducking though the shattered window pane.

The scout turned one way then the other. 'Where are they? Where the-'

'Rock! Here!' Across the street, Katya yelled and gestured with her hands for them to come.

As they got nearer to the others in the shelter of an old bank building, Marie saw the younger scout, Chappers, lying on the floor. He was covered in blood. His own.

'Oh, thank God,' the eldest scout said. 'You got out in time. He's hurt, Rock. We took the back way but a chunk of something landed on 'im.'

'I'm fine, Brynn,' Chappers groaned, holding a bunched up cloth to his head. 'Get me to the bikes and I'll be right. Clipped me was all.'

'Hush,' Nova said, stroking the man's bloodied hand. 'Save your energy for the dive, dickhead.'

Chappers laughed, then coughed, then fell silent.

***

The red phone box made for an excellent place for the young 'uns to wait it out until Leddy Rickett could get back. She ushered them in through one of the cracked lower panes, made sure they all had strips of cotton to cover their noses and mouths. The air was clearer here, but not clear enough in Leddy's mind. The little Faretheewell 'uns needed more protection than the likes of her.

'How long will you be?' one asked.

'Don't forget us,' said another.

'As if I could,' she replied, stroking their soft cheeks.

She felt their fear but also their trust, which hurt her more. They surely knew who she was now. They'd seen her fly, heard her wings, knew her name as something other than Cerulean. These sweet things weren't stupid, and many of them were more than old enough to figure it out. And yet they trusted her to help them. To save them. To take them home.

'The people need me,' she said. 'Stay and I'll be back for you.'

'Quick as a blink?' a tiny one said.

'Quick as a blink.' Leddy booped the almost-baby's nose with her finger. 'Watch for me,' she said. 'Stay safe.'

And the little 'uns pressed up against the phone box's square panels of glass and watched in awe as their powerful hummer friend darted off across the city.

***

They covered Chappers head to toe with a fire blanket from a box on the wall inside the bank. It didn't make sense to take him with them. None of them wanted to use the phrase 'dead weight', but that was essentially what he was. They could argue for a recovery team at a later date and request resources to bring his body in when things settled. If any of them made it back to the East, of course. The young scout, they knew, would understand.

The tremors had eased but still this place felt wrong. Too quiet. Too easy. The skyscrapers, the air, the ground beneath their feet.

'Was it us?' Kat asked as they readied themselves to leave the bank and set back toward the pharmacy and their dive gear.

'Absolutely not,' Brynn said. 'They did this, the bastards.'

Marie wondered who the 'they' of that statement was, who were the bastards he spoke of? Presumably goblins or hummers or the South. Were these terms interchangeable? And if not, who was really in charge? She hadn't pieced it together yet. All she knew for sure was that when it came to them and us, in Diamond, there were a lot more them than us.

She wondered, too, what it was they'd done (*They did this, the bastards*) and thought to ask Brynn about it, but got the distinct impression he didn't know either. Only that they–whoever *they* were–had done something terribly bad.

The four surviving scouts and Marie headed back along Third, walking almost the length of the Grosvenor building before bits of twigs and brambles and other dead greenery began drawing their attention upward.

'What the fuck?' Nova said, throwing her arms up, ducking her head.

'Christ, what next?' Brynn said. He studied a twig he'd picked off his shoulder where it had landed, threw it down. 'You see any trees around here, Marie?'

She did not.

Brynn looked to the Grosvenor's peak, where it kissed the black plumes of cloud belched by the smoke stacks. 'Then where'd you suppose all this came from?'

As the five stood staring up at the great steel and glass skyscraper, something stood out from the falling scrap: a small shape moving differently to the rest, and Rock was the first to put a name to it, to the figure he'd know anywhere.

'It's Rickett,' he said of the hummer coming in to land some way ahead, knowing the others knew as well as he did who that was.

'What's she carrying?' Kat said.

They hurried to where the fairy had landed. There, Leddy Rickett held in her arms another, smaller figure, grey in appearance, scorched and ruined, as if made of smoke and ash. She laid them down and looked at the five people as they approached.

'Is it alive?' Nova said.

'She,' Leddy corrected. 'Yes, she is alive. Just. I caught her as she fell.'

'Is she one of yours?' Brynn said.

'One of mine? Can you be more specific?' Was she a hummer? Leddy thought. Is that what the old man was asking? Or was this broken thing woodland born? She couldn't feel his intent, which took her off guard.

Ordinarily she'd know from the vibrations of a question, the warmth or lack of it in the asker's eyes. But not this man. There was no intent behind his words. No judgement. No fear. Only curiosity, it seemed.

'I meant is she kin to you. And I meant no offence by it,' the scout reassured.

'Yes,' Leddy said after a moment. She looked at the face of the unconscious fairy in her lap. 'I believe she might be.'

Then, from the pavement behind the group a shriek got everyone's attention. They turned to see yet another fairy limping as fast as her tiny legs could carry her, one wing pert as it ought to have been, the other in a sorry state, hanging loosely down her back like a worn raincoat on a peg.

'Get away from her,' the fairy cried out.

Leddy saw the face, knew exactly who it was, and could barely fathom it. 'Broadleaf, is that you?'

'Get away,' Broadleaf said again, nearing them now, but keeping her distance from the abomination on the floor. 'It's not safe. It took me, was going to kill me. Back away from the evil thing. Back away.'

'She's not hurting anyone,' Leddy said. 'Look. She's out cold.'

'Then leave it. Let it die here in the street.'

'I can't do that, Broadleaf. It's Mae, Mae Skylark, Pappy's daughter.'

Broadleaf paused, and Leddy Rickett could feel a fear and rage rising in the young Faretheewellian, and she sensed that Broadleaf had seen the wings she worked hard to keep covered in the hollow, had noted the size and strength of them, had recognised the size and strength of the one she'd thought of as green, green as the forest, not blue like the skies of the North, the hummers, the destroyers of all she held dear.

'You,' Broadleaf said, in a low rumble of a breath. 'You,' she said with a fierce hatred of everything her eyes now gazed upon.

'I'm so sorry,' Leddy said. And she was. So very sorry.

'What's happening,' Marie muttered.

Nova gave the subtlest shake of her head: *Not now*.

A moment later and the young fairy hurled herself at the hummer on the ground, knocking Leddy free of the unconscious Mae and sending her reeling backwards.

'Broadleaf, stop,' Leddy said.

But the fairy pounded and lashed at the hummer, thumped her fists against her muscular form.

And after a while, Leddy Rickett let the punches land, allowing the Faretheewell native to manifest her anger and loss and grief into the swing of an arm, the kick of a foot. She laid on the road and gave into the hurt and took it until Broadleaf had nothing more to give, to release, to offload.

'Should we-' Marie began.

Still no, was the look in Nova's eyes.

Marie looked over at Rock. He stood like a coiled spring watching the fight play out, apparently wrestling with diving in to help, to part the scrapping pair. But at some point he seemed to give up on that idea, apparently realising, as Marie herself had, that the hummer could end things any time she liked, could overpower the weaker fairy with ease, and was instead choosing to take the beating. There was a word for that: penance.

Finally, the weaker of the two fairies slumped down onto the tarmac beside the hummer and the barely alive Mae Skylark. She sat cross-legged and studied her own feet, picked at her fingers, let the others think what they would. Leddy felt the rage in Broadleaf subside, if only out of exhaustion. It was enough for now.

'Ladies,' Brynn said. 'Forgive me but we do need to go. Only so long we can stay in this air before we all suffer.'

Leddy nodded.

'Don't think I'm going back with them,' Broadleaf said, still looking down at her feet. 'I'm not sharing a hollow with traitors.' She didn't need to clarify. Everyone was aware she was referring to Rickett and the Skylark creature.

'I'm sorry. There are no woods left for you to go back to,' Brynn said. 'You'll come with us. Stay with us until we can figure out where it's safe for you.'

Leddy stood, then. 'How are we to do that? Our kind aren't known for our ability to swim. And the babies?

What of them? And her father?' she pointed at Mae. 'I left him back there. I'm not leaving him to perish.'

Broadleaf snorted. 'Like you give a shit.'

Leddy ignored her, instead keeping her eyes trained on the scouts. 'I won't leave him, Rock. I won't.'

Rock wiped the sweat and grime from his top lip, looked up and down the empty boulevard. 'How many little ones?' he said.

'Six...no, seventeen.'

'And the other? Pappy, you say? Where exactly?'

'A large hollow on the border with the plains.' Near where we met all those times, she wanted to say. Where we had our chats and where your feelings grew. Where I felt your eyes upon me and where I wondered quietly to myself how it might be to use a token, to become a person so we might look eye to eye with each other, walk hand in giant hand.

'I know the place.' He checked his watch.

'What ya thinking, lad?' Brynn said.

'Right,' Rock said, after a moment. 'Here's what we're going to do.'

16. DEBRIEF

On this day 9th April 1994

Some thoughts drift into being while others come to us fully formed in a way that suggests they always were. Today I had one such thought. It was upon casting my mind back to a conversation with my dear friend Johan in which we discussed the monarchy of this land, that I got to attributing a similar line of logic to other areas of my life, and more specifically the situation I find myself in at home.

The queen of old, he said, the one they mourn, was pulled toward another place (which by his description I took to mean Yorkshire). She would leave to spend time there, and in doing so would essentially abandon the needs of her people for the sake of her own happiness. He spoke of a 'back door', a gate not officially recorded, told me I passed it sometimes when the gate is positioned in such a way as to take me a certain route through the forest.

He described where it led to—a waterfall, a hidden place of green, a cave—and I knew it immediately, having been there many times, both alone and in the company of my daughter.

I was put in mind of the Evers boy, lost around the same time. That hidden place was not so far from where the child had lived as to prevent one as young as he from getting there under his own steam were he so motivated. The authorities searched, as I understand it, finding evidence of his being there (a burned down candle, crumbs of food and the like). But no boy, just like no queen, both vanished.

I wondered then if it was their intention to be lost, to walk or fly away from those who knew them, and it shocked me how profoundly relatable a desire that was.

I recalled Barbara and how I leave her behind every time I step through the gate, how much easier it becomes for me to rationalise, how much less the guilt gnaws at me, how little I pine to be back with her again with each return journey. Dare I say, how little I care?

When I record my endeavours in these pages I tell it as if I do these things for us, as if I seek out meaning and purpose for us both. I frame my inadequacies (because I fear that is all they are) as a search for enlightenment. When in the cold light of day I know were it not for my daughter I would surely have walked away from my marriage and ended all of our torment by now.

And so to the thought, that perfectly formed thought that has filled my head since it occurred with such suddenness and completeness, the notion that our memories are nothing more than the lies we tell ourselves to justify the people we have become. I wonder if all I remember is as it was, or if it is just how I would like it to be remembered. How I need to believe it was in order to go on. It seems I have developed an acute awareness of bias, and an understanding that if I am fallible to the mis-recording of information, a flawed witness you might say, then who else? Who else?

I ponder the question and find myself doubting the veracity of all that had been said before.

***

Marie closed the journal. Her palpable disappointment in her father was matched only by her mental and physical exhaustion. She shuffled down in the bed, the cool of the sheets refreshing after a warm shower. Outside, the dark ocean rippled with starlight from the surface, not the spiral galaxy she knew but another array, bright and colourful and glorious just the same.

The silvery thread of the dive rope trailed up from the module where the circular shadow of a moon pool sat underneath. She studied the length of it from end to end but there was nothing there but rope. Nobody pulling themselves hand over hand, no scout, no Rock, no sign.

A knock at the door.

'Hey, how you feeling?' The medic, Genevieve, acted as if she was just passing, as if she hadn't made a special trip from her on-call room to check up on Marie.

The scooter ride from the city felt now as if it had happened to someone else, the two women scouts riding in tandem on one bike with Brynn and Marie on another, while Rock went to find Pappy Skylark in the West. They knew it would be close. Only so much gas in those tanks, so much mileage in the solar stores of a scooter. Still, he wouldn't hear of it playing out any other way. A stubbornness Marie couldn't help but respect.

She held up the small alarm clock as if to ask: how long, now?

To which the woman in the green lab coat let out a deep breath that said: too long.

Genevieve felt for Marie's pulse, smiled reassuringly. 'Get some sleep. Nothing you can do. If anyone can make it back-' The medic let her words trail off.

'Don't think I can,' Marie said.

But as Genevieve dimmed the light, Marie closed her eyes and felt the minutes pass in a blink. When she woke all was quiet but for the ticking clock. In the deep waters of the ocean something glinted anew. A fish? A sub?

A person. No, two people. One carrying the other down the silvery line of rope.

She leapt out of the bed and pressed the intercom, fumbling with the button until she heard the static sound that told her it was open to the other end.

'He's there! He's there!' The only thing she could think of to say at first. 'Rock's on his way down the rope! I can see him.'

'Yes, we know,' came the reply. 'Thank-you, Ms. Fisher. It's all in hand.'

She dashed back to the window and saw a flurry of men and women in the moon pool room. Some were waiting inside while others had geared up and were kicking through the water toward the scout, who carried the other dive suit strapped facing outwards, piggyback-style, on his tanks.

Marie counted the number of floors up and across, doing her best to memorise the direction she would need to go, and bolted from the room grabbing a robe from the back of the door, dropping the journal into a pocket as she went.

***

She got to the dive room just as the second suit, the one not containing Rock, was being hauled from the water. The scout had already removed his helmet and stood hunched by the wall sucking at the air like he'd not taken a breath in days. The others were leaving him be, letting him recover. Brynn, however, had his own way of communicating his relief and simply went over to Rock and mock-punched him a couple of times on the arm.

Dale Senior stood with a group of others. They overlooked Marie, so taken were they with the scout's return, which allowed her to listen in on certain exchanges she doubted she would otherwise have been a party to.

'No, sir. No further sightings. Last squad spotted heading due North.'

'When these guys were still there?'

'Yessir.'

'The South?'

'No movement, yet, sir.'

'And the quakes?'

'Looking into it, sir. Possibly natural in origin or catastrophic mechanical failure.'

'But we can't rule out an act of malicious destruction or terrorism at this time?'

'No, sir. We can't.'

They cut the conversation short as Brynn and another man stepped up and unclipped the dive helmet from the other dive suit, twisted it and lifted it off. As the suit deflated, out fluttered over a dozen young forest fairies, cautious and blinking in the artificial light, followed by Pappy Skylark, Broadleaf, and last of all Leddy Rickett with the limp form of Mae Skylark draped unconscious in her arms.

The fairy group flew up to a corner and hovered there, wide-eyed and watchful.

'Hello, my friends,' Dale Senior said, keeping a distance, sensing their discomfort. 'You are welcome here. Anything you need just let us know.'

'Thank-you,' Pappy said, which appeared to calm everyone, although it took a while longer for them to lower themselves from the ceiling in order for them to be shown to a room of their own.

***

Later, some of the same people gathered in the monitoring lab with the screens: Dale Senior, Rock, Genevieve, Marie, Brynn, and the older of the fairies, while the little ones slept. Another couple of the Eastern folks were there, also, operating the screens and analysing data, but mostly minding their own business.

It hadn't occurred to Marie how strange it was that at no time had anybody asked her to leave. It was only as Dale Senior rolled a chair up next to her and sat, everyone else allowing him the silence to speak, that she realised that it wasn't an oversight on their part. That she was in the room for a reason.

'We have images,' Dale Senior said. And Marie didn't much like the soft lilt of his voice, the apologetic curve of his brows.

'Just tell me.'

'The goblin. The "fetch" as you called him.'

Marie waited.

The man went on.

'One of our fixed cameras–we put them up to measure the destruction of the woodlands. Research stuff. You know.'

Marie just looked at Dale Senior, who'd paused, her face asking the question: *And?*

'Anyway,' Dale Senior continued. 'One of the cameras on the live feed picked up the West gate. Well, easier I show you than try to explain it.' He nodded to the technician operating the nearest screen, who pressed a switch that made the moving image come to life.

Marie saw a barren patch of dead forest just like she'd seen for herself before stumbling across the central plains, before being picked up by the dust devil that turned out to be Rock on a solar scooter, before falling into the ocean of the East.

After a moment, the space they were looking at flexed and contorted, then from nowhere the gate appeared, wrought iron bars, ornate frame, the portal's diaphragm a twinkling universe of light.

'There she is,' Pappy said, a fondness in his voice, like the gate was a much-missed friend.

Marie also felt a twinge of emotion at the sight of it, a deep-seated and somewhat unexpected longing to go home.

But then a figure emerged through the sheen of lights, a squat and hunched silhouette dragging something out into the dead forest. It took her a moment for her mind to make sense of what she saw on the screen. It was the goblin, and he was dragging a body, dumping it out in those woods.

He went back, then, through the gate, and another minute or so later emerged again with a second body, dumped that alongside the first, before going through the gate a final time, just before the gate itself disappeared, the barren forest around it filling the space it had occupied.

Rock nodded to the technician who duly paused the moving image.

Marie looked at the crumpled shapes on the ground. 'One of those Shaun?'

'We reckon,' Dale Senior said. 'Other is likely that vicar you told us about.'

'And the goblin. He's in my world now? You haven't seen him again?'

'Can't be sure,' Brynn said. 'Gate jumps all over the shop. Coulda come through any time and we wouldn't have seen him if it weren't in the eyeline of our cameras. Best guess? He made himself at home in the West.'

Marie thought about what was being said. 'Goblins are the South, you say?'

'That's right.'

'Wouldn't he go back there?'

A fleeting glance between Rock, Brynn, and Dale Senior told Marie there was more to this than they were willing to share with the group, or perhaps just with her.

'Suffice to say,' Dale Senior said after a pause. 'That's one goblin who's burned his bridges.'

Fine, Marie thought. Whatever. 'I'm going back,' she said.

'Not through that gate you're not,' Rock said, pointing a finger at the screen where the two bodies lay motionless beside a splintered tree trunk within the frozen frame.

'No,' Marie replied. 'Not through the gate.'

This sent a flicker of confusion across the faces of the people. Not so the face of the hummer, who upon hearing Marie's resolute tone stood from her position next to the screen. The older fairy, too, Pappy, moved closer.

'There's another way,' Marie said. She pulled her father's journal from the pocket of her robe, riffled through the pages until she came to the entry she'd read earlier, an entry she'd read several times over, in fact, that hadn't clicked in her mind until just now.

She showed Dale Senior the page. He read it and passed it around for the others to see.

'It doesn't say where, though,' Rock said. 'Could be anywhere.'

Leddy Rickett took another step forward. 'The well,' she said.

And no sooner had the words been spoken than Marie remembered the wish token she found as a child, when she'd wished above all else for her mother to be happy. 'The well,' she said, echoing the hummer.

And she knew it to be true.

17. WHERE TO NOW, BIGGUN?

The fetch, the goblin fetch, who'd gone by many names and many faces, relinquished his wait for the girl. She was not coming back, he decided. Not soon enough, anyway. Only so long he could stay in a form of his choosing and revert he did until able to guzzle down his latest catch. Out of powder. Out of tricks.

And so he turned to the shitterbug, dead as a burned out tree troll, the filthy thing itself now reverted, unable to hold its own shape as a biggun without the life in it to do the magicking. He pinched the thing between clawed fingers and dropped it in the pan, boiled it up good. One time he would've chewed it raw, but time spent in this place had altered him, softened him some might say, and nowadays he had a taste for the finer cuisine.

'Oh, Hubert,' he mused, stirring the thing around.

Then, harpooning the body of it out of the water with a long handled fork, he surveyed the ugly object, glad it would guzzle better than it looked, and he crunched off the head and the torso, chewed it quick, swallowed it hot.

Where to go from here? he thought. Not back if he could help it. Undesirable was that.

They weren't allowed the bones there. Only the flesh. A crime punishable by a hanging was theft of that sort. No value in the meat, the viscera, a by-product of processing. Waste it was and waste they could have.

The old woman would know by now, he realised. An old woman who wasn't a woman any more than he was a vicar or a man. She might also revert to form now this one was gone, which would set him at a disadvantage. She'd come looking, she'd fight, and might even win.

The gate? he thought. Perhaps. But it was an option of last resort.

The bones, though. Oh yes, the bones. That was the best part, an invigorating hit, the source of the good stuff. And the goblin, the fetch goblin, who'd gone by many names and faces, devoured it with the most absolute, the most divine pleasure.

Crunch, crunch, crunch.

18. ASYLUM

In the early light, the foss had yet to see its first visitors. Weekdays, most folks were at work or school. It would be the retirees, the rambling crowd with their egg and cress sandwiches, their flasks of tea, that would likely show their faces to explore the green and dip their toes in the pool today. Not too busy and certainly not busy for a while yet.

Marie ducked through the tunnel, feeling for the rocks above her head as she went, her way lit only by a glow summoned by one of the children whose gift was that of light.

'Let's pretend we're explorers!' they told the little 'uns to quell their fear. 'Just a game,' they said.

The little 'uns in turn played along with the ruse to quell the fear of the old 'uns, until they reached the end of the tunnel, a wall as stone-solid as the rest.

'Where now?' Marie said.

'Keep going. It's there,' Pappy told her. 'Trust me.'

So she did, and she reached a hand into the stone and into the falls on the other side. She felt the cool water sploshing through her fingers, enough so as she believed it possible, and pushed herself forward and out and through, until she stood waist deep in the pool below. She kept the small cage she carried under her jacket free of the rushing waterfall, kept the small thing inside dry. 'It's clear,' she said.

The others followed, carefully flying to the side so as not to get their wings wet. They spied the cave and headed for it. The cave that once housed a frightened boy who once trapped a queen in a jar. Inside they saw the etchings and scrawls of others across the walls of the cave. Others like them. Others hoping for sanctuary, to be safe, to be recognised as free from tyranny.

Broadleaf, surrounded by a fluttering gaggle of the babies, gasped. 'Green Skulls,' she said, touching her hand to the scratched words written long before most of them came to be: *We are here*.

Pappy sat quietly aside his daughter, close enough to gently stroke her foot though the bars. In the cage, Mae Skylark sat grey and motionless, her sister's useless dead wings hanging limp, eyes open and watching, not seeing, not truly seeing, as far as her Pappy could tell. But that was enough for now. She was here. She was alive. And that was enough.

'The people will come,' Marie said. 'They mean no harm. They come here to look, that's all, and to enjoy the green. Shouldn't bother you any. But if they do-' she glanced out the cave entrance to the forest and the stream that wove through the valley away from the foss, the wilds that to her eyes didn't look a million miles away from the forests of Faretheewell as she remembered it from her childhood. 'You've got plenty of places to go.'

Leddy smiled. 'Be careful out there,' she said as Marie climbed out of the gaping cave mouth. 'A goblin holds a grudge like you wouldn't know.'

'I will. You just worry about those little ones.'

And with that she scrambled down the outside, splished through the stream, and headed the way she knew would take her toward civilisation. The very same way she'd walked a hundred times with her father. The way home.

Marie got to the small village pub just as they were setting up to serve their brunch menu. She apologised for not having any money, told them she'd fallen in a river and lost her mobile and purse, a tale that was easily believed given the state of her. The barman said of course she could use their phone. Of course there was no charge. And she thought hard about who to call, how to find their numbers, given nobody remembered phone numbers anymore.

The only number she could think of was her own. The day she'd gone up in the attic to read her father's journals she'd left her mobile on the bed right before the vicar frightened her out of the back door and sent her bolting through the hedgerow. She punched the numbers into the handset and listened to it ring.

Please, God, she thought. Please let someone hear it. Please let someone answer it. And on the fourth or fifth ring, they did.

***

The silver Jag pulled up outside the pub around midday. Marie saw it through the narrow windows, thanked the barman for the use of the phone and the drinks and bar snacks he's kindly given her as she waited, and went outside, picking up speed on the stone flag path to the road where she met Olive with a powerful hug, not letting go for a full minute.

There were so many things to talk about, but there was time for that later. For now, Olive wanted to get Marie home to Darkwood where she could wrap her up safe and warm.

'Gone done a runner,' Olive said of the fetch, the goblin, the vicar, Shaun, whoever the fuck he was. 'I checked the house and the garden. He's not there, love, promise. And should he come back he'll get one heck of a shock. Quite like to see him try, if I'm honest.'

Marie didn't ask how Olive got in the house. She assumed the old woman had a key given to her by Barbara. Village life was like that, all watching out for each other. She was only glad that she'd been there when Marie rang.

'I'm sorry about Hubert,' Marie said, some ten miles out of Marble Falls. She often found that a car was a good place for such conversations, the kind where you didn't want to look in someone's eyes as you mentioned the difficult things, the uncomfortable things, things that no matter how difficult or uncomfortable needed to be said.

'Aye, me too.' The older woman lifted a pendant from the chain around her neck–a cylindrical charm that Marie had always seen but never really noticed– and kissed it. 'Good 'un was Hubert. Real good 'un. He'll see us right a while longer, though. Don't you worry about that.'

Marie wanted to ask what she meant, to ask how she and Hubert had come to know each other and what their relationship was. She wanted to say the word 'historian' to see how Olive would respond. But she was exhausted and the memories of what she'd seen were already beginning to gleam a little less brightly in her mind's eye. She'd sleep tonight, and tomorrow she would no doubt remember a little less, care a little less about the concerns that presently gnawed at her like fire ants.

She watched the woods and hedgerows pass in a blur. She thought of how her mother chose to forget, made a point of it, allowing the bad things to fade even if they never truly did, oftentimes wriggling their way into her subconscious whether she wanted them there or not. She thought of her father's need to document, to never forget, to always record, to pass on the knowledge, himself acting as a historian of sorts.

'Can we make a quick stop on the way back?' Marie said.

'Course, love.'

And they did, at the shop in the village where Marie was afforded an easy smile and credit reserved for locals by the woman behind the till, who knew her mother well, had known her family for years. After a brief exchange, Marie came out with a pint of milk and a loaf and an empty journal the cover of which was the dusty green of oak leaves on late summer boughs, along with a packet of cheap biros. She would not forget. Not this time.

While perusing the shelves of the narrow and low-ceilinged shop, she'd noticed something in the inside pocket of her jacket, something heavier than the fabric it nestled in. She'd reached in, pulled out a handkerchief, opened it up. There inside was the silver coin from the box she'd found among her father's things, the object that shocked her across the room the last time she'd touched it. She'd assumed it lost in the oceans of the East. It wasn't pulsing or vibrating or calling to her. No voice spoke of faltering hands. It just sat there in the handkerchief in her palm.

It was then she remembered something Genevieve had said in the undersea habitat, as the medic helped pull the dive suit up and over her clothes in readiness for the final climb. A casual utterance that Marie hadn't noted as anything other than a passing quip, something about being careful what you wished for. And she thought of how the woman in the green lab coat had held her hand and her gaze a moment longer before the conversation moved on.

She wrapped the coin up again, slipped it back in her pocket. She would return it to where she found it first of all, and she would do her best not to forget, to write it down, to document the things that faded with every passing breath. But she wouldn't write about this part of the story, this memory, the silver coin, because some things she knew were safer kept from the world at large. From the goblins and their ilk. Better they didn't know about that.

Darkwood came into view down the lane as they turned the final corner and headed along the stretch of road that coasted by the cottage. Marie had never known Olive to drive. This had always been Hubert's car, his pride and joy. But the older woman was doing a grand job of it, nonetheless. They parked up on the verge and Olive turned in her seat, resting her hand on the younger woman's arm. 'You want me to come in with you?' she said.

'No, that's okay. Gotta face the ghosts sometime. I'll be fine.'

Marie took the milk and bread, the book and pens, felt the weight of the coin in her pocket just to be sure, then climbed out of the car. Olive gave a wave as she pulled away.

When the coin was safely nestled in amongst the piles of books in the attic, Marie pushed the ladders back up and closed the hatch. She went downstairs and sat on the sofa where her mother had laid to watch her game shows. She was strangely at ease in the room, opposite the wood burner with a hot cup of tea and a slice of bread and jam. The memories came fast, then, of Barbara and her father around her in this place, this wonderful place that felt more like home than at any other time she could recall.

The police would come and ask questions about Shaun, that much she knew. She would think of what to say if and when they did. She wondered if anyone else had seen him here, either as the real Shaun or as the fetch version, and tried to work out how that may help or hinder her case were they to choose to pin his disappearance on her.

She didn't yet miss him. Funny that. But then, he hadn't been *her* Shaun for a really long time. Not the man she'd married on a beach only months after meeting him, while travelling the globe, while running away. The more she thought about it, the more she questioned, had he ever? Or had the man she married in fact been a kind of fetch? Had he played a role to fill her need, revealing his true self only later, and for that Shaun–*the real Shaun*–to be a total and utter twat? Likely he did.

Never trust a goblin, she thought, and the words raised an unexpected smile on her lips for the first time in she didn't know how long.

She took a bite of bread and jam, peeled the plastic from the brand new journal and spent a while doodling foliage and tiny winged things around the edges of the cover. She would paint them later, she knew. Would make art of it.

She opened the book to the first sheet of lines and put the date at the top, then crossed it out again. What to write? How to say all she wanted to say, the story she wanted and needed to tell? She tore out the page, crumpled it small, threw it over toward the wood burner where she'd use it to light the fire later.

She pictured her father's journals and their occasional missing pages and wondered how many rewrites he'd chosen to do, how many false starts there had been? The torn pages she'd assumed to be taken by another, more malevolent presence, she now realised was most likely nothing of the sort. Sometimes, she thought, you just need to start over.

She lowered the pen to the next blank page and freed her mind and allowed her hand to write whatever it wanted.

'*On this day*,' she began.

19. FOREVER BURN

Below ground, a secret inferno, a rich and expansive and ancient seam of black, simmers crackling red. There, the work is done by this burning line, creeping ever inward, relentless and undiscriminating, inching along from the city outer where a goblin did as he was told, hit the switch, watched it boom.

Pockets of shale gas catch and blow when touched by the constantly moving burn. They shatter upward their shrapnel stores. The heat of it, the smoking stench of it, hints at death for some, a glorious future for others. It crawls beneath the city, self-sustaining, now. The ground it eats, it weakens and carves out, making the castles above sway and creak and threaten to tumble. Which in time they will, one by one, into sinkholes of ash and crash like corpses to the deadland.

Those glorious plumes once coughed out by man-built stacks instead now exhale from the very soil, between fault lines and up waste pipes into the air, as it should, as it must, to continue the work and change the landscape and ready the core world of Diamond for the blessed day:

The coming of the South.

<u>About the author</u>

Elinor Taylor lives and writes in beautiful West Yorkshire, UK, with her husband and son, and her dog, Alice.

<u>Also by Elinor Taylor</u>

The Smallest of Sparks
Volumes 1&2

Storms in Jars
(as E.J. More)

<u>With Hugh Howey</u>

The Balloon Hunter
Death to Anyone Who Reads This